THURSDAY'S CHILDREN

THURSDAY'S CHILDREN

Flash Fiction from
512 Words or Fewer

by Curtis C. Chen

The following stories are fictional. No actual person, organization, or event is depicted.

All of the stories in this collection previously appeared on the *512 Words or Fewer* web site (512words.blogspot.com) between October, 2008, and August, 2013. The following stories were first published in *365 Tomorrows*: "Love Lucy," 2007; "Ghosts of Earth," 2006; "Birthdays," 2006; "Antique," 2006.

Edited by DeeAnn Sole

Cover and interior art by Natalie Metzger (www.thefuzzyslug.com)

First Printing: 2014

ISBN-13: 978-0615955216
ISBN-10: 0615955215

www.curtiscchen.com

Monday's child is fair of face,
Tuesday's child is full of grace,
Wednesday's child is full of woe,
Thursday's child has far to go...

— *English nursery rhyme*

CONTENTS

INTRODUCTION
by Laura Mixon

It's my pleasure to introduce you to Curtis Chen's excellent new collection of science fiction, fantasy, and horror flash fiction, THURSDAY'S CHILDREN.

Flash fiction, for those not familiar with the term, is usually defined as a story of 1,000 words or less. In this case, each story is 512 words or shorter in length. The book is organized into six thematic parts. There are 117 stories in this collection, and each stands alone, but as you read, you'll have a sense of a larger whole.

Flash fiction has its roots deep in the past. Many are familiar with the "baby shoes" story ("For sale: baby shoes, never worn"), often falsely attributed to Hemingway, which appeared in the early 1920s. "The Eensy Weensy Spider" and other very short stories for young children have been around forever; poetry, music, and short works throughout the centuries have evoked story as well. In recent years, demand for entertainment delivered in ever-smaller bites has soared, thanks to the rise of social media and our shortened attention spans, and flash fiction writers such as Curtis have risen to the challenge.

Telling a story in so few words is much, much harder than Curtis' apparently effortless prose will have you believe. Fiction, especially in science fiction and fantasy, requires the reader to understand a world often far different from ours. To work as fiction, it must also have an element of the unexpected, and must tell us something about what it means to be human. To achieve all this in so few words is the mark of a skilled storyteller, and to achieve it over and over, across such a broad range of subjects and subgenres, as Curtis has done, is impressive as hell. He takes us to worlds in turn bizarre, terrifying, exhilarating, hilarious, and awe-inspiring.

Reading these little story bites is as easy as eating M&M's or potato chips—once you get started, you'll first and foremost be diverted and entertained. But as you read, you will find yourself pulled to a deeper level. Curtis' characters and concerns are deeply human, and those undercurrents make this collection a very satisfying read. He takes on science, religion, family, technology, cultural identity, people exposed to unknown terrors, people overcoming impossible odds—sacrifice and selfishness—isolation and inclusion. These are stories about women and men, heroes and villains, victims and survivors. This, above all, is a collection of tales about people you'll come to care about.

In short, you are in for a treat. Buckle up and enjoy the ride!

Laura J. Mixon (M. J. Locke)
December, 2013

Laura J. Mixon is the author of six science fiction novels, including UP AGAINST IT (as M. J. Locke), and a periodic instructor at the Viable Paradise SF/F writers' workshop. Visit her web site at www.feralsapient.com.

Thursday's Children

THE END

August 23, 2013

God woke up on Saturday morning, went downstairs to check on her animals, then stomped into the kitchen. Satan stood at the counter, fussing with the French press.

"What happened to my terrarium?" God asked.

"I didn't touch your pets," Satan said without turning around.

"They're not pets," God said. "And that ecosystem is very delicately balanced—"

"Okay, eco-sphere, whatever." Satan carefully filled his insulated travel mug. "Your aquarium was blocking the screen. I had to move it so we could watch the game."

"You moved it next to the wine cooler," God said. "Interior temperature dropped by half. Most of the reptiles are dead."

"Are you sure they're not just hibernating?"

"Oh, you're a herpetologist now? And would it kill you to clean up after your little boys' club meetings?"

Satan frowned at God. "Geez, what crawled up your ass and died? Is it that time of the month again?"

"I'm going to forget you said that," God said. She glared at Satan's suit and tie. "You really need to go in today?"

"Yes," he said. "Conference call with Asia. Time zones. Can't be helped. Don't worry, I'll be back before seven."

"What happens at seven?"

"Oh, for Pete's sake." Satan grabbed his briefcase. "Dinner with Lucy and Geoff! Reservations at the Garden? Remember?"

"Yeah." God fidgeted. "Sorry I've been distracted this week."

"It's been more than a week," Satan muttered, and slammed the front door shut.

God ate two granola bars and drank a bottle of water, then returned to her experiment. The mammals which had survived last night's big freeze were quite resilient, and she wanted to see what would happen if she made them more complex.

The phone rang at five-thirty. God put it on speaker, but had trouble understanding what her husband was saying. It sounded like Satan was driving.

"I'll be ready to go soon," God shouted at the phone.

"No," Satan said. "Listen! There's been a change of plan. I didn't want to do this over the phone, but—this marriage is not working."

God was only half-listening. Her attention was focused on extracting bone marrow from a sedated male specimen, which she could use to create a female clone. "I'm sorry I've been busy. I'll take tomorrow off, I promise."

"That's not the point! Dammit, how do I say this?"

"Just hang up," came a female voice through the speaker. "She doesn't care."

God frowned. "Is that Lucy?"

"You had your chance, honey!" Lucy said. "He's mine now!"

"Okay, stop," Satan said. "You're making it worse."

God put down her instruments. "Where's Geoff?"

"Probably still at the office," Satan said. "Look. Baby. I'm sorry, but I can't do this anymore. I need someone who's more attentive, more invested in our relationship."

"You should have sucked his dick more!" Lucy said, giggling.

"Really not helping!" Satan said. "I'm sorry. We're leaving. This is the end."

The line went dead. God turned back to her work.

"No," she said, watching as the male and female shared a piece of fruit. God smiled. "This is just the beginning."

SHIBBOLETHS

December 10, 2010

The rain started the same day the animals started talking. Noah was sitting in his office, staring out the window at the gray clouds, when the female pig with an Australia-shaped blotch on her right ear trotted into his open doorway.

"I don't want to go with Ricky," said the pig.

"Who's Ricky?" Noah asked.

"Whoa!" The pig stumbled. "You can understand me?"

"Yeah," Noah said. "Why didn't you ever talk before?"

"I've been talking for years!" the pig said. "Okay, hold on. Repeat back what I say exactly: *multi-variable calculus equation.*"

"Multi-variable calculus equation," Noah said.

The pig nearly fell over. "How long have you been able to understand our talking?"

"What do you mean, 'our talking?'" Noah asked. "You don't mean all animals can talk?"

The pig snorted. "Okay, don't go anywhere! I'll be right back!"

"Where would I go?"

The pig ran away. Noah looked out the window. Lightning flashed in the distance, and fat raindrops slapped against the glass, distorting the skyline of the distant city.

"Okay, I'm back!"

Noah turned to see a camel hunched in the doorway behind the pig.

"We have camels?" Noah asked.

The pig nudged the camel's leg. "Go on, say something! Let's see if he can understand you, too!"

The camel looked at the pig with baleful eyes, then said, "A radical government may be toppled by a reasoned populace."

Noah repeated the phrase.

"Bloody hell," the camel said. "How long has he been able to understand us?"

"I don't know!" the pig said, hopping up and down. "I just came in here to tell him about Ricky, and he could understand me!"

"Ricky," the camel said, with obvious disdain. "Why do you hang out with that wanker?"

"He's not so bad. I just don't want to spend forty days at sea with him, you know?" The pig ran over to Noah's desk. "There are other male pigs, right? I can get a new partner?"

"Not my department," Noah said. "You need to ask Eliza about that."

"Right!" the pig said, and ran off. The camel stared at Noah.

"Can I help you with something?" Noah asked.

"Did you see that ludicrous display last night?" the camel asked.

"What?"

"Chelsea and Everton," the camel said. "What was Ancelotti thinking?"

"Is this sports?" Noah said. "I don't really follow sports."

"Typical." The camel shook its head and retreated back down the hallway.

Noah picked up the telephone and dialed a four-digit extension. When the woman at the other end answered, he asked, "When did the animals start talking?"

"How long has it been since you left your office?" Eliza asked.

"Don't change the subject," Noah said. "Are they actually talking, or am I hallucinating again?"

"Interesting," Eliza said. "Why do you think you might be hallucinating?"

Noah hung up the phone and ignored it when it started ringing. He looked out the window. The rain was coming down harder now, in glowing sheets of luminescent green. He was pretty sure that wasn't supposed to be happening, either.

FREE ADVICE
June 28, 2013

I wait an agonizing fifteen minutes in line for the right maker window to open up. Gods aren't used to waiting for anything, you understand; and the bored smiles I get from the hostess in a flimsy *Naiad* costume are infuriating.

At least I know my own disguise, as a potbellied business drone, is working. Normally a woman would be all over me within seconds. Especially the married ones. It's a curse to be the god of betrayals.

Finally, the diner at window three rolls off his stool, and the hostess waves me over.

The boy working window three can't be more than sixteen years old, but his hands are nimble and quick. He could be one of mine. I order *Thunnus* sashimi to start and watch as he makes art out of the preparation.

Cut, dip, form, assemble; his grace honors the once-living ingredients and the patron who demands this sacrifice. It's a quaint ritual, designed to give mortals a simulation of receiving worship. I don't begrudge you that need, but it is only a shadow of what real adulation feels like.

The boy bows his head when presenting the wooden slab, adorned with three perfect portions of fish. He doesn't look up as I consume the offering. The textures and flavors unravel magnificently in my mouth, and it almost feels like a sin to swallow.

I compliment the boy, order an *Arachne* roll, and ask: "Did you grow up on the island?"

He stiffens, but doesn't pause his dance, spinning inside the tiny booth to retrieve a soft-shell crab, turning back to fold it into his next edible creation. "Long time ago, sir. Live here now."

"Ever visit back home? Friends, family?"

He pauses, knife in mid-air, and glances at me. "Got no family since the war, sir. No friends, neither."

The knife descends, slicing through the seaweed-wrapped bundle. "Not even Kritodemos?"

He stops the blade and looks up. His hands move to grip the edges of his counter, and I see them shaking. "How you know that name?"

I smile at him, a god's smile, and I know it calms him, even if he refuses to soften his stare.

I pull out the hundred-drachma note the man in the alley gave me. The hologram of Zeus glitters in the light. You'd never know it was counterfeit if you didn't have a god's eyes.

"He's here," I say to the boy. "Paroled last week. He will arrange a chance meeting soon, be surprised to run into you, want to catch up. You'll go along. Why not? It'll feel just like old times. You'll wonder how you ever had any fun without him. But he will betray you at the first opportunity."

I slide the cash across the counter.

"I can't accept," the boy says.

"A generous gratuity," I say. "Take it. You're right, islander: you have no friends. Only the gods."

After a moment, he snatches the money and hides it in a pocket, faster than even my eyes can follow. Nimble and quick.

CREATION BLUES
May 22, 2009

"You there! Cake or death?"

Patrick blinked with surprise. "Um, cake?"

The clerk grinned. "Just seeing if you're awake. All right, come on through."

Patrick trotted quickly through the open doorway and into an empty corridor. He limped forward, following the glowing signs, and once again regretted not bringing his cane today. His wife had called it foolish pride. She was probably right.

The interview room was just as featureless as the corridor. Even the desk and the examiner's suit were a flat, off-white color, making it look almost as if a disembodied head and two hands were floating in the air.

Patrick handed over his application papers and sat down in the white chair. In his dark dress uniform, he felt like an invader, the germ in a sterile laboratory.

"Right. I see you've ticked the 'non-lethal' and '*Homo sapiens*' boxes," the examiner said. "Those two features are naturally opposite. How do you intend to reconcile them?"

"Mutually repellent biological auras," Patrick said. "No species may harm its own kind. I've described the mechanism on the 505/B."

"Interesting." The examiner flipped through Patrick's forms. "That covers proximate cause, but what if, for example, someone drops a hammer onto someone else's head?"

"That's negligence," Patrick said. "Not homicide."

"Fair enough. And how do projectile weapons fit in?"

"No individual may cause *intentional* harm to another," Patrick said, rubbing his knee. "Accidents may be tragic, but they're not malicious."

"What about evolution?" the examiner asked.

"What about it?" Patrick asked.

"Well, how does speciation affect your aura mechanism? Let's say your *Homo sapiens* eventually mutate into a new, biologically distinct but physically similar species which exist contemporaneously with their ancestors. It's happened before—like Neanderthals, or *Homo erectus*. Would those two species be able to kill each other?"

"I hadn't thought about that."

"Well, you must consider these things when you're a god," the examiner said. "It may not technically *be* homicide, but it would certainly *look* like it, wouldn't it? One hominid cracking another's skull? And if they're both sentient, does that mean it's murder?"

"I don't know," Patrick said, his face feeling hot.

"Don't feel bad," the examiner said, selecting a rubber stamp. "Most applications are rejected initially. Just last week I had a bloke in here wanting to create a miniverse where faster-than-light travel was possible. Wasn't happy when I told him he had to actually do the math on a 447/A."

Patrick shifted in his seat. His leg throbbed with a dull pain.

"Now, your problem's a bit simpler," the examiner said. He stamped each of Patrick's forms with a blood-red REVISE AND RESUBMIT. "You've basically got magic in your 'verse; you just need to work out the logical rules, and the computers will take care of the rest."

Patrick took the forms back.

"Best of luck," the examiner said. "And by the way, thank you for serving."

Patrick nodded. His walk back down the corridor seemed much longer than before.

NOT AS WE KNOW IT
December 21, 2012

"Here we go." Renfti pushed the button. "End of the world."

Sarlmon watched the flashing red color spread across the map on the wall display for a second, then sat down at the control station next to his student. "You seem confident of the outcome."

Renfti folded her hands and smiled. "I've studied this species for a long time. They're quite gregarious—almost pathologically so. Cut off their social contact, and they start losing their minds."

Sarlmon nodded. "An interesting hypothesis."

"I've tested it with several small groups," Renfti said. "Same results every time. The key is to isolate them, remove all objective evidence from external sources, then initiate a dominance struggle. It never ends well."

"But to reproduce that on a large scale?" Sarlmon asked. "Surely you can't expect these beings to self-isolate everywhere. Cultural and geographical differences will provoke different responses across the planet."

"Some things are hard-wired into the brain." An alert popped up on Renfti's console, and she tapped at her controls. "Survival instincts remain, because the genes are selfish. Civilization alters the dynamics and causes instinctual responses to have undesirable results..." She frowned. "That's unusual."

"Let me guess," Sarlmon said, "something unexpected in one of the large population centers, probably a coastal city."

Renfti gaped at him. "How did you know?"

"My dear, you are not the first candidate who's ever tried to defend this thesis." Sarlmon waved at the wall display. "Show me the data, please."

The map zoomed in, and one shaded area resolved into clusters of pulsing red dots. As Sarlmon and Renfti watched, one particular cluster moved upward, accreting other red dots.

"This doesn't make sense," Renfti said, poking at her controls. "An anomaly. One bad datum. It won't affect the outcome."

"How many individuals in that cluster?" Sarlmon asked.

"The computer estimate is..." Renfti shook her head. "That can't be right."

"How many?"

"Nearly a thousand!" Renfti hammered at her controls. "There must be some mistake. They couldn't have self-organized that quickly; communication issues alone would be insurmountable—"

"They're moving." Sarlmon pointed at the screen. "Where are they going? Can you overlay the radar scan?"

"Yes, Professor. There." The display flickered, and the translucent blue ghosts of buildings and structures appeared, cobalt-tinged jars around the teeming crimson fireflies. "Oh no. No, no, no..."

"Let me guess," Sarlmon said. "A launch facility."

A large red sphere blossomed in the base of one of the blue structures, and alarms began sounding all around the two scholars. Renfti screeched. Sarlmon slapped his override and began programming a transfer orbit.

"I don't understand!" Renfti wailed. "It should have worked! All the simulations were positive!"

"Nuclear-capable societies are always complicated," Sarlmon said as he piloted the ship out of weapons range. "I'm afraid your experiment is over, my dear. They've seen us. It's the military's problem now.

"Oh, stop blubbering. Your next course will be Earth history. Learning how we survived our nuclear age should help you understand how to make things go wrong on these undesirable alien worlds."

THE SAINTS ARE COMING
October 31, 2008

The platoon waited, lying flat against the dirt slope as the sky darkened above them. Billy pushed his palm into the ground, feeling the damp soil. The enemy was bringing a storm. They always brought weather. They weren't exactly subtle.

"Weapons free, boys!" he called down the line. The soldiers responded with a chorus of clacking noises, chambering rounds and disengaging safeties.

Billy looked around just as a bolt of lightning seared the valley, painting the silhouette of someone coming up the hill. Billy shouldered his P90 and jammed the butt into his armpit, hard, until the soreness there burst into pain. They'd run out of caffeine and glucose three days ago. He tried to focus his eyes.

Shuffling noises approached. The soldiers flanking Billy turned and lifted their rifles over the sandbags.

"Messenger!" came the voice, just before a boy in camouflage fatigues stepped into the light. "Bravo Company messenger for Sergeant Armstrong!"

"Stand down," Billy said. Lightning stabbed the ground, closer than before. "Get in here. You're staying until the storm passes."

"Maybe even longer," somebody muttered as the messenger climbed into the trench.

"Milo, I will cut off your tiny hairless scrotum!" Billy shouted. A few boys chuckled. It was a ritual.

The new boy held out his message with shaking hands. Billy took the plastic card, verified the bar code, and passed it to Jackson, the radioman.

"What's your name?" Billy asked the messenger.

"Private Michael Thibodaux, sir."

"Don't call me 'sir.'" Billy frowned as Thibodaux wiggled a loose tooth with his tongue. A baby tooth. "How old are you?"

"Everyone fights," Thibodaux recited.

"Sarge?"

Jackson held up a deciphered display film. His round eyes looked even bigger than usual. Billy read the message and caught a whimper before it left his throat.

"Platoon!" Billy called. "Circle up and switch to infrared scopes! Eyes on the treeline!"

"Who is it, Sarge?" one of the boys asked, moving closer.

Billy hesitated, then said, "Francis Assisi."

"We're fucked," Milo said.

"I thought EPA napalmed all the animals around here!" said another boy.

"Yeah," Billy said, "I guess that didn't stop him."

"What, zombies again?"

"This isn't the city. We've got room to fight." Billy pointed to Thibodaux. "Now somebody get him a weapon!"

"Oh, my sweet Rapture..." Milo sang. "Halle-fucking-lujah."

More laughter. Rituals kept them sane.

Something boomed in the forest. Billy swung around, his heart racing. The wind blew a smoky odor—almost like barbecue—into his nostrils.

"Anybody see anything?" "Trees are moving—" "Oh shit! Ten o'clock! *Ten o'clock high!*"

The saint stood fifty feet tall, towering over the treetops. Flying, flapping shapes followed him and circled his head. The beatific glow of his skin illuminated dark smears on his friar's robes. His huge, watery eyes found the platoon, and he gestured with one massive finger. The flying things descended.

"Cover! Cover!" "Are those birds?" "They don't got no feathers!"

"Fucking miracles," Billy grumbled. "OPEN FIRE!"

Their weapons barked. Saint Francis of Assisi roared, and the corpses of wolves obeyed him.

It started raining then.

Curtis C. Chen

JUST ANOTHER FISH STORY
November 18, 2011

I had the story, bit by bit, from various people, and, as generally happens in such cases, each time it was a different story.

You may say that is to be expected when temporal anomalies are involved; but we—that is to say, humanity as a species—have adapted remarkably well to dealing with the multiple realities which exist side-by-side, in parallel most of the time, intersecting only briefly, with unpredictable results each time.

The first account I had of the incident was from my dog, Bartholomew, an Irish setter who had wandered into this timeline some years ago.

"It's raining fish out there," Bartholomew said as he entered the house through the kitchen. I waited until he had shaken himself dry in the alcove to respond.

"Do you mean that literally, or is this another of your canine metaphors?" I asked from my seat at the table, where I was enjoying a mid-afternoon repast of toad in the hole.

"Literally, of course," Bartholomew said, lying down in his doggie bed.

I would have questioned him further, but he had already fallen asleep, no doubt exhausted from a long day of chasing automobiles and navigating wormholes.

The next to report on the unusual weather was our housekeeper, Nancy, who returned from her weekly trip to market at the stroke of eight.

"Fuck a duck!" her strong alto reverberated from the foyer. "It is raining motherfucking cats and dogs out there!"

"Do you not mean fish?" I inquired, leaning out of my chair so I could see from the parlor into the hallway.

"Not unless you know some fish with hair and legs and teeth and

16

shit," Nancy said. "Now please excuse me, I'd better put away these goddamn birds before they thaw."

I rose and stepped over to the front window. There was, indeed, a torrential downpour outside, but the fading light made it difficult to discern what the various wiggly objects falling from the sky might be. Moreover, as is the way with many incursions from other realities, the objects tended to disappear—I believe "phase out" is the technical term—when they contacted other solid matter in this reality.

There was a knock at the front door.

I opened the door. The being which stood before me was quite unprecedented. The overall shape of it was humanoid—bipedal, at any rate—but it wore no clothes, and instead of a single contiguous external integument, its outer skin appeared to be a wet mass of overlapping fish, varying in size and species, with the occasional crustacean or mollusk mixed in.

"Good evening," the creature said in a perfectly clear baritone. "Apologies for the intrusion, but I presume you are Doctor Robert Coombs, the renowned water-surgeon?"

I raised the two fluid appendages which had replaced my arms during my only excursion to another plane, and formed the extremities into a fringe of the thin, dexterous tendrils I employed in my work. "The same. How may I help you?"

"Not just myself, Doctor," the fish-being said. "Our entire homeworld is in dire straits."

THE WREN AND THE HEN
AND THE MEN IN THE PEN
October 9, 2009

Every morning, the wren descended from the baron's airship to visit with the hen in the barnyard. The hen neither desired or encouraged these conversations, but, confined as she was within her coop, could do little to prevent their occurrence.

On this morning, the wren shouted from far across the barnyard, "They're here! Can you see them? They're almost here!"

"Go away," said the hen, delivering her customary greeting.

The wren hit the ground and tumbled into the wire barrier around the chicken coop. "The baron's getting at least a hundred interns! They came by rail but the baron had to send trucks to bring them from the station to the north pasture!"

"I suppose that explains all the construction," the hen muttered. The humans had been running their machines day and night, building fences and towers and inexplicable metal things. "What are 'interns?'"

The wren said, "I don't know. But they're humans! I think they're like visitors. They're going to stay here in the baron's care!"

"Great," said the hen. She could hear the rumble of engines approaching. "More mouths to feed."

The farmer emerged from his house carrying an empty basket and stomped over to the coop.

"Morning, Rosie," he said. The hen ignored him.

"We're getting interns!" the wren shouted.

"None of my business," said the farmer, opening the chute at the bottom of the coop. "A little light today, Rosie?"

"Winter's coming," said the hen.

"You let me know if anyone starts shutting down for the season," the farmer said. "We just fenced off some new ground in the north pasture. Girls might enjoy the outdoors if they're not producing."

The hen knew Thirteen and Twenty-Two hadn't laid in almost a week. But no hens ever came back after being relocated.

"I'll let you know," said the hen.

The farmer turned and walked back into the house.

"You're not laying anymore!" the wren said to the hen.

"Shut up," said the hen.

"You could relocate with the other hens—"

"I said shut up!"

The hen snapped her beak. The wren hopped backward and cowered.

A caravan of trucks rolled up to the edge of the fence at the north pasture. The hen could see most of the enclosure behind the edge of the barn.

The baron's guards prodded a line of thin, bald men into the enclosure. The bald men all wore gray, and there were human symbols painted on their clothes and foreheads.

One of the bald men staggered and fell. The nearest guard ran up and began kicking him. The other bald men did nothing. They didn't even try.

The hen watched and wondered when the baron had decided to treat these men more like animals than humans. She also wondered how long it would be before the baron decided that even animals should be treated like property.

"How far can you fly?" the hen asked the wren.

The wren puffed out his chest with pride. "I've flown all the way to the ocean!"

The hen braced herself and said, "Tell me about it."

VAMPIRES OF NEW YORK
November 19, 2010

The thin girl in the silver bikini unwrapped her wrist slowly, as if she were doing a striptease. She must have been new. Max hadn't seen her in the club before, and he spent a lot of time in the club.

"I don't need the show, honey," Max said. "I'm just here for a drink."

The girl stopped and shrugged. "Whatever you say." She yanked the rest of the bandage off unceremoniously and held her wrist valve over Max's goblet, releasing a steady trickle of dark red liquid.

"You a vegetarian?" he asked. There was a faint grassy aroma to the girl's blood.

"I thought you just wanted to drink."

There goes your tip, thought Max.

The girl pulled a new bandage out of the dispenser attached to the table. She put a thumb over her valve to stop the flow, then wrapped the bandage around her wrist and turned away. She didn't even offer to let Max lick the blood off her thumb.

"Kids these days," he muttered.

"Talking to yourself again?" said a voice behind him. "Not going senile, are you?"

"You should be so lucky," Max said.

Josef walked around the table and sat down. "I swear, these chairs get less comfortable every time."

"Maybe you're losing weight."

"Don't you start with me. My doctor keeps telling me I can't drink positive. You believe that? I say he can tell me what to do when he's a hundred and twenty years old." He turned to flag down a waitress.

"Why do you keep dragging yourself to that free clinic?" Max asked. "Why don't you join a health plan like a normal person?"

Josef scowled. "Max. How can you ask me that? We both lived in the ghettos, we both went to the camps, how can you even ask me that?"

"It's not the same, Josef."

"It's never the same," Josef said. "They always find some new way to kill us."

Max shook his head. "Things are different, Josef. This is America."

Josef snorted. A blond waitress stopped next to him, and he smiled up at her. "Hey, sweetheart, what's on tap today?"

"A-positive, A-negative, B-pos, B-neg, O-neg," the waitress recited, chewing gum and clearly bored. "Soup of the day is beef and barley."

Josef grumbled. "Nothing AB? What's her name, the brunette with the curls?"

"Called in sick," the waitress said. "I can get you a plasma mixer."

Josef made a face. "Please don't. A-positive, make sure she's an omnivore. I can't stand that grassy vegetarian aftertaste. I want a girl who enjoys a good hamburger once in a while, you understand?"

The waitress nodded. "Stacy. I'll send her right over." She dropped a napkin on the table, then sashayed off toward the bar.

"Oh, look at that," Josef said, ogling the waitress' backside. "I tell you, Max, it's a damn shame we didn't get turned when we were younger. The things I'd do if I still had a twenty-nine-year-old body..."

"Please," Max said. "You'll ruin my appetite."

SECRET STASH
March 22, 2013

"The coffee was poisoned?"

Samantha didn't say it like a question; she said it like she didn't believe me. That just made me angrier.

"You want to talk to the doctor here? The alchemist?" I said, feeling the edges of my phone dig into my fingers. "Jake is in a fucking coma."

"Why weren't you affected?"

"Mom and Dad," I said. "Remember all those tinctures and potions they made us drink every morning? 'For luck, for protection?' We're immune to plant toxins and the most common thaumaturgic reagents."

"So you know what the poison was."

"We'll know in a few hours."

"Good," Sam said, sounding distracted. "I assume you want to stay there with Jake. I'll call Lee and ask him to send someone else back to the house."

I wasn't sure what to say, but I had to say something. "What?"

"Is it not Lee? Who's your supervisor these days?"

"What the fuck," I said, "are you talking about?"

Sam sighed. "Who should I call at your office to redeploy agents to the house? Just tell me, Rachel."

"You're not calling anyone," I said. "I'm waiting for the toxicology report, and then I'm getting a warrant and a SWAT team and breaking down that old geezer's front door."

"No, you're not," Sam said, in the tone of voice which asserted her older-sister-ness and which I hated down to my very bones. "The priority here is repatriating those artifacts. Look, don't worry about it. We'll send another team to negotiate—"

"I'm going to say this one time." I spoke slowly and clearly. "My partner is in a coma. Strickland poisoned us both. He is going down. We can seize the goddamn artifacts after he's behind bars."

"No, no, no," Sam said. "Once those jars are in a DC evidence locker, they become part of a criminal investigation, and it'll be hell to get them out of the system. No. We get Strickland to sign the papers as a free citizen; we remove the jars legally and *quietly*; and we avoid an international incident."

"And *then* we arrest Strickland for assaulting a federal officer?"

Sam hesitated before answering. "We can talk about that later."

"Don't fucking bullshit me here, Sam."

"Look," she said, "you want the truth? Strickland's going to ask for immunity from prosecution. He knows what he did, and he knows the value of those artifacts. He knows he has leverage."

"And my hands are tied here, Rachel. The Prime Minister of Egypt sat in the Oval Office and looked Marshall right in the eye and—"

"Oh, so it's 'Marshall' now?" I said. "Not 'Mr. President?'"

"*So* not the point right now, Rachel."

"You know what?" I pictured Sam sitting behind her giant wooden desk, and I focused my hatred. "Call whoever you want. I bet I can beat them back to Strickland's house with a black-and-white. Let's have a little race. Just like old times. Whaddya say, Sammy?"

"Rachel!" Sam said. "Do *not*—"

I hung up on her and headed out of the hospital.

THE RULE OF THREE
July 13, 2012

"Reload!" Janelle reached behind her and grasped empty air. "Reload, dammit!"

"No more speedloaders!" Traci shouted. "Use the shotgun!"

Janelle cursed, holstered the revolver, and swung the Remington off her shoulder and forward into both hands. She leveled the barrel at the abomination that was shambling toward them.

Thick, syrupy blood oozed from its neck and face, where four of the revolver rounds had torn through the gray flesh. At least one of those bullets must have gone through the brain—what was left of it, anyway.

So why is it still walking?

"There's only one," Janelle said. "This is a waste of ammo!"

"Seriously?" Traci said.

The zombie raised one skeletal arm toward their barricade. Janelle fired the shotgun, and the skull disintegrated with a sickening noise.

She lowered her weapon. "We need to get out of here."

"Finally, we agree—WHAT THE FUCK!"

Two clawlike hands appeared on top of the barricade and pulled up the rest of the undead body. The neck was a gray-red stump, leaking blood in weak spurts. The zombie drew itself up on top of the barricade.

Janelle fired again, and again, taking off both of the zombie's hands at the wrists. But it had already levered itself over the barricade, and tumbled onto the floor.

"It's still moving!" Traci said. "Why the *fuck* is it still moving?"

The zombie dragged itself to its wrists and knees and began crawling toward them. Janelle backed up, pressing herself against the wall next to Traci. *We don't have enough ammo for this.*

Something buzzed loudly from the doorway, and all the lights in the building went out. Janelle cursed and aimed the shotgun at where she hoped the zombie was.

But the shuffling had stopped. She heard clicking noises.

"Flashlight's dead," Traci said. Something snapped, and then a yellow light appeared.

She tossed the glowstick onto the floor, where the zombie lay sprawled, motionless.

"The hell?" Traci said, kneeling.

"Don't get too close," Janelle said.

"No worries, it's off now," came a voice from the doorway.

Janelle brought the shotgun up just as a flashlight went on, pointed at the ceiling, revealing a tall woman wearing police body armor. Both her hands were raised above her head.

"We're all friends here, now," the stranger said.

"That buzzing noise," Janelle said. "You did something to the zombie?"

"EMP. And it's not a zombie. That's why it didn't stop after you decapitated it."

"So what the hell is it?"

"It's a robot."

Janelle grimaced. "I'm not in the mood for jokes."

"No joke," the stranger said. "Nanotechnology gone wrong. Real bad news."

"That seems... implausible," Traci said.

"That ain't even the weird part," the stranger said.

"So what *is* the weird part?" Janelle asked.

"You know about the aliens, right?"

Janelle gaped. "Aliens."

"Yup," the stranger said. "Honest-to-gosh, invasion-from-outer-space, flying-saucer aliens. Seen 'em with my own eyes."

"I do not believe this," Janelle grumbled.

"Well," Traci said, "they do say that bad news comes in threes."

Janelle shook her head. "Please shut up now."

INTERVIEW WITH A GATEKEEPER
June 14, 2013

I open the door, I close the door. That's all. I don't look inside, I don't go through. You could not pay me enough to go through.

They say what's on the other side always changes. It's different for every person, and different every time that person opens and closes the door. Sometimes it changes on *both* sides, and the person who went in never comes out. We give them forty-eight hours. Then we have to send the next one in.

It's busier here than you might think. Anyone above a certain national security clearance has to open the door. Every President since Carter has had to at least look inside before taking office. Sometimes they step through, but we never close the door on them. Can't take the chance that he'll disappear. Even if he freaks out— well, that's why we have them do it, right? To see if they can handle it.

No. We have no idea how it works. Every now and then, the eggheads come by with some new sensor they've cooked up. They're always disappointed when they leave. And they always argue about who has to open the door.

See, the door knows who's opening it. It has to, right? Because it shows you something that will scare the shit out of you specifically, and only you. It also knows if there's more than one person looking inside. If there are two or more observers, it does nothing—open it and you see the back wall there. The door works for a single person at a time, and it's eyes-only—no photos, no video. If you try to record what you see, it just doesn't work.

And isn't that almost scarier than the door being a portal to weird-ass places which don't exist? It implies that the door can tell the future. It doesn't decide to *stop* working *after* you open the door and pull out your phone to take a picture; it doesn't work at all in the first place. It knows what you're going to do.

But here's the other thing. You see how they installed the door here? It opens toward you. It doesn't work if you open it from the other side, pushing the door away; it only works if you pull it open.

Now think about the doors you have in your own house, like your front door. You *pull* the door open when you're *inside*. You push when you're entering the house, pull when you're leaving.

So here's my question. We can open the door and go through—*out*—to whatever bizarre reality it's created for your own personal torment. But every time we do that, what the hell might we be letting back into our world?

I'm pretty sure we won't like the answer, whenever we finally find out. But that won't be anytime soon. Meanwhile, you know, it's a paycheck. I'm not rigging elections or doing illegal domestic surveillance or anything morally questionable like that.

I open the door, I close the door. That's it.

TRANSPORT
July 9, 2010

"I'm going to let him out of the bag for a minute."

"Do not let him out of the bag."

"Just for a minute."

"Do not open that bag!"

The armored truck's front left tire hit a pothole, and Derek cursed as he bounced in the driver's seat. The heavy vehicle, swathed in steel and doused with drag-inducing kinetic wards, handled like a drunk beaver on stilts.

Jay, the younger man in the passenger seat, craned his neck to look at the man-sized lump wrapped in sackcloth and chained to the floor of the rear compartment.

"Are you sure he can breathe in there?" Jay asked.

"You do remember what his power is, don't you?" Derek replied. "He's a persuader. He influences people, gets them to do what he wants."

"Well, that's why we're wearing these, right?" Jay lifted the diamond-shaped pendant around his neck. "Besides, if he were controlling me, I'd probably just pull my gun on you."

Derek grunted. "It's not that simple. He doesn't pull your strings like a puppetmaster. He gets under your skin, into your subconscious. Makes you think you believe things you don't. You don't even realize you're being influenced. Guys like this don't leave fingerprints."

"Guess we're lucky to have caught him at all, then." Jay cocked his head. "Did you hear that?"

Derek kept his eyes on the road. "No."

"Sounded like coughing."

He unbuckled his seat belt and leaned toward the doorway. Derek took one hand off the steering wheel, grabbed the roll bar behind his head, and yanked the wheel over hard. The truck swerved, knocking Jay's head against the passenger side window. The truck flipped onto its left side, scraped down the road, and shuddered to a stop.

Jay's unconscious form had fallen onto Derek and pinned him. Derek flexed his fingers, tracing sigils in the air. A blue cloud appeared and levitated Jay's limp body into the rear compartment. Derek disentangled himself from his seat belt and the airbag which had deployed from the steering column, then climbed through the doorway.

The prisoner stood on the wall which was now down, both arms lifted by the shackle and chain holding him to the vertical floor. His head, still bagged, wiggled from side to side, but stopped when Derek hopped down into the compartment.

"What's going on?" the prisoner called out.

Derek didn't answer. He looked down and moved his fingers again. Jay's right arm stiffened, lifted a key off his belt, and clumsily unlocked the shackle around the prisoner's left wrist.

"You gave him a dead charm," the prisoner said. "You're a controller, too! You breakin' me out, bro?"

Derek drew his sidearm from its holster, cocked it, and aimed at the prisoner's chest. "Killed while trying to escape."

"What?" The prisoner jerked back. "Wait! Let's talk about this!"

"Say hello to my daughter for me," Derek said.

He pulled the trigger once, twice, three times, and then it was over.

GIRLFIGHTCLUB
October 22, 2010

"Can't fight if you don't eat," the guard said.

Galena stared at the puddle of gruel on her tray. "Maybe I don't want to fight."

"Don't fight, don't live."

"Catchy. Can I get that on a t-shirt?"

The guard tossed a spoon into the cell. "Eat."

Galena choked down the food. It wasn't supposed to be appetizing. It was designed to prevent starvation. Nobody was allowed to die outside the arena.

The lights went out at midnight. Galena counted to one hundred, then silently rolled out of bed and felt her way over to the corner of her cell.

Her fingernails caught on the edge of the loose brick next to the toilet. She was just starting to pry it out of the wall when she heard an unfamiliar shuffling noise. It was headed directly for Galena's cell.

She coughed loudly to cover the sound of her pushing the brick back into place, then summoned a belch to mask the noise of pulling her pants down and sitting on the toilet.

A small, bright light clicked on and shone in her face. She squinted into it and crossed her arms over her crotch. "What the hell!"

"Galena Moritz?" It wasn't the guard. It was a woman.

"Sorry, Miss Moritz is currently indisposed," Galena said. "If you'd like to leave a message—"

The flashlight beam swung up, illuminating the visitor's face. Galena's mouth hung open.

"So you recognize me," Aurelia Langwies said. "Good. Put your pants on and let's go for a walk."

"You want to trade places with me?"

They were walking around the darkened exercise yard, illuminated only by moonlight.

"Pay attention," Aurelia said. "You take my place in the ring. I go into hiding. The quod thinks you've escaped and replaces you with another plebeian."

"Great plan," Galena said. "I love it, except for the part where I get caught and executed."

"Nobody will ever see your face," Aurelia said. "I have a reputation as a recluse. I arrive in full armor, and I never unmask."

"What if I get injured?" Galena asked.

"You're too good for that."

"It's not about being good," Galena said. "I watched Kalium go down last week after slipping on a piece of fruit. My luck won't last forever."

"By contract, only my personal physician can treat me. Both he and my agent are in on the plan." Aurelia stepped closer. "I know about your child. That's why I came to you. I knew you'd understand why I'm doing this."

"Because you're insane?"

"None of us fight by choice," Aurelia snapped. "And if I don't fight, my family suffers. Do you understand that?"

Galena nodded, thinking of her son. "I'm not left-handed."

Aurelia smiled. "I'm going to take a blow to the head in my next bout, and the concussion will affect my mental state."

"And your height?"

"Oh, honey," Aurelia said, "I wear lifts."

Galena chuckled and looked up at the moon. She knew the charade would never survive a whole nine months, but any freedom was better than none.

GODWIN'S BACKSTORY
April 22, 2011

The elevator ride up to the seventh floor seemed to take forever. Michael's hands weren't cuffed, but the three armed guards behind him and Denford made it clear that Michael was not a welcome guest.

Michael said, "Do you remember the first time you learned about 'Godwin's Law?'"

Denford kept staring straight ahead. "I thought you only reported to the old man now."

"I'm not reporting," Michael said. "We're just chatting."

Denford didn't reply.

"I hear it happened on the Russian Far East desk," Michael continued. "A local sport diver sensed Teutonic wards all over a shipwreck near Sakhalin. Nothing of obvious intel value, so nobody was very interested at first—except one World War Two enthusiast, an up-and-coming CIA supervisor named Theodore Godwin.

"It turned out that his division was trying to set up a completely unrelated operation near Vladivostok, and the only reasonable way to get their agents on site was by submarine out of Japan. But it was a high-risk, low-reward situation, and nobody wanted to stick their neck out for it. Godwin really believed, but he didn't have the clout to make it happen.

"Anyway, a few days later, another wire comes across the desk with new information about the Sakhalin shipwreck, and guess what? Somebody who saw the diver's photos is pretty sure that was a Nazi vessel, and there could be military artifacts on board. Maybe even some of Hitler's amulets.

"Well, all of a sudden, everyone and his dog is rushing to greenlight a recovery operation, and Godwin says you know, as long as we're out there near Sapporo with a submarine anyway, why don't we just go ahead and run this op that my division's been trying to clear for the last two months?"

Denford finally turned to look at Michael. "Yeah, I know the story. There's nothing in the shipwreck but barnacles and fish skeletons, but the old man lucks out and snags some prize intel on Soviet Fleet deployments. He gets on the fast track to director."

"And nobody could ever prove that Godwin doctored those shipwreck reports, or persuaded someone to do it for him, but that's irrelevant. The real lesson was, if you can draw some kind of line, no matter how thin or how convoluted, that connects your proposal to Hitler, your chances of approval magically and dramatically improve." Michael shrugged. "Godwin's Law."

The elevator stopped, and the doors opened. Denford and Michael marched forward, followed by the guards.

"Was there a point to all that?" Denford asked. "Or were you just running your mouth?"

"We're never going to catch Hitler," Michael said. "We missed our chance in 1945, and it'll never come again. But he's actually more valuable this way.

"As long as there's still some mystery surrounding him, we'll want to know more. And some people can use that. They can sell the question without ever worrying what the answer is going to be."

The double doors to the director's suite opened.

"Sometimes," Michael said, "we don't really want to know the answers."

POKER FACE
August 31, 2012

"It's a trick," Adkins said. "He's reading your expressions or something, looking for reactions to what he says. Like some fake carnival psychic."

"It ain't a trick!" Berk said. "Rosebud, close your eyes."

"Fine," Roseler said, and closed his eyes. "McCue's looking for a... *four* to make a straight flush. Anderson wants a jack for three of a kind, or a five for two pair. And Gray..." He opened his eyes. "Gray's a good poker player."

"What do you mean?" Berk asked. "You can't read him?"

Roseler nodded. Gray's face was as still as stone, but more than that, his mind was masked. Roseler could tell there were thoughts moving inside that head, but he couldn't get a good sense of what they were; it felt like looking through a fogged-up window, or trying to hear voices behind a thick door.

This was obviously not just a put-on for the card game. But Roseler wasn't going to tell on Gray. Not yet, anyway.

"It takes some practice, but anyone can do it," Roseler said, not taking his eyes off Gray. "You don't think about your specific cards. You look at them, and then you forget about them."

"How the hell do you play when you don't know what you're holding?" Adkins asked.

"Think about it. You don't see anyone else's cards, right? You're guessing at what they have based on what they *do*. So you just need to decide what you're going to do in response. The cards don't enter into it at a certain point. It's all about psychology."

"But you can tell if someone's bluffing," Gray said. "Right?"

"Sometimes," Roseler said.

"Officer on deck!" Adkins shouted. All five sailors jumped to their feet as Ensign Young stepped into the doorway.

"As you were," Young said. He thumbed the stack of file folders he was carrying. "I'm looking for Seaman Gray and Seaman Roseler. And I trust this is just a friendly game of cards here."

"Yes, sir! Just playing some bridge, sir!" Adkins said, a little too quickly.

Young looked around. "Five for bridge?"

"We're teaching Rosebud," Berk said.

"He's terrible at bidding," McCue added.

"Well, you'll have to work on that later, Roseler," Young said. "Master Chief needs you and Gray to come help with a thing."

Roseler frowned. "Um, why the two of us in particular, sir?"

Young shrugged. "Some kind of magic thing. Your intake files here say you both tested positive for aptitude."

Gray stiffened, and Roseler felt his own stomach knotting up.

"That may be, sir, but I've never had any formal training," Roseler said.

"Me neither," Gray said. "I don't know how useful we would be—"

"I'm sorry, did I give the impression I was making a request?" Young snapped. "Report to Master Chief Erickson, and he'll tell you what's up. That's an order. Got it?"

"Yes, sir," Roseler and Gray replied in unison.

"And take these files with you. Dismissed." Young pushed the files into Gray's arms and turned to the other three sailors. "So, you boys play Hearts?"

RHYMES WITH PORK
May 28, 2010

You are in a small windowless room. To the north is a blank door. An orange cat sits in the middle of the floor.

The cat rubs up against you.
> **open door**

You can't reach the door. The cat is weaving between your legs, impeding your forward motion.

The cat meows at you.
> **push door**

You can't reach the door.

The cat is yelling at you now and scratching your leg.
> **kick cat**

The cat skillfully dodges your foot. Also, you're a dick.

The cat continues yelling at you.
> **pet cat**

The cat nuzzles your hand and continues yelling.
> **feed cat**

You don't have any cat food.

The cat won't stop yelling at you.
> **inventory**

```
You are carrying:
1 half-eaten sandwich
1 back issue of Wired magazine
2 large tomatoes
1 keycard
> look keycard
```

DRUNK HULK NOT KNOW WHAT YOU MEAN
```
> examine keycard
```

The keycard is a flat plastic badge of the type issued
by many tech companies. The employee photo looks like
one of the dudes from Flight of the Conchords. There's
no company name.

The cat is still yelling at you.
```
> use keycard
```

Use it on what?
```
> use keycard on cat
```

The cat licks the keycard, then continues yelling.
```
> give sandwich to cat
```

The cat sniffs the sandwich, makes a face, and backs
away, yelling.
```
> give tomato to cat
```

Why would a cat want a tomato? Get real.

The cat is still yelling at you.
```
> read Wired
```

You flip through the magazine. It's the one where they
talk about Google.

The cat is still yelling at you.
```
> look sandwich
```

DRUNK HULK THINK YOU FAIL KINDERGARTEN
```
> examine sandwich
```

For some reason, you have a half-eaten ham and cheese sandwich sealed in a zip-top bag. It's hard to tell how old the thing is, but that fuzzy white stuff all over the bread can't be a good sign.

The cat bites your ankle.
> **grab cat**

The cat deftly avoids your clumsy grasp.

The cat is still yelling at you.
> **tear magazine**

You rip several pages out of the back issue of Wired.

The cat is still yelling at you.
> **crumple pages**

You crumple the torn magazine pages into paper balls.

The cat is still yelling at you.
> **throw balls**

You toss the paper balls across the room, one by one. The cat stops yelling and watches with great interest, leaping into the air to intercept each projectile, then batting it around the floor.
> **open door**

The door doesn't have a handle or knob. You can't open it.
> **push door**

The door won't budge.
> **pull door**

The door doesn't have anything for you to grab onto.
> **use keycard on door**

You swipe the keycard across the blank surface of the
door. After a moment, you hear a beep, then a click.
The door pops outward slightly.
> **push door**

The door swings open to reveal a second windowless
room. There is a gray cat sitting in the middle of the
floor.

The gray cat starts yelling at you.

WHO DIED?
May 24, 2013

If you tell me, I can bring him back. Or her. Whoever it was. Tell me.

Oh, no. Stop. I'm sorry, I wasn't clear. It has to be your first. Yes, the very first. Your first experience with death. It may not have been a human; perhaps it was a pet, a goldfish or dog or—no? All right. But it must be your first.

I'll know if you're lying. It only works if you tell the truth. It has to be the first. The first death which made it clear to you that death is real, permanent, pervasive, inescapable. Your first. That's the only one I can bring back.

That doesn't mean it has to be someone who was close to you. That's the other thing everybody gets wrong. It's not the first person who died and affected you in some deep, traumatic, emotional way. No. It's simply your first death, the one that exposed the reality of dying to you.

Yes, they do often coincide, and those stories are as horrible as they are pedestrian; the young child who loses a parent, we've all heard that one, haven't we? But the good news is, I can do something about it. I can bring that parent back. If that was your first death.

Well, of course there's a price. Isn't there always? That's how this works. The price, in this case, is your memory.

Oh, not your entire memory. Heavens, no! That would be unspeakably cruel. I only take that single memory, of your first encounter with death. That moment of revelation, when you understood that the Reaper was whispering around every corner, waiting for each of us at the end.

I take that memory, and you get your dearly departed back.

Of course, there will be certain side effects. That knowledge of death, of what it does and how it affects us, has informed every decision you've ever made since you acquired it. You would have been a very different person without it. And once I take that memory, you will be different.

Not different in any noticeable way; not at first. You'll still be you, with the same personality, the same fears and foibles as always. But you'll not have the same understanding of death any longer. You'll have to go through that experience again. You'll have to relive your first death.

Maybe it will be easier this time, better; maybe it'll be worse. Who can say? Some actually desire that opportunity, that second chance to grasp the ineffable.

But in any case, you'll have your dead back. That's the important thing, for most; they're willing to sacrifice to save that person. They're willing to plunge themselves into the unknown for the guarantee of seeing their long-lost loved one, alive again.

Oh, I can't tell you what happened to any of the others. Also part of the bargain, I'm afraid. You don't get to play the odds. You must decide with only the information I've given you.

Have you decided? Excellent.

So, tell me: who died?

FRIDAY THE THIRTIETH
October 29, 2010

The first postcard simply said "Have a killer birthday," with a photo from an old cemetery on the other side. No signature, no return address. I figured it was a joke, one of my old sorority sisters who'd seen my Facebook post and felt like messing with me.

The next few were the same kind of thing: "One day closer to dying," "Nobody lives forever," stuff like that. All with pictures of cemeteries in New England.

It wasn't until they started writing the messages in blood that I began to worry. I know because I scraped off some flakes, snuck them into the hospital where I worked, and tested them. Human blood, type A negative. No joke.

I had expected to get some weird stuff. It was one of those stupid ideas you have late at night, after drinking a little too much and maybe smoking something not quite legal. And yeah, I'll admit, I was feeling lonely. I was turning thirty in less than a month, and I didn't have a boyfriend or a decent career or a pony.

So I decided I'd ping my friends, ask them to send me postcards for my birthday. My parents moved around a lot when I was younger, so I knew people all around the world. I didn't specify what people should write on their cards. I figured I'd let them exercise their creativity. I just wanted to feel loved—or at least liked.

I posted on Facebook, sent a few mass e-mails, and waited. I got some nice postcards, but after a week of also getting a creepy graveyard image every day, I wasn't looking forward to the mail so much as dreading it.

After the tenth postcard—the one which talked about how many pints of blood are in a human body, and how many square feet of wall that could paint—I called in sick and sat by the window and waited for the mailman. He showed up around eleven o'clock. I

42

walked up just as he was pulling out a plastic bin full of catalogs and credit card offers.

"You got anything for number twelve?" I asked.

The mailman turned and stared at me. "Hello. Have we met?"

"Apartment twelve," I said. "I'm expecting a postcard."

He smiled. "Ah, it's you. Of course." He turned back to his truck.

"Listen, aren't there federal laws against tampering with mail?" I asked. "Or sending hazardous materials? I only ask because I've been getting postcards written in blood, and that seems, I don't know, like it might be not okay."

The mailman turned back to me, grinning and holding a single postcard. His eyes glowed red, like coal embers inside his skull.

"I'm just the messenger," he said.

He thrust the postcard into my hands and disappeared in a plume of smoke.

After I finished freaking out, I sat down on the ground and looked at the postcard. The picture showed Edgar Allan Poe's gravestone. The message said:

Happy Birthday! You have been chosen. Enjoy the cake!

I'm really not looking forward to the cake.

Curtis C. Chen

QUESTION OF THE DAY
August 12, 2011

"How do you want to die?"

He was just a minor demon, from the look of him: one who could only affect very specific objects or events. They'd infested inner cities all over the world in the last few years. Not usually dangerous, just a nuisance.

What made me stop walking was the way he'd asked the question: not as a threat, but very matter-of-factly, almost like a presenter on some chat show. I looked over his rough horns, brick-coloured skin, and tattered clothes. Black hooves poked out the bottoms of his trouser legs.

"That's quite an unusual question," I said.

The demon blinked at me. "It's the only power I have. To affect how a human life ends. You'd think more people might be interested—I mean, you're mortal, aren't you? You've got to die someday. Why not have some say in how it happens?"

I knelt down and dropped a few coins into his battered tin cup. He nodded thanks at me.

"The thing is," I said, "most people don't like to think about dying. They'd like to believe they'll live forever."

"You're telling me," said the demon. "Smoking, having unprotected sex, driving automobiles—some of you are honestly just asking for it, all the time. Thought I'd have more takers. Turns out I got stuck with a bloody worthless power."

"So how does it work?" I asked. "Let's say, for example, that I wanted to die while shagging a supermodel."

"I'm not a bleeding genie." The demon looked rather offended. "It's not the Make-a-Wish Foundation here. I can only affect natural causes, within your own body, right? Say you don't fancy dying of cancer; I can guarantee you die of some other disease."

44

Something clicked inside my brain. "Hang on. So if I say I want to die of old age—"

"No, it's got to be a specific ailment."

"All right, let's say smallpox then. You're saying if I ask for that, you can fix it so I won't die of anything else? I'd be able to, for example, smoke all I want and not worry about lung cancer, guaranteed?"

The demon wrinkled his snout. "Well, there is a bit of a catch."

"I knew it." A lot of magic had escaped into the world—along with the demons—when Hell froze over, but it was all pretty dodgy.

"You wouldn't die of lung cancer, but you might still get it," the demon said. "You'd still suffer the symptoms. It's not a free pass to live recklessly, without regard for your health."

"Well, what good is it then?"

"I never claimed it was any good." The demon shrugged. "It's what I can do."

I stood up and pulled out my wallet. "Well, thanks for the chat, anyway. Never actually spoken to a demon before." I dropped a fiver in his cup. "Best of luck."

He smiled and scooped the cash out of the cup. "Cheers, mate. You change your mind, you know where to find me."

I shook my head and walked away.

IT'S NOT THE HEAT, IT'S THE STUPIDITY
June 18, 2010

The elastic snapped and flew out of Maria's hand before she could wrap it around her hair. She cursed and held her ponytail in place while searching for another elastic. If she let go, the hair would fall and stick to her sweat-soaked skin.

Maria continued walking to keep the air moving over her skin. It hadn't rained for weeks. She looked forward to getting back to her apartment and sitting in front of the ancient air conditioner. Noisy, but it worked.

There it is. She pulled a hair elastic out of her back jeans pocket and tilted her head down to tie up her ponytail. The pavement curved right. Just a few more minutes, a quick jog up the always-stuffy stairwell, and she could cool off.

Just a few more weeks, and she'd be out of the city forever.

Somebody whistled ahead of her. "Lookin' good, *senorita!*"

Maria looked up. Three *cholos* sat on the front steps leading into her building, one of them built like a tank, another adorned with tattoos, the third holding an unlit cigarette between his lips. All three wore blood-red bandanas.

Perfect. That's just perfect.

She slowed her pace and lowered her hands to her sides. The men watched her—not looking for threats, but ogling her figure. Maria had considered the risks when choosing her outfit this morning, but her desire for comfort had outweighed her modesty. She stopped a few feet from the nearest *cholo* and turned out her pockets.

"That's all I got, guys," Maria said, holding out two dollar bills and her go-phone. "Take it or leave it."

Non-Smoker stood up, shaking his head. "Don't want your phone. But we sure gonna take something. Ain't that right, boys?"

"I like what I see," Tattoo grunted.

"I'd like to see a little more," said Tank.

Seriously?

Maria looked up and down the street. Empty. Chances were somebody would notice three gang-bangers raping a woman in broad daylight and probably call 911...

"Look," she said, "I'm not going to fight, but can we at least go inside? This is my building. It's got AC."

"Hey, no problem," Non-Smoker said, stepping aside. "Anything to make your experience more... pleasurable."

They snickered as she walked up the steps and unlocked the door, then followed her inside. She waited until she heard the door click shut again.

"Damn!" said Non-Smoker. "You need to talk to your landlord, girl, because this air is *not* conditioned—"

Maria whirled around with her wrists together and palms forward, her fingers curved around an invisible ball. She whispered three syllables, and a wave of energy rippled from her hands and through the *cholos*. The three bodies smashed up against the closed door and turned to ash. Their clothes and bandanas fell into a dusty heap.

Three more souls, Maria thought. *I'm never going to get out of this damn city.*

On the bright side, the spell had been endothermic, taking heat energy out of the surrounding air. She actually had a pleasant walk up the stairs for once.

WHAT YOU SHOULD KNOW ABOUT WATER RITES
February 20, 2009

A familiar prickling under Chiwetel's chin woke him. He always wondered why Ekon liked to curl up there. Chiwetel slid a hand under the hedgehog and gently rolled him away.

Chiwetel sat up, shivering. He pulled two sweatshirts on over his damp t-shirt. He hadn't been prepared for this city. One minute the sun was shining, and the next there was rain. Chiwetel had never lived in such a place.

He scooped up Ekon with both hands and walked out of the grove to a public fountain. Chiwetel pulled a crumpled paper cup from his jeans, filled it, and held the cup while Ekon drank. After breakfast—dry bread for Chiwetel, berries for Ekon—Chiwetel slung his backpack over his shoulder and tucked Ekon inside his sweatshirt pocket.

The exterior of the Conservatory of Flowers glittered, its Victorian architecture unlike anything Chiwetel had ever seen in person. It was like a dollhouse, ornamented and precious.

The woman in the foyer took Chiwetel's wrinkled five-dollar bill with mild disgust on her face. He could feel her watching as he went inside. He didn't care what she thought of him.

He walked through the doors into a different world, humid and green.

"Good morning!" said a man wearing coveralls and a name tag.

"Hello," Chiwetel said. His heart was pounding. Why should this old gardener make Chiwetel more nervous than a truckload of rebels with automatic weapons?

Chiwetel hurried into the next room. He walked without stopping, past the exotic orchids and ferns, and through the door marked *Aquatic Plants*.

A pool of dark water filled the room. Plants that looked like large, green, upturned jar lids floated at one end. They were circular, as wide across as a man was tall, with flat edges folded up to reveal sharp red spines beneath.

Chiwetel slipped Ekon onto the nearest giant lily pad—*Victoria amazonica*, the sign said—and held both hands over the little one when he squeaked. Chiwetel knelt down and unpacked the supplies. A lock of hair. A tiny tooth. A bag of dirt.

He piled everything on a leaf ripped from the nearest vine, grabbed a rock from a bonsai display, and smashed his ingredients while chanting in a dead language.

The old gardener came in and shouted as Chiwetel was dumping powder around Ekon. Chiwetel finished drawing the circle, dropped the leaf, and pulled the gun out of his waistband. The man wouldn't know it wasn't loaded.

"Stay back," Chiwetel said.

The man stopped and held up his hands. Ekon looked up and squeaked.

"What the hell?"

Chiwetel wasn't sure if he was sweating, or if it was just the humidity. "Do not interfere," he said.

"I don't even know what—"

A flash of light blinded them both, and the man rushed forward. Chiwetel let him take the gun and leaned over the pool to look down at the lily pad.

Lying there, naked and dark-skinned and human, was an infant boy. He gurgled and smiled. Chiwetel felt his face dripping wetness into the pond, causing ripples.

Curtis C. Chen

Thursday's Children

REUNION
May 8, 2009

The girl standing on Ellen's doorstep is drenched. She looks like a wet cat, her dyed red-and-purple hair flattened against her small head. Cold wind blows past her into the house as Ellen stands there, frozen.

"Are you Ellen Montgomery?" the girl shouts over the storm.

Somewhere behind Ellen, a tea kettle whistles.

"Ellen Montgomery!" the girl repeats, enunciating as if she thinks Ellen might have a hearing problem. "Is that you?"

"Yes!" Ellen says. "Yes, that's me."

"Can I come in, please?" the girl asks, her voice a little more respectful now.

Ellen says, "Who are you?"

The girl says, "I'm your daughter!"

Neither of them drinks her tea. Ellen's cup sits on the table, steaming away its heat, while the girl—she says her name is Theora—cradles her cup with both hands, still shivering.

Ellen shakes her head as she flips through the contents of the folder, the papers and films still curled and warm from being hidden beneath Theora's hoodie.

"Where did you get all this?" Ellen asks.

Theora shrugs. "It wasn't easy. I mean, the DNA I did first, that was easy—I just sent away for one of those heritage-testing kits from NatGeo, right? And then I knew I was adopted."

"I'm not sure what I can do for you," Ellen says.

"I just wanted to meet you," Theora says. "And warn you."

"Warn me? About what?"

Theora's face is an unreadable mask. Ellen wonders if that's a natural expression, or if the girl's been practicing for a long time.

Theora takes both hands away from her teacup. Ellen lunges forward to catch the cup before it hits the floor, but it hangs there in midair. Then it rises. Ellen watches it float up to Theora's eye level.

"That's not—" Something sparks inside Ellen's head, and she crumples to the ground, unconscious.

When Ellen wakes up, she's got a splitting headache. She sits up on the couch and sees Theora on the floor.

Ellen feels a sharp pain as she turns her head. She touches the back of her neck and feels a patchwork of bandages. Her hand comes away sticky with not-quite-dried blood.

"What did you do?" Ellen asks Theora.

The girl holds out her left hand. Her palm has been stained red by the tiny tangle of wires she's holding. Ellen can see a small bulb at the center of the mass, like a spider with too many legs.

"They lied to you," Theora says. "They can't do a permanent memory wipe. This thing was suppressing your recall. My biological father had one too."

"You met Michael?" Ellen asks. "You found him?"

"Yeah," Theora says, looking down. "I couldn't remove his implant before it—I couldn't get it out in time. I'm sorry."

Ellen feels like she should cry.

"We need to go," Theora says, standing up.

"Go where? Why?"

Theora starts to reply, but Ellen can't hear her. A vivid flood of sounds and smells and sensations is filling her head, blotting out the present with the past.

MONEY FOR NOTHING
August 9, 2013

"Don't know why you're wasting your time with the lottery," Rutina says, watching me twirl the ticket between my fingers.

It's because I know something you don't, Ruti. And I can't tell you my secret. It's too dangerous.

I don't know if this will work. It's a long shot, but even if it doesn't pan out, I'm only out a few bucks. And, you know, a third of the money goes toward public education. Hopefully including basic math skills.

The TV announcer shouts something—I'm only half listening, focusing my attention on the Lotto ticket, the object I want to push. Out of the corner of my eye, I see white balls spinning inside a metal cage.

"Maybe turn it down a bit," I say. "We just got Wally to sleep." A crying baby will definitely affect my concentration.

"Tevs." Ruti lowers the volume.

I have no idea what I'm doing. If I do win the lottery, how much luck does that count for? What's the price? Because I don't *make* the luck I push onto things—I *steal* it from somewhere else. And I'm always hoping it comes from someone I don't care about.

Ruti punches me in the arm.

"Ow!" I glare at her.

"Did you win or not, weirdo?"

I look up. I read the numbers on the TV screen, then compare them to my ticket. I read them again. And again.

"Well?" Ruti says.

"I did it," I say. "I won."

"Hey, Ollie! You're on TV!"

I rush out from the kitchen where I'm helping Ruti's mom with the dishes. Ruti's bouncing excitedly on the couch. Of course the news chose the worst possible photo of me, the one with my hair in those stupid curls, but the big number floating beside my dopey face softens the blow.

Six zeros. Two commas. More money than I've ever imagined.

And sure, a lump sum payout will be only half that amount, and income taxes will eat half of that, but that still leaves eight figures. Over a hundred thousand dollars, tax-free, every year for the rest of my life.

As soon as I finish doing the math, I'm reminded it's all too good to be true.

When I regain my senses, I'm kneeling on the floor, crying. Ruti is next to me, holding me upright.

"Ollie, what's wrong?" she asks. I point at the TV. "Who is that?"

"Dead," I sob. "He's—supposed—to be—dead."

Ruti's mom crouches down and puts a hand on my shoulder. "It's okay, Olivia. We'll figure this out."

"Mom?" Ruti says. "Do you know what she's talking about?"

Mrs. Alwen nods. "I haven't seen him in years, but that looks like Olivia's birth father."

So this is the price. This is what I have to live through to win the lottery.

Jesus, we're all going to be at the award ceremony, all four of us together. I don't know if I can do it. Mom sure can't. And I don't know how we're going to keep Steven from killing him.

BACHELOR OF SCIENCE
January 9, 2009

"Brandon, can I see you in my office?"

Brandon sighed and locked his computer before standing up. The other engineers on the third floor were always eager to prank someone who hadn't properly secured his workstation.

He followed his new manager down the hall casually—without delay, but not too fast, lest anybody think he actually *wanted* to talk to David, who kept telling everyone to call him "Dave," as if that would make him seem like more of a pal.

David had sat down at his desk and was typing. He nodded at Brandon as he walked in.

"One second," said David. "Would you mind closing the door?"

Brandon turned around. The engineer sitting across the hall raised his hand and made a slicing motion across his throat. Brandon held up one finger and closed the door.

"Thanks," David said as Brandon sat down. "Don't worry, it's nothing bad, I just wanted to discuss a personal matter." He faked a smile, as if that would ease Brandon's concerns. "HR says you've worked here for six years, but only been promoted once. Why is that?"

Brandon rolled his eyes. "I like my job."

"Someone with your talents could have a more interesting career."

"Writing kernel code for cell phones?"

David smiled, and it was the first genuine emotion that Brandon had seen on his face. "No. I'm talking about what you can do with your mind. Your powers of persuasion."

Brandon shot to his feet, knocking his chair over, and backed into the office door.

"We don't have a name for it," David said, standing up and

walking around his desk. "It's not 'telepathy,' and 'mind control' is inaccurate and cheesy."

Brandon closed his fingers around the door handle. He stared at David and concentrated.

"See, I know what you're doing." David folded his arms and leaned against the wall. "You can *influence* people, and right now you're trying to make me forget. It's not going to work, because I have the same power—and I've been trained."

Brandon gritted his teeth. "What do you want?"

"I'm here to recruit you."

"For what? Some government bullshit? Not interested."

David laughed. "Well, we can do this the easy way—"

He gasped and fell to his knees. Brandon ran over and caught David before he did a face plant onto the carpet.

"Here's the thing," Brandon said. "I have more than one superpower. I'm guessing you don't, otherwise I wouldn't have been able to stop your heart." He lowered David to the floor and made a show of checking his pulse. "Sorry, but I'm sure you would have killed me, or worse. And I need the head start."

He jumped up, threw open the door, and yelled, "Somebody call 911!"

People swarmed out of their cubicles. Brandon asked where he could find a first aid kit, knowing full well that the closest one was with the receptionist on the first floor. He grabbed his backpack and ran for the stairs. He didn't know when he would be able to stop running.

SWEET NOTHINGS
December 31, 2010

Amy concentrated while holding the piece of candy, thinking: *You're not fat. Stop cutting yourself. You are not fat.*

The girl on the other side of the counter was wearing long sleeves, but Amy had seen her bare wrists when she turned to point something out to one of her friends. The older scars were horizontal, across the width of the girl's arm; but the newer, brick-red scabs were diagonal slashes, turning ever closer to fatal.

"Here's a free sample of our Milk Bordeaux," Amy said, identifying the candy in the tiny paper cup as she slid it across the top of the counter.

"Thanks," the girl said, picking up the candy between her thumb and forefinger.

You're not fat, Amy kept thinking. She was pretty sure her power to imbue objects with thought impulses only worked as long as she was touching them, but it couldn't hurt to try.

She forced a smile while ringing up the girl's purchases. Amy's face was starting to feel sore from feigning holiday cheer. After the teenagers had left, Amy rubbed her jaw muscles with both hands.

"Long day?" said a male voice.

Amy looked up and saw Joe leaning against the doorway and smiling at her. His mall security uniform was rumpled, as always, but Amy knew that was just an act; when push came to shove, the stern looks he could summon far outweighed his informal appearance.

"At least it's Friday," Amy said. "Free sample?"

"Nah," Joe said, patting his midsection. "I get enough of that at home."

"Right," Amy said, smiling. "I forget your wife's got that cottage industry—"

An arm appeared over Joe's left shoulder, and the attached hand closed around his throat. Joe made a gurgling noise and jerked forward and to the side.

Amy saw the owner of the arm, a stocky bald man wearing a gray suit and dark glasses. The man's other arm raised a menacing black pistol to the side of Joe's head.

"Step out from behind the counter," the man said.

Amy couldn't say anything for a second. "M-me?"

The man looked annoyed. "Yes, you! Amy Washington! Get out here before I—"

As suddenly as the man had appeared, he stopped talking. His hands twitched, and Amy was afraid the gun would go off; but then his entire body went limp, and he crumpled to the floor. Joe fell forward, also unconscious, and Amy rushed around the counter to help him. She froze when she saw the woman.

The woman—tall, blond, imposing—stood behind the collapsed man. She had one hand inside her jacket, which she slowly withdrew as Amy watched. The woman held both hands up, palms out, empty.

Another man, younger, with brown hair and an angular face, came jogging up and skidded to a halt beside the blond woman.

"I can't believe that worked!" the younger man said to the blond woman. "Were you actually touching him?"

"Discuss later," the blond woman replied. She looked at Amy. "Miss Washington, you need to come with us."

EKPHRASIS

December 24, 2010

"My art is not a weapon," Glenda said to the soldier.

The man in the khaki uniform smiled, and his blue eyes twinkled in the afternoon sun. "We'd never call it that, Miss Knopp. We like to think of it as a force multiplier."

"I don't know what that means."

The soldier leaned forward. "Something that increases the effectiveness of our troops beyond their numbers. For example, GPS. Knowing exactly where you are grants a huge tactical advantage."

Glenda nodded, only half understanding but wanting the soldier to think she actually cared.

A door opened behind her, and Jeff walked through the living room of the small apartment on his way to the kitchen. "Sorry," he said, in a tone of voice that indicated he really wasn't. "Don't let me interrupt."

"Not at all," the soldier said. "I was just explaining to Miss Knopp that the Army doesn't want to weaponize her artwork."

Jeff refilled his coffee mug and headed back to the office. "You're still the military. She doesn't like the military. And neither do I."

The door closed again, making more noise than it needed to.

"You'll have to excuse Jeff," Glenda said. "He's from Berkeley."

"I don't care what your boyfriend thinks, Miss Knopp. I'm asking you to help your country."

"By killing people?"

"I can guarantee you, if you allow us to use your artwork, that it will never be used offensively," the soldier said. "In fact, you can help us deter violence. We air-drop information leaflets into the Middle East—"

"Propaganda."

The soldier shrugged. "Right now, most of it gets ignored. But can you imagine if each leaflet had your artwork on it? Images that would compel people to look at the paper, read the words, and *believe* them?"

"I get final approval on the design," Glenda said. She wanted the soldier to think that she was getting as excited as he obviously was.

"Excuse me?"

"I'll only agree if I get to approve all the propaganda messages," Glenda said. "You'll need original brushstrokes on every piece anyway. It doesn't work with mechanical reproductions."

The soldier smiled. "I think we can work that out."

She made some additional, minor demands, asked for double the money he was offering, and otherwise kept pushing until his eyes stopped twinkling. Then they shook hands—his palm was cool and dry—and the soldier said he'd send over the paperwork right away.

"You've made the right decision, Miss Knopp," he said as she showed him to the door. "Your art will save lives."

She closed the door behind him. When she turned around, Jeff was standing in the kitchen, watching her expectantly.

"So?" Jeff asked. "Did he go for it?"

"Oh yeah," Glenda said, hugging her boyfriend. "I thought he would balk at the price, but I guess the Pentagon's got a big budget."

"I still don't trust them."

"Of course we don't trust them." Glenda smiled. "That's why we're not telling them about your music."

IRREMEDIABLE
October 8, 2010

"So what's your superpower?"

Nathan turned to the man standing behind him in line. The stranger was wearing a green jumpsuit with yellow trim, and a green balaclava that covered his entire head except for his eyes. It must have been hot as hell under there.

"I don't have any powers," Nathan said.

"Well, aren't you kind of in the wrong line, then?" The green man chuckled as he spoke, as if he were telling a joke and expected Nathan to also find it humorous.

"The receptionist downstairs told me to come up to 4-B."

"Let me see your paperwork," the green man said, holding out one hand.

Nathan didn't feel like arguing, and he didn't want to find out what might happen if he refused. Costumed avengers weren't the most psychologically stable people in the world. He handed over his forms and watched as the green man squinted at them.

The clerk called for the next in line, and they all edged closer to the window.

"Wow. Sorry, man. I didn't know." The green man handed the forms back to Nathan.

"It's okay." Nathan folded up the paper and stuck it inside his jacket. "At least I survived."

The green man inched closer. "I hope I'm not prying, but—if you don't mind talking about it—what did it feel like? To lose your powers, I mean?"

"I was unconscious," Nathan lied. "I just woke up, and they were gone."

The green man nodded as if he understood, even though he couldn't possibly understand what Nathan was going through.

"Harsh, man."

The clerk called out, and the man in front of Nathan walked up to the window, a shiny blue cape fluttering behind him.

"So listen," the green man said, "I'm kind of in a situation myself, here. I used to be part of this organization, but lately we've been having, you know, creative differences. You know how it goes."

Nathan nodded and avoided eye contact.

"Anyway," the green man continued, "I've been thinking about hanging out my own shingle for a while. But"—he lowered his voice, as if divulging a secret—"I can't fly, so I can't really go solo."

"Why are you telling me this?" Nathan said.

"Have you ever considered being a sidekick?"

The clerk called for the next in line. "I can't fly, either," Nathan said. "As you know."

"Well, not right now, obviously, but the gem's effects aren't permanent." The green man leaned close to Nathan and whispered, "If it makes a difference, I do swing both ways."

He winked, and Nathan controlled his urge to punch someone in the nose. "I gotta go."

"Think about it!"

The clerk at the processing window was a surprisingly attractive young woman. Nathan wondered, as he handed over his paperwork, if this was really the best job she could get.

"Thank you," she said, filling in her part of the form with a red pen. "So, what's your superpower?"

Nathan gritted his teeth. "I'm a people person."

HUMBUGGERY
December 17, 2010

Lewis stared at the shifting swarm of tiny, six-legged, black beads inside the clear plastic box and wondered where his life had gone wrong.

"You're going to take over the world... with ants?"

"Pay attention," said Mentarian. Lewis had never learned his current employer's real name. In fact, Lewis had never seen Mentarian's face. The old man always wore goggles, and rubbed his bald head with his vinyl-gloved hands, making a squeaking noise like two balloons being rubbed together. It set Lewis' teeth on edge and reminded him of his worst childhood experiences.

"The insects are just one of my many tools," Mentarian continued. "Tell me, Lewis, what do ants do that no other creature can?"

Lewis fought the urge to roll his eyes. Mentarian indulged in long Socratic dialogues—not just in the lab, but also during heists and battles. Lewis suspected that was why none of Mentarian's plans ever succeeded, and why he had agreed to take on an intern. Lewis was yet another person Mentarian could talk at.

"I don't know," Lewis said. "Find unattended picnic baskets?"

Mentarian frowned, creasing his brow above his comically huge goggles. "I'm getting a little tired of your attitude, Lewis."

"Only a little? I'll have to work harder then."

"Is this all some kind of joke to you?" Mentarian snapped.

"You really don't want me to answer that."

The bald scientist stomped around the table to stand toe-to-toe with Lewis. Mentarian shoved a gloved finger into Lewis' face. "You serve at my discretion. If this course of study is *unfulfilling* for you, I can find another intern who is more receptive to my teachings."

Lewis thought about biting Mentarian's finger, but the

entertainment value would be outweighed by the council's disciplinary measures. There were better ways to get reassigned. Like bringing up the one question his introductory paperwork had said never to ask Mentarian.

"Why do you wear those stupid goggles?"

Mentarian took a step backward. "I can see you're not in a studious mood. We'll continue this tomorrow." He turned and walked away.

Lewis followed. "You know they make you look like an idiot, right? People might take you more seriously if you wore a better costume."

Mentarian whirled around and pointed at his face. "These are not a fashion choice! This is a necessity."

"Are you horribly disfigured?" Lewis asked. "It can't be that bad. Come on, you're supposed to take sidekicks into your confidence." He reached out and grabbed the goggles.

"No!" Mentarian clawed at Lewis' arms, but the old man wasn't nearly strong enough to prevent Lewis from lifting the goggles.

What lay underneath those dark lenses was the last thing Lewis ever saw.

"I swear, Mentarian," the council inspector said, "you go through interns like other people go through toilet paper."

Mentarian shrugged, placed a water dish inside the box of ants, and closed the lid. "You know what they say. Gotta kiss a lot of frogs."

"Or ants?"

Mentarian grinned. "At least they're useful."

SLEEPMONGER
January 30, 2009

INT. CAFETERIA - DAYTIME

Most employees eat lunch here. It's early, so there aren't many people yet, but JACKSON is still sitting in a corner, eating alone, avoiding company. He's a large man, clearly obese.

TODD walks over excitedly, carrying his own lunch tray.

                    TODD
          Is this seat taken?

JACKSON's mouth is full, so he nods his head. TODD sits down anyway.

                    TODD
          So, about the other night--

JACKSON points a knife at TODD.

                    JACKSON
          Please shut up. You haven't
          told anyone, have you?

                    TODD
          Of course not! I gave my word.
          But I've been thinking. I know
          you need to eat a lot, but
          maybe if you figured out
          precisely how much, you
          wouldn't be so, well...

                    JACKSON
Thanks. I was afraid I might
go a whole day without someone
mentioning my weight. Can you
please leave me alone?

                    TODD
But you've got an amazing
power!

                    JACKSON
It's not amazing. It's
useless. Go away.

                    TODD
Look. You've been hiding this
all your life, yeah? You've
never embraced it. You've
never tried to use it.

                    JACKSON
I can't use it. I can't
control it.

                    TODD
Maybe you just need a bit of
practice.

                    JACKSON
It's too dangerous.

                    TODD
Jackson, with great power
comes great responsibility.

                    JACKSON
If you ever say that again, I
will stab you.
          (sighs)
I'm going to tell you one
thing. And then you're going
to stop bothering me. Right?

TODD
Depends on what you tell me.

JACKSON
I discovered my... "ability"
when I was twelve years old.
Christmas. My parents were
driving me home from the mall.
We had waited in line for
hours to see Santa. I was
tired. I wanted candy. They
wouldn't allow it. They were
going to feed me a proper meal
when we got home.

TODD
You were hungry. Oh my God.

JACKSON
I hadn't eaten since
breakfast.

TODD
And you... your parents fell
asleep? In the car?

JACKSON
I saw my dad slump over the
steering wheel. Then our car
went off the road. I don't
remember much else.

TODD
Jesus.

JACKSON
So you understand why I'm not
keen to experiment with this.

> TODD
> I'm real sorry about your
> parents, but you need to know.
> What if this building
> collapses, and it takes hours
> for them to dig us out? What
> if they can't get near us
> because you can't control your
> ability, and they all keep
> falling asleep? How many
> people might die then?

> JACKSON
> You must be a lot of fun at
> parties.

> TODD
> I just want to help.

JACKSON sighs and looks around the cafeteria.

> JACKSON
> We don't talk about this here.
> We go someplace else.

> TODD
> I totally agree.

> JACKSON
> I pick the place. You drive.
> You pay.

> TODD
> (hesitantly)
> Can we perhaps set an upper
> limit on the cost of these
> meals?

> JACKSON
> (quoting)
> "Don't get cheap on me now,
> Dodgson."

Curtis C. Chen

TODD frowns, trying to place the quote, then snaps his
fingers and smiles.

                    TODD
          Jurassic Park. Brilliant!
          "Louis, I think this is the
          beginning of a beautiful
          friendship."

JACKSON rolls his eyes. He's already regretting this.

Thursday's Children

NOTHING UP HIS SLEEVE
May 21, 2010

Maurice saw Beatrice waving the no-rabbit signal behind her back. That was bad. No rabbit meant no real magic, and mere tricks and illusions weren't going to impress the potential investors in the audience.

Maurice stepped up and put his palm on Beatrice's upper arm, giving the cue for their first trick. She looked at him with raised eyebrows. He nodded. She inhaled through clenched teeth, then curtsied to the audience and exited stage left.

Maurice started slow, doing more talking than conjuring; he pulled handkerchiefs from a hidden pocket, lit a flash-paper button off his jacket with a concealed striker, compressed soft foam balls between deft fingers. The audience *ooh*ed and *aah*ed, as expected, but these sleights of hand were not Maurice's true talent. They were merely a reliable warm-up, a way to stall for time while Beatrice prepared the apparatus and he prayed for his power to manifest.

All too soon, Beatrice wheeled a small platform to center stage. On the platform was a glass terrarium, and inside the terrarium was a single Venus Flytrap. The plant took up most of the rectangular space, half a dozen thick stalks topped by pairs of oval flaps, spiked at the edges and joined by a red membrane. Two of the traps were closed.

The audience murmured as Maurice explained the peculiar nature of the carnivorous *Dionaea muscipula*, how it trapped and digested its insect prey. He indicated the two closed traps and described how the plant had been fed shortly before the show—he did not specify how shortly, for Beatrice had done it only after his on-stage signal—and how he had to act quickly to perform his rescue.

Maurice gestured to Beatrice, and they each took one end of the terrarium, lifting it to show there was nothing underneath, no hidden compartment in the platform, no devices buried in the dirt. Then they put the glass case back down, and Beatrice stepped aside while Maurice waved his hands over the plant, loudly reciting gibberish.

After a moment, the Venus Flytrap quivered inside the terrarium, and one of the closed traps twitched open. Inside, a single fly righted itself, unstuck its wings, and rose into the air.

The audience applauded, and Maurice smiled at Beatrice with relief. His happiness was short-lived, as he saw her eyes grow wide.

Maurice looked down and saw more insects emerging from every open trap on the plant—flies, beetles, wasps, even spiders. They crawled over the green stalks, buzzed around the enclosure, collided against the glass walls and mesh ceiling.

The audience cheered. Maurice beamed at them and presented the spectacle with a flourish of his hands, as if it was all part of the show. He blinked away the sweat which had trickled from his forehead down to his eyes. The moisture and the stage lights blurred his vision into a multicolored haze.

"The rabbit!" he hissed at Beatrice. "Bring it out! Now!"

THRILLING HEROICS
July 27, 2012

"Sign here. And initial here. And here..."

Pamela watched as the other lawyer, McBride, flipped pages and pointed over his client's shoulder. The plaintiff, Charles Lucas, made a show of using both bandaged hands to hold the pen as he scrawled on the document.

Another flashbulb went off behind Pamela, and she heard a grumbling noise from the fourth person at the table: her client, Dyna-Gent. She leaned over to him.

"Just keep it together a little longer," she whispered.

"You didn't tell me there would be so many reporters," Dyna-Gent muttered, his eyes narrowed behind his mask.

"You should be happy. You're big news."

"I'm being sued."

"Hey, no such thing as bad publicity, remember?"

Dyna-Gent grimaced and folded his arms. Across the table, Lucas finished signing, and McBride slid the settlement papers across the table.

"All yours, Miss Kirk," he said with a smile that was clearly for the cameras.

"Thank you," Pamela said. "But before my client signs, he has a brief statement."

"An apology, I hope," McBride said.

The grumbling grew louder. Pamela grabbed the glass of water to her left, the one she'd poured earlier, and held it in front of Dyna-Gent's face. "Take a drink and count to ten," she said under her breath.

Dyna-Gent glared across the table as he took the water from Pamela. He tipped the glass back, taking a huge swig, then did a magnificent spit take, drenching Charles Lucas—and causing blue electrical arcs to appear all over his body.

"What did I just drink?" Dyna-Gent bellowed at Pamela.

"Salt water!" she said, pointing at Lucas. "Which happens to be an excellent electrical conductor!"

Dyna-Gent looked at Lucas and smiled. "Of course."

"This is outrageous!" McBride said, getting to his feet.

"I'll tell you what's outrageous," Pamela said, standing up. With her heels, she had a good inch and a half over McBride, and that would play on camera. "It's outrageous that your client is pursuing this fraudulent lawsuit against a respected community defender! The fact that Mr. Lucas is himself super-powered invalidates any claim of damages he has against Dyna-Gent."

"Not so," McBride said. "My client is suffering the after-effects of the explosion which triggered the incident in question. He was not super-powered before that unfortunate—"

"Oh, really?" Pamela pulled a file folder out of her briefcase and slapped it down on the table. "Then why did metro police detect a massive electrical surge in Mr. Lucas' basement, when public utilities recorded no matching drain on the city grid? Where did all that electricity come from, Mr. Lucas?"

"Don't answer that!" McBride snapped. Lucas' mouth hung open, and blue-white sparks jumped between his teeth. "The accident affected my client's genetic structure—"

"Give me a break. DNA doesn't work like that," Pamela said. "We'll see you in court."

She waved at Dyna-Gent, who stood and followed her out of the room.

"My hero," he said, patting her shoulder.

Pamela allowed herself a smile. "Just doing my job, citizen."

FEARLESS

May 13, 2011

"The doctor must have stepped out," the smiling receptionist said as she walked Alex into an empty office. "Would you wait here, please?"

"Do I have a choice?" Alex said.

"Oh, don't be nervous—"

"Do I seem nervous to you?"

The receptionist continued smiling. "Your consultation is entirely confidential. Doctor Gottlieb's very good. I should know; I'm a former patient."

"Let me guess," Alex said. "Agnosia implant?"

The receptionist turned to look down the hallway. "Oh, here he comes now."

Doctor Gottlieb exchanged hellos with the receptionist, then entered the office and closed the door behind him. He pulled a reader tablet out of his white coat and sat down at his desk.

"How can I help you, Miss... Burstyn?"

"It's *Officer* Burstyn." Alex held up her badge.

Gottlieb put down the tablet. "I'm sorry, Officer. Do you have a warrant?"

"I'm not here on official business," Alex said. "But it's funny that would be the first thing out of your mouth."

Gottlieb folded his arms. "My patients value their privacy. I perform a lot of sensitive procedures, often involving personal issues—"

"Yeah, I know. That's why I'm here. I want an MGR-5 enhancile."

The doctor blinked. "Excuse me?"

"MGR-5. Metabotropic glutamate receptor five?"

Gottlieb frowned. "You've done your homework. Most people just call it 'the backbone implant.'"

"That could be any number of treatments," Alex said. "I want the gene therapy."

"You'll still need an implant to regulate stress hormone production—"

"And a wire down my spine, yeah, I know."

Gottlieb leaned forward. "There are side effects. Impaired judgment, for example, which could be an issue in your line of work."

"Which is why you'll prescribe drugs to treat those side effects."

"All this will be very expensive."

"I can pay."

"And if you ever want to have children—"

"I don't."

They stared at each other.

"Anything else you want to say to try and talk me out of it?" Alex asked.

"Just this," Gottlieb said. "Medical science has achieved some miraculous things. But everything we do to the human body is still just a hack. The backbone alters a fundamental biochemical response. We evolved to feel fear for very good reasons. I urge you to think very hard before deciding on this."

"Do you know what happened to me last year?"

Gottlieb shook his head.

"My best friend died," Alex said. "He died five minutes after I asked him to marry me. He died because some mincer wanted his wristwatch, and I was afraid I'd get a hand cut off if we fought.

"I would have traded my arm if I knew it would save Ethan's life.

"I didn't want to make a rash, grief-fueled decision, so I waited. Thirteen months. I did the department-mandated therapy, I passed the psych eval. I know what I want. I want to move on, but I don't want to forget.

"I don't ever again want to see somebody die because I was too scared for my own well-being to do something to save them. Now are you going to help me, Doctor?"

HIGHER
May 27, 2011

The girl didn't look happy. Her eyes were red, like she'd been crying. Her forearms were bandaged, and her wrists and ankles were secured to the bed rails with heavy straps.

She was also floating about an inch above the mattress.

"You have noticed that she's levitating, right?" Gottlieb said.

Humphrey rolled his eyes. "Of course we noticed. That's why we called you for a consult."

"Because you've been dealing with a lot of strange cases lately," Iskra said, handing Gottlieb a patient file. "And we're honestly not sure what's going on here."

Gottlieb looked through the observation window at the girl for a few more seconds, wanting to form an opinion before any of her records could bias him toward a particular diagnosis. Then he flipped through the file.

"Where are her parents?" he asked.

"Her mother's with the police," Humphrey said. "The officers found some controlled substances in the apartment when they responded to the 911 call."

"No father on record," Iskra added. "The mother's a sex worker. Got herself fixed after the first unwanted pregnancy."

"But she didn't have an abortion," Gottlieb said.

"Not for lack of trying," Humphrey said.

Gottlieb looked up. "You pulled the mother's file?"

"Yeah. Cops wanted to know if she was clean."

"And why don't I have it here?"

Humphrey frowned. "It's not medically relevant."

"I'll decide that for myself," Gottlieb said. "You want me to consult, you get me all the facts. What kind of sterilization procedure did the mother undergo? Was it surgical?"

"Artificial menopause," Iskra said.

Gottlieb blinked. "What?"

"Endocrine regulation, using a combination of—"

"I know what it is," Gottlieb snapped. He looked at Humphrey. "A teenage girl starts floating in midair, and you don't think it could be hormone-related?"

"That was the mother, not the daughter," Humphrey said. "Implants aren't hereditary. And she didn't even have the procedure until after her daughter was born."

"How soon after the birth? Did she breast-feed her daughter?" Gottlieb asked. "What kind of endocrine implant did she have? Was it HPG axis-limited? Was there a nanotech component to the treatment? I need to see that file."

Humphrey scowled, said, "Doctor Iskra can get it for you," and walked out of the room.

"Nice to see you haven't lost your touch," Iskra said, shaking his head. "I'll get you the mother's medical records. Any ideas in the meantime?"

"Has the girl—what's her name?"

"Caitlin. Caitlin Kearny."

"Has Caitlin complained of nausea, dizziness, or vertigo?"

Iskra nodded. "All three. Do you know what's causing it?"

I hope not, Gottlieb thought. "Is it persistent, or does it come and go?"

"She says it happens whenever she gets intoxicated—usually just alcohol, though she's admitted to marijuana use, too. The discomfort also seems to coincide with her, um, levitation episodes."

Shit. "I'm going to need blood and tissue samples."

Iskra frowned. "What are you testing for?"

I can't tell you that. "I don't know," Gottlieb said.

STRONGER

June 3, 2011

"He needs a new skeleton," Gottlieb said.

Schumann glared for a moment, then turned his broad shoulders and sat down behind his office desk.

"In private," Schumann said.

Gottlieb closed the door and dropped the file on the General's desk. "I'll need your authorization for the procedure—"

"I'm not going to authorize the procedure," Schumann said.

Gottlieb blinked. "This is a medical emergency."

Schumann shook his head. "You need to remember who's in charge here, Doctor. I know the guy's your friend, you have history together, but this program is not your own private research lab. If I can't make a case for the operational benefit of a procedure, I can't authorize the funds for it. That's the bottom line."

It took Gottlieb a moment to unclench his jaw. "The *operational benefit* is that Paul Wilson doesn't die. Or is the United States government no longer in the business of keeping its citizens alive?"

"There's no need for insults, Doctor," Schumann said. He pushed away the file on his desk. "I've seen the updates. Wilson's condition isn't life-threatening. He'll be on his back for a few days until you figure out how to turn down the implants, and then you'll fix him."

"This isn't—" Gottlieb heard himself getting louder, and stopped before he started yelling at a three-star general. "Paul Wilson's enhancile is not purely technological. He has received gene therapy which alters the fundamental biochemical makeup of his muscles. We had to do that in order to keep the *myasthenia gravis* from destroying his soft tissue."

"I'm not an idiot, Doctor." Schumann stared right through Gottlieb. "Wilson's muscle growth is regulated by the implants. You can tune those to keep him from hulking out."

"We've been trying," Gottlieb said. "It's not working."

"Make it work."

"You tell me how to create some new amino acids and I'll get right on it."

Schumann sighed, opened the file, and scanned through it. "You've done this type of skeletal enhancement before?"

"Dogs and ponies. Literally," Gottlieb said. "But the principle is the same. It will work. I just need a signature."

Schumann closed the folder. "I'll sign on one condition. You need to put Wilson into the field."

Gottlieb shook his head. "He's not ready. We need to—"

"Don't bullshit me, Doctor," Schumann said. "You've released enhanced soldiers onto the battlefield two weeks after surgery. Wilson's been here for years."

"He's not a soldier. He doesn't—"

"I'm not asking him to be a soldier. I'm asking him to serve his country using his unique talents." Schumann opened a drawer and pulled out a reader tablet. "And he won't be alone."

Gottlieb frowned. "What are you proposing?"

"This isn't a proposal, Doctor. This is an order." Schumann pushed the tablet to the edge of his desk. "I'm putting together a task force. FBI's bringing in the candidates now, and they're shipping out as soon as you examine them and certify them fit for duty.

"This department's been making superheroes for three years. It's about time we started using them for something."

FASTER

May 20, 2011

Gottlieb didn't even see his office door open and close. He blinked, and then there was a man standing next to the bookshelf.

"Can I help you?" Gottlieb asked. It was his standard greeting when he had no idea what was going on. Which seemed to be happening more and more these days.

The man's face seemed familiar. Gottlieb squinted. The man appeared blurry, almost as if he were... vibrating?

"I want my money back," the man said. His voice quavered, like an audio sample being alternately sped up and slowed down.

"I'm sorry," Gottlieb said. "Are you a patient here?"

The man disappeared, then reappeared on Gottlieb's side of the desk. He grabbed Gottlieb's coat and lifted him out of his chair.

"I'm one of *your* patients!" the man shouted. "Don't you recognize the monster you created, *Doctor?*"

Gottlieb raised both his hands in a gesture of surrender. "I'm sorry. Your face—it's—"

"Oscillating?" the man said. "Yeah. My whole body, actually. Forty-five hertz, give or take, depending on my mood." This close, Gottlieb noticed an undertone beneath the man's quavering speech—a low buzzing, like an ungrounded electric appliance. "Don't you remember doing this to me? Or am I just another experiment to you?"

The face snapped into focus for a split second, and Gottlieb recognized the man. "Mr. Kendall? Herman Kendall?"

Kendall's grip relaxed. Gottlieb lowered his hands slowly.

"What did you do to me, Doc?" Kendall asked, his voice winding down.

Gottlieb slipped both hands into his coat pockets, finding his panic button in case he needed to summon help. "Please, sit. Tell me what happened. As I recall, you wanted a synaptic enhancile."

Kendall zipped around the desk and sat down. Now that Gottlieb knew what he was looking at, he could almost visually track Kendall's accelerated motion.

"It didn't work," Kendall said. "Or maybe it worked too well. I don't know. At first, it did what you said: helped me think faster, sped up my reflexes. I was unbeatable on the court. But then I started losing control."

"I warned you," Gottlieb said softly. "It was a highly experimental implant."

"I know!" Kendall stood up. "I know you said there would be side effects, and I was ready for that, but this—" He pounded his temples with his fists. "Nobody's going to let me compete now! You gotta take it out, Doc!"

"We discussed this," Gottlieb said. "The enhancile is a permanent change to your physiology. I can try to tune it, but there's no way to remove it without killing you."

Kendall sat down again. "Jesus, you might as well. My life is over anyway."

Gottlieb picked up a reader tablet from his desk and thumbed it to the personal files he'd been looking at earlier.

"Maybe not," Gottlieb said, holding out the tablet. "There are some people I'd like you to meet."

On the tablet screen were photos of a heavily muscled man, a scowling woman in full body armor, and a teenage girl floating several feet above a sidewalk.

FIVE FOR FIGHTING
October 26, 2012

Gottlieb checked his watch again. "Can't you work any faster?"

"I thought faster was *his* job." Caitlin nodded at Herman while continuing to pelt the computer keyboard with her fingertips.

"You'll tell me if there's a problem, right?"

"Sure."

Herman paced on the other side of the console, a man-shaped blur streaking back and forth across the room. In the far corner, underneath a metal stump, Paul cradled the remains of a security camera.

"You okay, Paul?"

Paul didn't look up. "I couldn't feel it. No pain. Nothing. It didn't even break the skin."

"The presentation is unusual," Gottlieb said. "But interactions between your gene therapy and these implant drugs are poorly documented—"

Paul flattened the camera between both palms, then let the metal pancake fall to the ground with a clatter.

"I was supposed to be strong. Not indestructible." He looked at Gottlieb. "They're never going to let me go, are they?"

"Paul—"

Gottlieb's earpiece chirped. "Escape route looks clear, Doc," Alex said.

"Okay, get back here." Gottlieb had failed to discourage Alex from running off by herself, and failed to convince Herman to follow her into the ventilation ducts.

"In a minute. Something else I want to check out," Alex said.

"We're on a schedule here, Alex," Gottlieb said. "And we have very specific mission parameters."

"Listen to you. 'Mission parameters?' I'm becoming aroused."

Caitlin snickered. Gottlieb ignored her. "Alex, I don't feel you're taking this seriously."

"It's a simulation," Alex said. "And we're doing great. Nothing here we can't handle."

"They're not just evaluating your physical skills," Gottlieb said. "They want to know if we can function as a team. And so far, we're failing spectacularly."

"What are you talking about?" Alex said. "We're like clockwork. Took out all the cameras in less than three seconds—"

"Paul went on a rampage," Gottlieb said. "And now he's freaking out because he's stronger than we expected. You rushed off before we cleared the room, Herman refused to go with you because he's claustrophobic, and I have no idea what Caitlin is doing."

The teenager smiled up at him. "I'm in your computer, hackin' your datas."

Gottlieb shook his head. "General Schumann doesn't think I can lead the four of you in the field."

"You've got other talents, Doc," Alex said.

"You're missing the point. If I can't convince Schumann that I can supervise this team, he's going to find someone else. Is that what you want? Some jarhead barking orders at you?"

Silence. Gottlieb allowed himself a triumphant nod.

"Jarheads are Marines," Alex said.

Gottlieb frowned. "What?"

"Schumann's an Army General," Alex said.

"She's right," Herman said. "My brother's in the Army. He'd be deeply offended if you called him a jarhead."

"I guess 'grunt' would be more appropriate?" Alex said.

"Or just 'soldier,'" Herman said.

"'Doughboy,'" Caitlin offered.

Paul said, "I've also heard 'dogface.'"

Gottlieb threw up his hands. "Really? *This* is what we need to discuss right now?"

"Hey, you get upset when people call you *Mister* Gottlieb," Alex said. "Words hurt too, Doc."

RUNAWAYS
November 25, 2011

Kaylee knows she can't throw the guy without killing him, or at least doing serious spinal damage; every surface in the subway station is some kind of hard flat or edge. So she settles for slashing his right leg, just above the kneecap, with one of the blades hidden in her leather gauntlets, and then running like hell. All I can do is observe from twenty-two thousand miles away.

Here's the thing about having your consciousness transferred into a solar-powered satellite in geosynchronous orbit: sure, you never have to sleep, you can see the entire continent at once, but that's pretty much all you can do. Watch. Even with a two-way broadband link directly into Kaylee's cerebral cortex, transmission delay plus reaction time means anything I tell her will be at least five hundred milliseconds out of date. And that half-second could get her killed.

So most of the time, I just keep my mouth shut and let her do her thing.

I watch, through Kaylee's eyes and the spotty subway securicam coverage, as she maneuvers through crowds of commuters. She knows I'll have better coverage once she's at street level, and she's probably figured the same thing I have from her first attacker's dress and approach: professional killer. Somebody's called down a hit on my little sister.

We knew it would happen someday. You can't run free in any city for long before the local mafia or union or PTA or whatever they call themselves wants a piece of your action. I hope she's ready for this.

"Another heavy on your six," I verbalize into Kaylee's speech centers. She won't hear the words so much as she'll think them, but she'll know the thought didn't come from herself. "Hoodie, ballcap, hand-cannon in his pants."

"Thanks, bigbro," she thinks back at me.

Her head snaps around, but she doesn't stop moving up the last stairway to ground level. The hitter behind her is younger than the first one, and better camouflaged; I only made him because of the weapon bulging in his waistline. He's smart, this one; not drawing on Kaylee until he absolutely has to, probably thinking he'll get close enough to put her in a headlock, use his size as advantage and use the piece for persuasion.

Kaylee skids to a halt at the top of the stairs, turns around, and screams at the top of her lungs, "Stop following me, you pervert!"

The crowds on both sides of the stairs, both going up and down, freeze in place. The hitter stops, too, and makes a show of looking around just like everyone else, working his disguise. That gives Kaylee more than enough time to draw her taser, line up a clear shot, and fire the darts right into the side of his neck.

The hitter gurgles and crumples in the middle of the parting crowd. Kaylee drops the taser, still discharging electricity into the man, and disappears into broad daylight.

"That's my girl," I think to myself, wishing I could still smile.

MUTINY
August 7, 2009

The planet screamed, but nobody heard.

José felt the cable wobble in his grip as Master Histian clapped. Histian always preferred to watch the destruction wrought by his weapons from outside the ship. José supposed it was one of the few remaining thrills which the old man could experience firsthand, with his own eyes.

It would be so easy for José to simply release the cable. But that would not be justice.

Long minutes passed before Histian stopped cackling and spoke: "Bring me in, boy."

José hoped it had been long enough. He took his time reeling in the cable.

"Magnificent, wasn't it?" Histian said when they were both inside the airlock. "Such a glorious demise!"

"Yes, sir," José said, sealing the outer door.

"Why must you always be so glum?" Histian asked, scowling. "Would it kill you to smile once in a while?"

José split his face in a fake grin. "Is this better, sir?" he asked through clenched teeth.

Histian's scowl deepened. The inner airlock door hissed open. José followed Histian into the ship, where they both climbed out of their pressure suits and then returned to the bridge.

"Show me the spectrographic analysis," Histian said, settling into his throne—it was too ornate to be called a chair—on the central platform.

The main screen lit up with a glowing array of graphs. José scrolled the display in response to Histian's grunts and hand gestures.

"Interesting," Histian said. "An unexpected spike in the ultraviolet. And that appears to be plasma filamentation." He leaned forward and steepled his fingers. "Tell me, boy, does this mean anything to you, or is it all just pretty blinking lights?"

José curled the fingers of his left hand into a fist. "I'm very happy for your success, sir."

"Of course you are," Histian sneered. "You're going to sneak an extra portion of beefmeat while I'm enjoying my wine tonight."

José kept his back to the throne, hiding his face and biting his tongue.

"Did you think I wouldn't notice?" Histian continued. "Do you think I depend on you for everything?"

"No," José said, pressing a button. "Just enough."

The door on the opposite side of the chamber slid open, and eight armored commandos entered. The first fired a barrage of stun pellets at the back of Histian's throne, pinning him down. The second commando launched a police net. The rest surrounded Histian's platform with their weapons raised.

The police net landed on the throne, trapping Histian. The webbing contracted and dug into his pale skin. He cried out in pain. José allowed himself a genuine smile.

One of the commandos stepped onto the platform and said, "Histian Winterfield, you are under arrest for theft and conspiracy to transport illegal armaments across stellar boundaries—"

Histian ignored him and glared at José. "You did this? Why? Why betray your master?"

José walked up to the old man and looked down at him. "You're not my master," José said in a low, quiet voice. "And I don't like you."

HAVE SPACESUIT, WILL TRAVEL
April 6, 2012

"Don't tell me how to fly!" Angel said. "I know how to fly."

"You know how to play video games." Carolyn's voice crackled through the helmet radio. "There's a difference."

Angel nudged the throttle with her right index finger. "Just give me a map reading, okay? We don't have a lot of time."

"Almost clear," Carolyn said. "Another fifty meters, then turn forty-five degrees up."

"Pitch," Angel corrected.

"Why do I need to learn made-up words when I can just say 'turn?'" Carolyn asked. "I gotta tell you which way to go anyhow."

"We'll have this argument later," Angel said. "Pitching up, four-five degrees, now."

She pulled back on the vertical stick with her left thumb. Her view changed from the gentle curve of the habitat ring to the angular mess of the cargo docks.

"Okay, I'm lined up." Angel brought up the HUD overlay in her helmet. "Range painting on. Where am I going?"

"Straight ahead of you, two lanes in. Bay ninety-five. The ship is all the way at the end."

Before Angel could ask whether that was the spaceward or homeward end of the lane, an alarm started blaring, and blinking red lights lit up her HUD.

"What's wrong?" Carolyn shouted.

"Wait one," Angel said.

She felt remarkably calm as she worked both joysticks and pressed lightly on the triggers to change her thrust vector. Carolyn was right: it wasn't anything like a video game. Angel felt the backpack rockets pushing against her body as they fired, three different arrows of force joining to shove her out of the way of the approaching freighter.

It wasn't until she was safely out of the lane that Angel felt her hands shaking and her stomach fluttering. All sorts of audio and visual alerts filled her helmet, now that she'd exceeded speed limits in controlled traffic space, but all she heard was the blood rushing past her ears—until her mother's voice pierced the noise.

"Angel Daria Chace!" She did not sound happy. "What in the name of all that's holy are you doing out there?"

"I'm helping Granma," Angel said, braking and re-angling herself toward the target ship.

"Did you steal that spacesuit? And—what?" Her mother paused. "*Angel!* Did you take your grandmother's *ashes?*"

"She wanted to be buried in space." Angel slowed her approach, then slapped the magnetic case containing her grandmother's ashes onto the side of a cargo container. "I'm sending her into the Sun."

"Angel, you get back inside right now! And where is your sister?"

The suit radio buzzed, and a new voice filled the helmet. "Unidentified pilot, this is Galen Traffic Control. Please stop maneuvering inside restricted space and meet dock authorities at airlock three-nine. Repeat..."

Angel's face hurt from smiling so much. She'd never been called a pilot before.

"...additional," the controller continued. "Please hold at airlock three-nine for the captain of that freighter who almost pancaked you. He says he 'wants to meet any cowboy who can dance like that in a three-pointed tin can.'"

DOWN TO EARTH
May 17, 2013

"They have telescopes," Perry said. "They've all got telescopes. Some of them are tracking you right now, feeding live video to public web sites. We can't shut down the entire worldwide amateur astronomy community. You can't de-orbit."

I hated not being able to see him. Several of the meteors—the smaller ones—had struck my helmet, knocking out the heads-up display embedded in the transparent visor. It was weird, hearing Perry's voice in my ear without seeing his face, and I wondered if it would have been better if one of the bigger rocks had smashed into my head. At least then I would have died in an instant, instead of now having to choose a terrible public demise.

"You think it's going to be better if I yank off my helmet and suffocate?" I asked. "Then the whole world gets to watch my corpse circling the planet for centuries. At least if I burn up, it's over in a few minutes."

"Do you want your husband to see that?" Perry said. "Do you really want your immolation broadcast live, in high-definition 3-D?"

"Fuck you, Perry," I said. "Lamont's smart enough to turn off his TV. You're worried about how this is going to affect the stock price."

There was a long pause. I stared down at planet Earth, huge and beautiful and still. I wondered how many people were observing me from the ground. They probably couldn't see my face through the polarized helmet visor—unless somebody was using a wide-spectrum receiver. Never underestimate the ingenuity of bored graduate students.

"We have another option," Perry said at last.

"Does it involve me not dying?"

He hesitated before answering. "I wish I had better news, Kayla—"

"Just tell me."

"Your spacesuit thrusters still have eighty percent of their reserves," Perry said. "We can give you a procedure to overload the primary fuel cell cluster."

I kept my face calm and hoped nobody watching from the ground could read lips. "You want me to blow myself up?"

"Just let me finish," Perry said. "It'll be quick. Over in less than a second, and any debris gets incinerated in the atmosphere before hitting the ground. We can program in a random delay, so you won't even know when it happens."

"You're so kind," I said. "And then the company gets to cover up the whole thing, pretend my suit was damaged in the meteor shower, and call this entire 'incident' a terrible, unavoidable tragedy."

"I'm on your side, Kayla," Perry said. "I'm sorry, but this is your best option now."

I squeezed my eyes shut, holding in my tears. "I want to talk to Lamont."

"What?"

"I want to talk to my husband."

"Kayla—"

"You get my husband on comms," I said, "or I start waving my arms in semaphore and spelling out exactly what happened for the whole damn world to see. You've got thirty seconds, Perry."

"That's not enough time!"

"Twenty-five seconds."

"Okay, okay!" The line beeped and went dead.

"Fucker," I muttered.

GET YOUR ASS TO MARS
June 8, 2012

My father died before I went into space, but he was the reason I made it there.

For years, he talked about visiting the Grand Canyon, but kept putting it off. There was always something more important to do. It became a running joke between us. Every birthday and Father's Day, I would send him another tacky souvenir I'd bought online, building up memorabilia from a vacation he'd never taken.

It was funny until my junior year of college, when he was diagnosed with stage three bone cancer.

That summer, I surprised him with a gift: two train tickets to the South Rim. It had taken me weeks to negotiate with his doctors, but we all knew he didn't have much time left.

He had taken up whittling, using a kitschy penknife I'd sent him the year before. The lacquered handle showed tracks from coyote, deer, sheep, and other mammals native to Arizona. The pawprints had inspired him to attempt to carve tiny versions of each animal.

He was fashioning an alleged mountain lion out of basswood while we waited for the train. His fingers kept slipping off the blade, but I said nothing.

"What do you think?" He held up the tiny chunk of maimed lumber.

I squinted. "You're getting better. That almost looks not like a mutant dog."

"Everyone's a critic." He laid the carving on its side. "Hold that, will you? I need to make my mark."

I don't know if it was the pain in his hands, or if the whistle of the incoming train startled him, but I saw a flash of light as the knife spun out of his grip and slid across the glass tabletop. Then I saw red.

"Are you okay?" I asked.

"I'm fine," he said, his voice tight.

"You're bleeding."

"What? No." He held up his hands and turned them over. There were no cuts or scrapes anywhere. "I'm fine, see."

I pointed at his chest. There had been one fuzzy red dot on his shirt a moment ago. Now it was expanding. Other dots appeared, turning the solid blue cloth into a gruesome polka dot design.

An ambulance rushed us to the hospital. The doctors refused to let him leave. I knew what they would tell me. My father wasn't going to see the Grand Canyon.

I sat with him that night, reading aloud from a book titled *Over the Edge*, which cataloged the outlandish ways people had managed to get themselves killed in the national park over the years. I had been saving it for his next birthday.

"See," I said, "it's a good thing we didn't go. You might have ended up dead. Or worse."

"Promise me you won't wait," he said. "Whatever it is you want, whatever you think will make you happy—don't wait until it's too late."

"I promise, Dad."

He smiled at me, and I held his hand as he closed his eyes.

I went to the Grand Canyon after my father died. I scattered his ashes there, and I kept my promise.

MARTIAN STANDARD TIME
March 13, 2009

Sean O'Reilly was the first human on Mars. He got to enjoy it for about three seconds.

"Well, here I am." Those were his last words, transmitted by radio to the whole world.

The three of us still inside the lander saw him stumble. We didn't know what was happening until he fell down, and his feet kicked up some dust. Then we saw the laser beams crisscrossing his body.

I wish I could have thought of something better to say than "Houston, we have a problem."

The sandstorm hit two minutes later, while Brian and I were wrapping Karen's pressure suit in reflective foil to protect her from the lasers. The storm lasted over forty hours. After it passed, Sean's body was nowhere in sight.

Once Mission Control gave us the all clear, Karen ventured outside in her silvered suit. She found three dead laser mounts bolted to nearby rocks. Two had been smashed open by storm debris, and the third had lost its power supply. She brought everything inside for a closer inspection.

"These are our lasers," Brian said. "The same kind we're carrying. This is exactly like our equipment."

"That's impossible," I said. "Our hardware is custom-made for each mission. Nobody else has this equipment."

Karen went into the cargo bay and brought back a large metal case. Inside were four cutting lasers identical to the three she'd recovered from outside. She picked up the least damaged Martian laser and compared it to each of the four in the case.

"What are you looking for?" Brian asked.

"Something else that's impossible," she said. "Serial numbers."

She put both lasers down and turned them for us to see. They had the same sixteen-digit serial numbers etched into their casings.

"This has to be a mistake," Brian said.

"We don't need to figure this out," I said. "We take pictures, send all the data back to Houston, and they can puzzle it out. We still have a mission to complete."

Brian squinted at the damaged laser. "There's something else etched on here. Looks like letters... 'seanor.'"

"What?" I said.

"That was Sean's username," Karen said.

"Below that there's a row of gibberish. And then a row of numbers." Brian frowned. "These are coordinates. Martian latitude and longitude."

"Let me see that." I examined the gibberish. It looked like a random sequence of letters, numbers, and punctuation.

"Son of a bitch," I said. "Sean could memorize anything. He always used randomly generated passwords. Said they were harder to guess, more secure."

I turned to a computer console, brought up a terminal window, and entered Sean's username, followed by the gibberish characters.

The computer logged me in and showed me Sean's private files.

"Son of a bitch," Karen said.

I held up the casing and pointed at the numbers. "What's at these coordinates?"

Brian switched the tabletop display to a map of Mars. "Unnamed crater, Arcadia Planitia. It's not on our list of sites to explore."

"It is now," I said. "Let's suit up and get out there."

BIRTHDAYS
October 17, 2008

When Stacy was twelve years old, she celebrated her father's thirty-third birthday. It wasn't actually his birthday. It was two weeks before his birthday, but he was leaving on a mission before then, so they had to have the party early.

Stacy thought the party was boring. There were a lot of grown-ups there, drinking smelly drinks that bubbled like soda but tasted bitter. She knew because she stole a sip from her father's plastic cup. He was talking to another grown-up at the time and didn't notice.

"It's only sixteen light-years," he was saying, "but we're not sure how hard we can push the new stardrive."

"And you got that relativity stuff to worry about," said the other grown-up. Except he didn't say "stuff"—he said a bad word.

Stacy ran into the kitchen to find her mother. She was hunched over the sink, alone, her shoulders twitching.

"Mommy?" Stacy said, tugging at her skirt.

Stacy's mother turned to look at her. Her eyes were red, and her cheeks were wet.

"Ready for your bedtime story?" she asked, smiling.

"I'm not sleepy," Stacy said.

"Okay, come on then," her mother said, taking Stacy's hand as if she hadn't spoken.

"Mom," Stacy said. "I said I'm not sleepy."

Her mother squeezed Stacy's hand even harder.

When Stacy was sixty-four, she celebrated her father's fortieth birthday. She barely recognized the man who embraced her as the waitress maneuvered her wheelchair into the restaurant.

"My little girl," he said, his eyes glistening.

The waitress brought a plate of food that Stacy wasn't allergic to. She toasted her father with apple juice. She felt tired halfway through dinner, but pinched her arm under the table to keep herself awake.

After all the other guests had left, the waitress brought a glass of warm milk for Stacy and a cup of coffee for her father. The coffee smelled good.

He asked about Stacy's mother, about how his family had been over the last half century. Stacy told him that her mother, his wife, had remarried. She'd waited after the explosion, when everyone thought her father's ship had been destroyed due to a stardrive malfunction. She'd waited four years, but she couldn't wait forever.

"She never stopped loving you," Stacy told her father. She showed him the family photo that her mother had kept until she died, and which Stacy still carried in her purse. It showed the three of them at the beach, sunburned and laughing. He cried quietly.

When they left the restaurant, Stacy's father helped her into a waiting taxicab. He noticed her coughing and asked about her health.

"I'm old," she said, forcing a smile. She didn't want to tell him about the cancer.

Four days later, Stacy got a call from the space agency. They had found her father dead in his hotel room. He had overdosed on sleep pills, washed down with a bottle of whiskey.

They said he hadn't felt any pain. Stacy knew they were wrong.

BY ANY OTHER NAME
October 12, 2012

They met, accidentally, in the elevator. It was a three-minute ride down from the board room level to the forty-seventh floor, and Julia and Mary were the only people who entered the car—first Julia, studying her tablet and oblivious to her surroundings, then Mary a few seconds later, doing the same.

Neither one noticed the other until it would have been too awkward for either to leave. The doors timed out and closed, and Julia sighed and touched the panel to start their descent.

They stared at their warped reflections in the closed doors until Mary couldn't stand the silence any more.

"Good board meeting?" she asked.

"Good enough," Julia said. "What were you doing up there?"

"Design group confab. Needed to use the holodeck."

"Could you please not call it that."

Mary turned to look at Julia. "Why don't you like my work?"

Julia frowned and glanced at Mary without moving her head. "I don't have a problem with your work, Mary. But we named it the Holographic Visualization Chamber for good reasons, not the least of which is avoiding a Hollywood lawsuit."

"And everybody calls it 'the holodeck' anyway." Mary edged between Julia and the doors, practically daring the other woman to meet her gaze. "Because that's what it is. And come on, 'HOVIC' doesn't exactly roll off the tongue."

"We need a unique name to copyright," Julia said, still not moving. "A descriptive name that tells people all over the world what it does, and doesn't sound offensive or ridiculous in any known language. Do you have any idea how much research goes into this?"

"Last time I checked, this company was sitting on ten billion dollars in cash," Mary said. "Why don't we just *buy* the 'holodeck' name from Paramount?"

Julia turned ever so slightly to face Mary. "First of all, they would never sell. It's like a patent. Once you get it, you never let it go; the most you ever do is license it for a short but renewable period.

"And second, if we went to them with that kind of proposal, they would—if you'll pardon my language—bend us over the conference table and screw us like a cheap whore." Julia narrowed her eyes. "Asking for something is a show of weakness. Asking means you want. And want can be used as leverage.

"That's why neither of us walked out of this elevator, even though we didn't want to be trapped in here with each other. Leaving would have told the other person we didn't want to bear the uncomfortable silence. And that knowledge could be used against us later—an annoyance, a threat, even an outright attack. Do you understand?"

"Yeah, yeah, I understand," Mary said, stepping back.

"Good." Julia nodded authoritatively. "That's all."

Mary folded her arms. "Geez, Mom, the uncomfortable silence would have been preferable."

The corner of Julia's mouth twitched. "You started it."

Mary smiled in spite of herself. "Nuh-uh."

"Yuh-huh."

By the time the doors opened on forty-seven, both women were laughing uproariously.

TO CRUISE OR NOT TO CRUISE
August 19, 2011

Liz's phone always seemed to buzz when she was in the middle of something that required two hands, like changing an IV or catheter. This time it was a protomyelin shunt. She clicked her jaw once to decline the call and finished locking Mr. Carton's collar back into place. He looked up from the bed and grinned.

"That your boyfriend again?" he asked.

"Probably," Liz said. "How's the shoulder today? Still sore?"

"Don't change the subject," Mr. Carton said. "He still trying to get you to go on that vacation?"

"Does everyone in this hospital know everything about my personal life?"

"I demand daily updates from the nurse's station. Answer the question."

Liz sighed. "He's afraid it's going to sell out. Apparently it's a very popular cruise."

Mr. Carton shook his head. "Don't go."

Liz frowned. "You're not going to tell me life is short? I should live with no regrets? All that stuff?"

"You're not an idiot," Mr. Carton said. "Cruises are expensive. And what do you get out of it? Some pictures, a sunburn, probably gain ten pounds 'cause you've got nothing to do but eat. And get ripped off by island tourist traps."

"It's even worse than that," Liz said. "This is an interplanetary cruise. No stops. One week to Mars, one week back—"

Mr. Carton sat up. "Are you insane? Trapped in an enclosed space for two weeks? You'll be lucky if you don't kill each other!"

Liz recoiled. "Calm down, Mr. Carton. Your neck—"

"Listen to me," he said. "I speak from experience. My wife, God rest her soul, convinced me to go on a road trip once. Ten days.

Trapped in the same damn car, eating together, sleeping together. We never spent more than a few minutes apart. It was miserable. I nearly divorced her. Hell, I almost left her by the side of the road more than once."

"Lie down," Liz said. Mr. Carton groaned as she helped him. "It can't have been that bad. Weren't you two married for a long time?"

"Fifty-two years, until the cancer took her. But I tell you, that stupid road trip was the toughest ten days of my entire life. If anything had gone wrong—a flat tire, a bad meal, the wrong hotel room... I thought about strangling her more than once."

"But you didn't," Liz said. "You stayed together."

"You're not listening," Mr. Carton said. "We got lucky. It could have ended then, and I wouldn't have had the good life I had with Corrine. Do yourself a favor. Don't risk it. You got a good thing going with this guy, what's-his-name."

"Barrett."

"What kind of a name is that? Don't get me started." Mr. Carton waved a hand. "Trust me. You'll be happier if you don't go. Just be satisfied with what you have, don't ask for more."

Liz pulled the covers up to Mr. Carton's chest and looked at her left hand.

"Get some rest, Mr. Carton," she said. "I need to go make a phone call."

WANT YOU GONE
November 4, 2011

On Tuesday, Cletus and LeeAnn Savier went missing.

"What do you mean, missing?" said Pauline Jemison, Chief of Security aboard the Princess of Mars Cruises flagship, *Dejah Thoris*. "We're half a million kilometers from the nearest planet or spacecraft. Where the hell could they go?"

"I'm just telling you what the cabin stewards told me." Jefferson Logan, the ship's cruise director, shrugged his broad shoulders. In addition to overseeing the cruise activity schedule, he also kept track of the associated statistics: how many passengers attended each show, how many booked which tours or excursions, who ate at which restaurant for which meal. The data helped him plan for future demand, and also alerted him to any unusual activity patterns. Like two passengers suddenly going unaccounted for.

"They booked a Royal Banquet at Mortimer's tonight, but didn't show up," Jeff continued. "Two stewards checked the room after calling. No sign of them."

Jemison raised an eyebrow. Mortimer's was the ship's most high-class restaurant, with a standing dress code and entrée prices that ran into the thousands. Nobody stood up a reservation at Mortimer's. "Newlyweds?"

"There's no notation in their booking." Jeff brought up the passenger records on his tabletop display.

Jemison saw the ID photos and said, "Wait a minute. *That's* Cletus Savier?"

"You recognize him?"

"His name's not Cletus. And I think I know where to find him."

Jemison stepped out of the airlock and engaged her magnetic boots on the exterior hull. She took a moment to look around the blackness, just to make sure there wasn't something funny going on inside the effective range of the ship's navigational sensors, then walked forward.

She found the missing couple standing just behind the avionics section, looking through a telescope on a tripod attached to the hull and aimed at *Dejah Thoris'* destination: Mars. They were wearing the two spacesuits which she'd found still checked into the amidships excursion lounge but physically missing from inventory. Jemison switched her suit radio to the common EVA frequency.

"I hope that tripod has magnetic feet, *Cletus*," she said, "otherwise you're getting billed for the hull repairs."

The spacesuited figure on the left turned, and a familiar brown face smiled at her through the helmet. "Good to see you, too, Chief."

Jemison nodded at the other person. "You going to introduce me to the wife?"

The second figure rotated around, and Jemison saw a pink face with twinkling blue eyes. The woman smiled and shook Jemison's gloved hand. "Hi! I'm LeeAnn. Cletus said we might run into one of his friends on board, but I didn't think he meant the crew."

"Oh, we go way back." Jemison squinted at "Cletus." "I remember the first time I caught him breaking half a dozen ship's regulations and interstellar laws."

"Oh, we can afford to pay the fines," LeeAnn said. "It's less hassle than chartering a private spacecraft, anyway."

Something occurred to Jemison. "Is 'LeeAnn' even your real name?"

The other woman winked. "It is this week."

Jemison grumbled. "Congratulations. You two are perfect for each other."

Curtis C. Chen

SO IS THIS A GAME OR NOT
March 16, 2012

The passengers weren't listening, and Hartz was getting frustrated. He tried using one of the phrases he'd heard McGregor saying over the last few days to get the group's attention.

"Now hear this!" Hartz shouted at the crowd gathered in Cargo Bay Two.

"Quiet!" said one of the passengers, a stout man with dark hair. He waved his hands to get the others to settle down. "This must be the next clue."

"This is not a clue!" Hartz shouted. "Your tour leader is dead!"

"What?" another man said, frowning.

"We're under attack," Hartz said. "The raiders breached our starboard hull, and McGregor got blown out into space."

"Somebody died?" a third man said. "The plot thickens."

"So you're going to be giving us the clues now?" Dark Stout asked.

"Stop talking about clues!" Hartz pointed at the doors in the back of the room. "I need everyone to go back to their cabins right now. Lock your doors and stay there until a crew member tells you it's safe to come out again!"

Nobody moved.

"So we'll get the next clue in our cabins?" Dark Stout asked.

"Maybe they hid something in there," a woman said.

"They couldn't have," another woman said. "Pavel and I were in our cabin all morning—"

Hartz stepped forward, grabbed Dark Stout by his collar, and yelled, "Do you understand English? You're in danger! The whole ship is in danger! Go back to your cabins and lock the damn doors!"

"Okay, okay," the man said, wriggling out of Hartz's grip and turning to the crowd. "I guess we're going back to our rooms, then."

112

"Don't know why they made us come here in the first place," somebody grumbled.

"It's part of the story," someone else said. "A new plot point. They had to make sure we all heard it at the same time, *obviously.*"

A woman with bright green hair tapped Hartz on the shoulder. "You're a wonderful actor. Are you available next month? My nephew's having his bar mitzvah—"

"Ma'am," Hartz said, "we can discuss whatever you like after the ship is safe, but right now, I need you to go back—"

The bulkhead behind Hartz exploded outward. A chunk of debris slammed into his head and knocked him to the floor, unconscious, seconds before a three-legged alien entered the room, brandishing an energy rifle.

"Holy cats!" one of the passengers said. "They really went all out on this game. These effects are fantastic!"

Others murmured agreement.

The alien waved its rifle and emitted a string of trilling noises.

"What did he say?" one woman asked another.

"I'm pretty sure that wasn't English," a man said.

Dark Stout stepped forward. "I've seen this type of puzzle before. We're going to have to translate the 'alien language.' I'll start. Somebody take notes!"

The alien was quite surprised when, instead of resisting, its new prisoners began engaging in conversation. It took longer than usual to herd them into their cells, but they seemed awfully happy about the whole process. It was all very confusing.

Curtis C. Chen

PHOBOS CRUISE CRAZY
September 9, 2011

"You handled that well," Barrett said as Liz pulled off her nitrile gloves.

"Good thing we're out of zero-gravity," Liz said. "There'd be blood everywhere—seriously, can you put the camera away for one second?"

Barrett snapped another picture. "You'll want to remember this later."

"I doubt that."

Liz stuffed her gloves into the biohazard bag being held by a uniformed crewman. She had to admit, there was no shortage of service personnel on board the *Dejah Thoris*. She could hardly turn around without someone offering to get her a drink or find her an activity.

Princess of Mars Cruises wanted none of its passengers to be bored. They did their best to reduce interplanetary travel time: the spacecraft accelerated for the first half of each voyage, then spun around and decelerated for the rest. That also meant a full day of zero-gravity at midway, which was the highlight of the trip for many people. Unfortunately, some less sober passengers forgot when they were back in gravity and continued moving as if they were still weightless.

This particular man, whose head wound Liz had just sewn up, had attempted to fly down a circular staircase. He was very definitely drunk.

"You're too young to be a doctor," the man slurred, failing to grope Liz with one hand.

She moved out of his reach. "I'm an ICU nurse."

"That's hot. Wanna have dinner with me?"

Barrett leaned forward. "No, she doesn't."

114

Liz heard a commotion. Another crewman, this one with stripes on his uniform, made his way through the crowd holding a red-and-white plastic case. He stopped next to Liz.

"I'm Doctor Sawhney," he said. "Are you the nurse?"

Liz nodded. "Pulse and respiration normal. Probable concussion, but the bleeding's stopped."

Doctor Sawhney knelt down to examine the drunkard's skull. "Excellent work, Miss——?"

"Chartier."

"Do you always carry a sewing kit?"

"No." Liz nodded at Barrett. "My boyfriend lost a button on his shirt, and we needed to fix it for the formal dinner tonight. We were on our way back to our room when we saw this idiot fall down the stairs."

"Get him to Sickbay. I'll be there in a minute," Sawhney said to the crewmen who were helping the drunkard to his feet. "Thank you, Miss Chartier. I'm sorry I was delayed, but we had a situation in the excursion area."

"What kind of situation?" Barrett asked.

"I'll tell you all about it," Sawhney said, "tonight during dinner at the Captain's Table."

Liz knew exactly how much one of those seats cost. "Oh, we couldn't possibly——"

"It's complimentary," Sawhney said. "For both of you. Who knows what kind of diseases Mr. Midlife Crisis back there is carrying, and how many people he might have infected if you hadn't been here. Please, I insist."

"We'll be there," Barrett said. "Thank you!"

Sawhney walked back to the elevators. Liz glared at Barrett. He shrugged.

"It's the Captain's Table! We might never have the opportunity to do this again."

Liz shook her head. "I sure hope not."

ON ORBIT
December 4, 2009

"Someone," Don said, "put poison in the Coke machine?"

"Well, technically, the poison was attached to the water intake," Thomas said. "It's a good thing Richard could taste the difference. And then complained about it."

"How is he, by the way?"

"Nic says he'll be fine. She doesn't want him going EVA for a few days, so I put David into the rotation. We're checking the rest of our water supply now, but it's going to take a while."

Don shook his head. His white hair pixelated with the motion; the low-bandwidth videophone wasn't designed to support much more than talking heads.

"Right." Don tapped at something off-screen. "We'll send more potable water rations in the next supply run. Anything else go wrong this week? Alien body snatchers? A new strain of drug-resistant bacteria?"

"That was a rhinovirus," Thomas said. "And no. That's all the bad news." He tried and failed to hide his smile.

"Oh, boy," Don said. "You did it, didn't you? You nailed Penny."

"Don! I'm offended." Thomas waggled a finger. "And Penny would be, too. She much prefers the terms 'banged,' 'knocked boots,' or 'played hide-the-sausage.'"

The white-haired man sighed. "Is this a space station or a soap opera?"

Thomas shrugged. "Hey, I just work here."

"Seriously, Thomas," Don said, "I can't have you sleeping with anyone in your chain of command. It's bad for morale, not to mention just plain unprofessional."

It took Thomas a moment to process what he heard. "Wait. What are you talking about? We're not even in the same department.

116

I'm Engineering, Penny's Bioscience—"

"You're being promoted," Don said. "Congratulations, Thomas; we're making it official. You're the new Station Chief."

"No." Thomas' finger came up again, this time threatening. "No. You can't do this to me, Don. You don't want *me* in charge. Cynthia! Give it to Cynthia. She's better at logistics anyway."

"Station doesn't need a log," Don said. "Station needs a leader. That's you."

"Oh, come on! Just because I happened to remember where the emergency supplies were that one time—"

"You know, most people are happy when they get promoted at work."

Thomas shook his head. "I'm flattered, Don, really I am, but this isn't what I want. Not right now." He couldn't stop thinking about Penny—her smile, her lips, her smooth, pale skin. He didn't want to stop thinking about her.

"Too bad." Don's eyes glittered under a scowl. "What everyone on station *needs* is more important than what you *want*. It's out of my hands anyway. The board voted yesterday. I'm just the messenger."

"I never wanted your job, Don," Thomas said softly.

"I know. Believe me, I know."

"'Chain of command,'" Thomas muttered. "What are we, a military shop now? Am I going to be issuing uniforms and sidearms next week?"

"I'm hoping it won't come to that," Don said. "But you've still got a—what's the term?—'locked room mystery' on your hands. We need to deal with that first."

"Yeah," Thomas said. "Let's hope it doesn't turn into a murder mystery."

HAILING FREQUENCY
April 19, 2013

Carranda waited for the captain to turn his head, then palmed the data chip from her control panel.

"Request permission to visit the head, Captain," she said.

Captain Bailey Numpshol, Hero of the Tenth Fleet, recipient of the Plated Crescent for Valor in Service, inclined his head toward the comms station, grunted, and waved his hand as a sign of approval.

Carranda bit her tongue to keep from saying something her career might regret later, stood up, and walked to the private lavatory in the starboard aft corner of the bridge. She waited for the overhead illumination to flicker on, checked the lock on the door, and then pulled the computer tablet off her equipment belt. She slid the data chip into the tablet's reader slot.

She hated the face that appeared on the screen a few seconds later, after her personal encryption key had unlocked the coded transmission from Central Command. She hated her nineteen-year-old self for agreeing to run an errand for a devastatingly handsome midshipman. One stupid task which had plunged her into the dark and twisted tunnels of political espionage, where she was now trapped.

"Hello, Lieutenant Vurzo," said the face. The audio was being piped directly into Carranda's cochlear implant. "First things first. Your transfer request has been denied."

Carranda cursed under her breath.

"I'm sorry," the face said, without a hint of apology in his voice, "but you're too valuable in your current posting. We need an asset aboard *Scamander*, and your bridge station is the perfect cover. You're right in the middle of the action, but nobody notices you."

She wanted to punch the man on her screen. She wanted to punch him in the nose and make him bleed. She wanted to do anything that resulted in a visible, tangible result.

Eighteen months aboard the *Scamander*, suffering under that arrogant bastard Numpshol, passing intel back and forth without ever knowing why or if her work was making a difference. Central Command said she was essential, but they said that to everyone. Sometimes right before they "closed the loop" to prevent any possible security breaches.

"Your next assignment will be somewhat complicated," the face said. "Encoded in the sideband of this transmission is a chemical formula. Follow the provided instructions to override the safety protocols in your personal food dispenser and synthesize the compound.

"Once you've manufactured the liquid, put a few drops in Captain Numpshol's morning coffee. The compound acts very quickly. He won't feel anything.

"Complete this task before *Scamander* reaches Paglaban. If you can't get Numpshol to ingest the compound, find some other way to remove him from command, permanently. We don't care how you do it. Just make sure Commander Jauneen Marfish is the acting captain of *Scamander* when you make contact with Paglaban. We need her in that center seat.

"That is all, Lieutenant Vurzo. Go and execute."

Carranda turned off the tablet. Central Command had never ordered her to kill before. Her stomach churned, and her legs felt weak. She might actually need to use the toilet after all.

Curtis C. Chen

FIGHT OR FLIGHT
February 19, 2010

"Does *anything* work on this damned ship?" yelled Admiral Lanec.

Another blast rocked the *Claudius*, and Lieutenant Halifax Ornan saw her shield power indicator drop to sixty-four percent. Hali willed her fists to unclench and guided her hands back to the controls.

"Particle beams still off-line," Hali said. "Auto-cannons are tracking, but—"

"Pea-shooters," said Lanec. "Where the hell is *Augustus?*"

"Checking now, captain," said Lieutenant Brotman, seated next to Hali at Navigation. Joseph Lanec was now in command of the *Claudius*, and by protocol, the crew had to address him as "captain."

Hali's gaze wandered over to the spot on the deck where Captain Adam Satut, her former commanding officer, had bled to death less than five minutes ago. His blood was losing its wet shine and drying to a dull, brick-like texture.

"Lieutenant Ornan!"

Hali's head snapped back up. "Yes, captain!"

"Repair status on particle beams!"

Hali's fingers thudded against her console. "Crews have replaced the energizer on Bank Two. Fifty seconds to full charge."

"Helm, maneuver us to the enemy's ventral approach," Lanec said.

Brotman hesitated. "Sir?"

"Get underneath them!" Lanec shouted. "Weapons, target their forward thruster array! Do you need me to explain that, too?"

"No, sir," Hali said.

From her seat at Communications, Ensign Terhun said, "Captain, I have the *Augustus*."

"On screen!"

A pale man with a thin mustache shimmered into view. "Admiral

120

Lanec?"

"Long story, Captain Etter," Lanec said. "I need you to disengage *Augustus'* navigational safeties and alter course to this heading." He nodded at Brotman. Hali saw coordinates flash across the secure ship-to-ship channel.

Etter frowned. "That's a collision course, Admiral."

"That's why you need to disengage your safeties."

"We're barely a quarter the size of that ship," Etter said. "And with their shields up, we won't even scratch their hull."

"You're not trying to damage them," Lanec said. "Your shields are still at full power. *Augustus* will just bounce off."

"With all due respect, Admiral, you're going to make my whole crew spacesick just to create a diversion?"

Lanec threw up his hands. "Do they not teach basic kinematics at the Academy anymore? You're coming at us at, what, point-one-cee?" Even Hali knew those numbers: ten percent of lightspeed, nearly thirty million meters per second. "Superior momentum! Do the math!"

A smile crept onto Etter's face. "Our speed trumps their mass."

"After we disable their forward thrusters, your impact will send them into a flat spin toward the planet," Lanec said. "If we're lucky, they won't be able to regain control before hitting atmo."

"Yes, sir," Etter said. "Disengaging safeties and changing course."

"Give 'em hell," Lanec said. "*Claudius* out."

The viewscreen blinked back to a tactical display. Brotman turned in his chair and said, "Brilliant strategy, captain! Using our ships as projectiles—"

"Save it for the debrief," Lanec said. "Weapons, is it peanut butter jelly time?"

Hali looked over her shoulder. "Sir?"

Lanec rolled his eyes. "I'll teach you the song later. Do we have particle beams?"

"Ten seconds, captain."

Lanec nodded. "You may fire when ready."

RESCUE GONE
July 22, 2011

Kevin's hologram materialized in the ship's mess. That was odd; skippers usually displayed rescue holograms on their navigation boards, to provide the most information they could during a limited connection time.

There were several people in the mess. Kevin nodded at the nearest crewman and said, "I'm Warrant Officer Kevin Rhee, beaming from Orion Rescue Buoy 73. What's the nature of your emergency?"

The crewman stood up, fidgeting. "We've had a hull breach."

"Can you show me a damage report?"

"Um, yeah." The crewman gestured to a small screen above a food dispenser.

Kevin walked over to the screen and read the display. "This says you've got two breaches, port and starboard." The locations didn't line up, so it couldn't have been a single, through-and-through meteoroid strike. "What happened?"

The crewman's eyes darted around the mess before he answered. "I don't know. I wasn't on duty when it happened. Sleeping! I was sleeping."

Kevin's right hand drifted to his left wrist, but he hesitated before hitting the kill switch. Regulations were fuzzy about what circumstances would legally release a rescue hologram from his obligation to aid a vessel in distress. And Kevin didn't want to risk innocent lives just because one sailor had drunk too much coffee.

A tall, shirtless man entered the mess. Tattoos covered his skin from the neck down. Just as Kevin recognized the symbol on the man's right bicep, his vision blinked, and he knew he was in trouble.

Kevin slapped his kill switch. Nothing happened.

The tattooed man walked up to Kevin's hologram and grinned.

"Welcome aboard. I'm Captain Branson."

The blink in Kevin's vision had been the local computer taking control of his holo-projection. Rescue communication protocols degraded gracefully that way, when circumstances made a continuous data stream impractical—like pirates intentionally jamming the signal.

"Warrant Officer Kevin Rhee," Kevin said. "Orion Rescue Corps, service number—"

"Save it," Branson said. "Tell us about Hemet Interstellar's trading routes."

Kevin shook his head. "I don't know anything about private cargo carriers."

"Do I look stupid?" Branson spat. "Let me explain your situation. You've been downloaded, and we've modified our hologram engine so you can feel things like this."

He slammed a fist into Kevin's face. An impossible, searing pain shot through Kevin's entire body. He yelped and stumbled.

"Painful, isn't it?" Branson said. "We can make you hurt real bad, for a real long time. Tell us what we want to know, and we'll turn off your program."

"Go to hell."

Branson raised an arm. Kevin disappeared before the punch landed and reappeared on the far side of the mess. A murmur rippled through the room.

"I'm inside your computers, remember?" Kevin said. "I can access every system tied to your auto-pilot, including comms and navigation. I can drive this ship wherever I want, and I'm already broadcasting your location to every law enforcement sloop between here and Saturn."

"You can't access shit," Branson said. "Your program's running in a sandbox VM. You're bluffing!"

The ship shuddered. Kevin smiled. "Am I?"

GUARDIANS
September 3, 2010

Thirteen brave soldiers storm'd into Mount Mars.
Thirteen brave soldiers cannot see the stars.
Thirteen brave soldiers are buried in dust.
Thirteen brave soldiers will do what they must.
— *colonial nursery rhyme, c. 2130*

Jennifer knew what to expect when she entered the cavern. She'd been fully briefed by the Security Council, but she still wasn't prepared for the tangible quality of the light that filled the space when the soldiers appeared. The translucent figures seemed to melt out of the rocks all around Jennifer, and each one shimmered like nothing else she had ever seen or imagined.

"Hello," Jennifer said. "I'm Envoy Wakefield—"

A ribbon of light shot up from the ground, enveloped Jennifer like a cocoon, and knocked her off her feet. The light wasn't quite solid—it didn't grip her body so much as it *interfered* with it, making her skin crawl where it touched and partially phased through her— but it was strong enough to lift her a few centimeters into the air.

One ghostly face, a woman, rose to Jennifer's eye level. She looked familiar—angular features and straight, shoulder-length hair— but Jennifer couldn't recall a name from the personnel files. A lot of records had gone missing during the war.

"What year is it?" the woman asked, in a voice that sounded like running water.

Jennifer struggled to breathe. "Who are you?"

"Answer my question," the woman said.

"I was told not to."

The ribbon of light disappeared, and Jennifer dropped to the dirt. She yelped as she landed and fell forward onto her knees. The ghosts started merging back into the rocks.

"Wait!" Jennifer said. She scrambled to her feet and reached for the woman who had spoken. Jennifer's fingers sank into the woman's shoulder, and she tried to remember her briefing on the hard-light projector. How long could she be in contact with a ghost before her cells started imploding? Was it three minutes? She'd have to risk it.

The woman struggled against Jennifer's grip, but she couldn't exert enough force on her own, and the other twelve soldiers had disappeared already.

"I'm here to give you an update on our research," Jennifer said.

"Save your breath," the woman said. "You envoys have been lying to us for years. Maybe even centuries. We know the war's over. We know Mars was bombed into a radioactive wasteland. We know the only reason you people even visit is so you can change the batteries on the alien hardware, to keep us trapped here, to keep the wormhole open."

"We're very close to being able to free you," Jennifer said.

"It's been almost a minute," the woman said. "Are you sure you don't need that hand?"

Jennifer released the woman's shoulder and yanked back her hand. The woman flew up toward the ceiling of the cavern.

"I'm telling you the truth!" Jennifer said.

But the woman was already gone.

Thirteen brave soldiers stand watch under Mars.
Thirteen brave soldiers protect ev'ry star.
Thank you, brave soldiers—what secrets you keep!
But one day, we promise, you will go to sleep.

Curtis C. Chen

126

Thursday's Children

UP IN THE AIR
November 5, 2010

Stratton's job is to fly, chasing a thin stripe of daylight across the planet. He was born in the air, and God willing, he'll die without ever setting foot on dirt. He doesn't question these circumstances. He doesn't wonder about the world below. Stratton just flies.

His partner's name is Victoria. They met for the first time three days ago, when the air tanker refueled Stratton's bomber and a devotion crew removed the body of his previous co-pilot, Marcus.

The ceremony was dignified and short. Stratton and Victoria stood side by side watched Marcus' body fall through the open bomb bay and disappear into the clouds below.

"How did he die?" Victoria asked.

"Unknown," Stratton replied.

Victoria frowned. "That's a little worrisome, isn't it?"

Stratton shrugged. He didn't understand why Marcus had suddenly started vomiting blood and then stopped breathing. It wasn't important exactly what had killed Marcus. It was important for Stratton to get back to work. Back to flying.

Now, Victoria completes her maintenance checklist and watches Stratton from the right-hand seat as he adjusts the flight controls for some approaching weather.

"Must get pretty boring up here," she says.

"In the cockpit?" Stratton asks, confused.

"In the sky," Victoria says.

Stratton struggles to understand what she might mean. He can't imagine anything boring about living above the clouds, watching a perpetual sunset, seeing stars twinkling on the edge of night. He can't imagine a better life than the one he has.

Victoria fills the silence. "I grew up in Rookly," she says. Stratton recognizes the name of the city from the bomber's land maps.

"Never thought much about the sky until I enlisted. I mean, we'd see the flights overhead, but it didn't really affect our everyday lives."

"Our work is important," Stratton says.

"Oh, I know that," Victoria says. "But it's just so far removed from everything, you know? That's why I joined up. I wanted to see the world from a different perspective." She's staring at Stratton. He can see her out of the corner of his eye. "What do you think? How does this compare to life on the ground?"

"Never been on the ground," Stratton says.

"You're kidding," Victoria says. "Come on! You must have been born on land, right?"

Stratton shakes his head. "My parents were Sky Corps. They lived on the *Patrick Hayden.*"

"The heli-carrier?" Victoria is momentarily speechless. Then she reaches across the center console and punches Stratton in the arm. "No way! You're messing with me!"

Stratton feels his face growing hot. He hates this woman, who talks too much and asks too many questions and touches him without asking permission. He wants her to go away. He wonders if what killed Marcus in that seat will kill her soon. Stratton can only hope.

"Yes," he says, "I'm messing with you."

Victoria laughs. "You're all right, Strat."

Stratton has nothing to say. He stares straight ahead, out at the sky, and watches the sunset for as long as he can.

GUARDS

December 18, 2009

"Asshole," Ivan muttered as the door closed.

"Geez, say it a little louder, why don't you?" Conrad said. "Those doors are bullet-proof, not sound-proof."

The small, circular room was empty except for the display pedestal, two consoles with chairs, and a trash bin between them. Ivan and Conrad were seated facing a holographic map of the base.

Ivan swiveled his chair around, lifted his forearm onto his console, and flipped up his middle finger.

"That's good. Real mature," Conrad said.

Ivan brought his other arm up and deployed his other middle finger as well.

"I'm going back to work now," Conrad said, ignoring the dance that Ivan's middle fingers were doing.

"Don't you ever get sick of it?" Ivan asked, withdrawing his hands. "Following orders all the time? I sure do."

"Probably shouldn't have joined the Army then."

"Didn't have much of a choice." Ivan slumped in his chair.

"Is this where you tell me a sob story and I pretend to care?" Conrad said.

Ivan slapped his console. A red light started blinking, and a shrill alarm bell sounded. "How about that? You care about that?"

Conrad worked his own controls and silenced the alarm. "What is wrong with you? Now we have to write up an incident report. After the duty officer chews us out for another false alarm. Are you trying to get thrown into stockade?"

Ivan pulled a candy bar out of his shirt pocket. He unwrapped it and had the bar halfway to his mouth when Conrad leaned over and snatched it away.

"Hey!" Ivan said.

"No food or drink," Conrad said, throwing the candy bar into the trash. "Regulations."

"That was the last nutty bar at the exchange," Ivan said. "You owe me."

Conrad grabbed his crotch. "I got your nutty bar right here."

Ivan leapt out of his chair and tackled Conrad. They fell to the ground in a tangle of fists and shouts.

The door slid open. The duty officer entered and shouted, "Attention!"

Conrad and Ivan separated, stood, and lined up against the wall.

"What is going on here?" the duty officer asked.

"He started it," Ivan said, pointing at Conrad.

"What are you, twelve years old?"

"Twelve and a half," Ivan muttered.

"WHAT DID YOU SAY?" the duty officer screamed into Ivan's face.

"Twelve and a half, SIR!" Ivan replied.

The duty officer turned to Conrad. "And what's YOUR excuse?"

"He had a candy bar, sir!" Conrad said.

"A candy bar," the duty officer repeated.

"A nutty bar," Conrad said. Then, after a moment: "They're the best."

The duty officer shook his head. "Okay. I'm going to write up both you idiots, and your CO can decide what to do with you later. Now sit down!"

Conrad and Ivan went back to their consoles. The duty officer walked toward the exit and stopped in the open doorway to give them one final dirty look.

"Kids these days," the duty officer muttered as he left. The door slid shut behind him.

"Asshole," Conrad and Ivan said in unison.

TUNNELLERS
August 27, 2010

"Tell me again how we're not going to get shot, killed, and/or court-martialed?" Rhee said.

"You worry too much," Murtry said.

"Tell that to Harmsa."

"Harmsa had a big mouth." Murtry glanced around the corner of the building. "Okay, it's time." Murtry pulled out a metallic starfish. "Grab one of these arms."

Rhee frowned. "Is this another teleporter?"

"Just touch it!"

Rhee put his hand on the device, and Murtry pressed down on its center. Everything around them rippled.

"Let's go," Murtry said, moving into the light.

"Guard!"

"Chill." Murtry pointed at the other end of the building. The guard there was frozen, the smoke from his cigarette hanging in the air like a translucent gray ribbon.

"So the starfish stops time?" Rhee asked, following Murtry to the door.

"Basically." Murtry pulled out his lockpicks. "Watch the smoke, warn me when it starts moving again."

He got the door open in less than a minute. They went through and closed it behind them.

The inside of the warehouse was empty except for a large, glowing oval of light floating a foot off the ground. It showed unfamiliar barracks behind a barbed-wire fence. They watched an old man walk into view.

"You think he can see us?" Murtry said.

The man turned to look at them. He threw himself against the fence, shouting.

"Yes," Rhee said. "Also, your starfish time-stopper has worn off."

"What language is that?" Murtry asked.

Rhee looked at the yellow, six-pointed star on the man's shirt. "Polish."

"Excellent observation, Airman Rhee," came a booming voice behind them.

Murtry and Rhee whirled and stood at attention. Colonel Cranston, the base commander, walked up to them, followed by two MPs wielding pistols.

"Airman Murtry," Cranston said, holding out his hand, "I believe you're holding some inventory from Hangar 18."

Murtry sheepishly handed over the metal starfish.

"You didn't think we'd have detectors for these things?" Cranston shook his head. "Now that your pal Harmsa's talking, we have enough to lock up all three of you troublemakers. But it would be a shame if the Air Force didn't get some use out of you first." He nodded at the oval. "What do you think that is?"

Rhee said, "Time machine."

"Close," Cranston said. "We've been calling it a 'side-portal.' It's an opening to a different time, and a different reality."

"Like a parallel universe?" Murtry asked.

"Exactly," Cranston said. "We should be able to bury something in the past and dig it up in the present, but we can't. The theory is that the portal branches to a completely separate future."

"I have a question, Colonel," Rhee said.

"Go ahead, Airman."

"What's the point of time travel if you can't change the future?"

"Research," Cranston said. "What if the South had won the Civil War? Or the Germans had assassinated Hitler in 1944?" He smiled. "We've got all kinds of thought experiments to try out. And who better to send back in time to tinker with history than two of our best liars?"

IN THE NAVY
January 11, 2011

Petty Officer Second Class Sandra Choe, Sandy to her friends, was bored.

The clock on the wall read 11:32. She had the whole day off, but she'd already read every book in the base library, and the next planetside shuttle didn't make another run for five and a half hours.

"I'm bored," Sandy said.

Her bunkmate, Charlene, grumbled in the bed above Sandy. "Why don't you go get some lunch? I hear it's cake day."

Sandy contained her excitement long enough to ask, "Will you be okay here by yourself?"

Charlene waved a hand over the edge of her bunk. "I'll be fine. It's just a rhinovirus. Go."

Sandy went to the cafeteria, where there was indeed cake. She selected the two largest, most frosting-laden pieces and sat down to enjoy them. Halfway through her second piece, two Master Chief Petty Officers came into the cafeteria and sat down within earshot of Sandy.

"Still can't fucking believe it," said the first Master Chief.

"Total fucking clusterfuck," said the second Master Chief.

"How the fuck do you misplace half a million dollars' worth of fucking armor?"

"And you fucking know that's coming out of our fucking budget."

"Fucking fucks."

The only unusual thing about this conversation was the discussion of missing equipment. Sandy, being a sensor tech, had never worked directly on armor, but she had calibrated plenty of sensor arrays to detect enemy armor.

After finishing her cake, Sandy found her supervising officer,

136

explained about the conversation she'd overheard, and asked for permission to search the base's cargo holds.

"Do you know how many fucking holds this base has?" her SO asked. "Waste of fucking time. But hey, if that's how you want to spend your fucking day off, go to town."

Sandy borrowed a portable sensor deck from her shop and began searching. The Gamma Accra orbital platform had grown "organically," as the PR flacks liked to say, and was in many places a maze of twisty passages. The cargo holds had been designed for access from space, not from inside the base.

It took her nearly an hour to locate and access the first hold. Sandy found nothing interesting in that one, or the second one. The third hold had several containers with more radiation shielding than necessary, but Sandy ignored them.

She found the missing equipment in the fourth cargo hold. It had been mislabeled—somebody had typed "5" instead of "4" on the manifest—but it was all there, a platoon's worth of armor pegging the needle on Sandy's sensor deck.

Her SO actually smiled when she reported her success.

"Well done, Choe!" he said, shaking her hand. "You'll get a commendation for this. Fuck, I'm putting you in for a fucking medal! Good work. Dismissed!"

Sandy went back to her quarters, where Charlene was snoring loudly. The clock on the wall read 16:04. The next shuttle didn't leave for two more hours, and there wouldn't be any new books in the base library until the next USO ship docked.

"I'm bored," Sandy said.

Curtis C. Chen

SACRIFICE
June 1, 2012

"Beacon!" The familiar, pulsating light pattern flashed across the left side of Semira's visor. "You see it, soldier? *Beacon!* Just over the ridge! Now *move!*"

Riddam didn't move. Semira shifted her weight and slid down the slope, bringing a cloud of fine dust with her. It wasn't until the next bombardment ignited a new set of fireballs that she saw why Riddam wasn't moving.

The armor had saved their lives on more than one occasion. It wasn't just weaponry, or defensive equipment; it also cleaned water, identified toxins in local flora, and processed and stored waste so hostile forces couldn't track the unit by their organic residue. But when push came to shove, it was still just a suit of armor.

Riddam's entire right side had been crushed by an enemy drone. Semira couldn't believe she hadn't heard the crash, but the evidence was right there, smashed into the hillside: gnarled metal beneath a cracked ceramic shell, detonation sensors in the nose melted into a black lump.

She flattened against the hill, lying above the wreckage and perpendicular to Riddam, their helmets close together. Riddam still had her lance pointed upward, and her eyes continued scanning the sky, but Semira knew that unfocused look. The armor sealed itself around any life-threatening injuries until a medic could unlock it, and it also pumped painkillers into the soldier's body until overridden.

"Here's what's going to happen now," Semira said. "I'm going to pull you out of this hole. We're going to get over this fucking hill. We're going to make it to that beacon. And we're going home."

Riddam chuckled. Her eyes were thin rings of pale green circling bottomless black holes. "Thanks for the pep talk, Chief," she said, "but I only got one arm and one leg right now. You go ahead. I'll

138

catch up after my limbs grow back, okay?"

Semira grabbed Riddam's shoulder plate and yanked. She moved, but not much. "Put down the lance and push, goddammit."

"Don't be stupid, Chief."

"That's an order!"

"Well, I'll see you at the court-martial, then."

Riddam turned her head, and Semira saw the other side of her face: red and black and other colors that sat wrong against Riddam's pale skin. She might have been pretty, in another time and place. Semira suddenly realized she'd never seen Riddam outside the armor.

Semira gritted her teeth. "You're going to fucking make me *live* with this, you little bitch?"

Riddam stared back, her expression unreadable. "Woof, woof."

It took Semira a moment to remember how to laugh. "You really want those to be your last words, soldier?"

Riddam smiled. "Meet you on the other side, Chief. Hoo-rah."

Semira climbed over the hill. She didn't look back. Even after she reached the beacon, even after the pod lifted off, she didn't look back.

DRIVE ON
July 8, 2011

Debra didn't want to run over the kid, but he wasn't leaving her much choice. Blocking a military convoy wasn't directly threatening, but it was suspicious. It also kept them from moving, and that was dangerous.

She tapped the horn. The boy's mouth flapped, but his words were lost in the noise of the crowd.

"Move!" Debra waved and pointed. The boy pumped his fist in the air. Sometimes Debra thought she'd get more respect if she drove a cart and mule instead of a Humvee.

Base Command had anticipated a protest when the VIP convoy left the airport, but not a mob. The street was clogged with locals chanting, waving signs, and throwing whatever debris they could find at the Americans.

Debra ignored the projectiles. Glass bottles would shatter against the Humvee's energized defense field, and metal objects like tin cans would get deflected. Organic matter sometimes made it through, depending on its composition and velocity, but D-fields had greatly reduced casualties and vehicle damage in the field.

"Attention," said the dash computer. "Vehicle has been stopped for more than sixty seconds. Please check surroundings for possible threats."

"Thanksalot," Debra muttered. Was this just another random crowd, or had someone staged an ambush? She waved at the boy again. He raised his middle finger at her.

Then she saw what he was holding in his other hand.

No. No no no—

Debra switched the horn to ultrasonic and blasted it, forcing everyone outside to move farther away—except the boy. He stared defiantly through the windshield.

His left hand twitched against the trigger plate taped to his palm.

"Sergeant!" came the voice from the backseat. "Is there a problem?"

Debra didn't answer. She was busy with the dash computer, inputting her security override so she could manually redistribute the D-field. The screen flashed yellow, and she stepped on the accelerator.

The Humvee roared forward. The boy threw up his hands and yelped as the front bumper knocked him down. Debra stomped the brakes a split second after the boy's head disappeared from view, then smacked a button to deploy the Humvee's armor skirt.

"Debra!" The voice from the backseat was louder now. "What's going on?"

Debra opened her mouth. A small stone cracked the windshield.

Several pounds of high explosives detonated underneath the vehicle. The force field which Debra had redistributed to the undercarriage shaped the blast downward. The Humvee bounced up, then fell and landed inside the crater with a jolt.

Debra silenced the motion alarms and reset the D-field coverage. A Coke bottle sailed down and broke apart above the hood, glittering green fragments hovering for a moment before sliding away. She felt numb.

You just saved lives, Debra told herself. *One dead instead of hundreds. Besides, if they court-martial you... at least you'll get to go home.*

A hand touched her shoulder. She turned and stared into the scowling face of Congressman Wright.

"What the *hell* just happened?" he demanded.

Debra smiled weakly. "Sorry, Dad. Looks like you'll have to do another press conference tonight."

ART ATTACK
February 13, 2009

"You can't smoke in here, sir."

Rodney sighed. "So where *can* I smoke?"

"The east wing patio." The nurse pointed to a map.

"That's the other side of the hospital."

"Yes, sir."

He grumbled and shoved the cigarettes back into his pocket.

"Have you tried the patch?" the nurse asked.

He squinted at her. "Great idea. I'll ask my physician."

"Of course," the nurse said. "Best to make sure there won't be any adverse interactions with your current medication. Sir."

Another voice behind him said, "Lieutenant Geyerson? You can go in now."

Private Jeremy Dean and his squad had been patrolling the Hindu Kush mountains when they found a cave filled with prehistoric wall paintings and heavily armed Taliban. Dean had returned to the US last week for surgery.

"Do you know why I'm here, Private?" Rodney asked.

Dean nodded. "The cave paintings, right?"

Dean had been taking pictures before the ambush. Gunfire had gouged away most of the painted rock, and Dean's photos were the only remaining record.

"You don't think they're prehistoric," Dean continued, "because it doesn't fit archaeological theory or something."

Rodney flipped through his case file. He noticed Dean folding his arms when one particular photo went by.

"Actually," Rodney said, "I'm wondering why your squadmates have all killed themselves."

Dean blinked. "What?"

Rodney fanned out the crime scene and autopsy photos. "Hallmark. Cheng. Barron. They're all dead."

Dean stared at the photos. "How? Why?"

"You tell me," Rodney said. "These men didn't show any signs of depression or PTSD, but they all committed suicide in the last week."

Dean shook his head in silence.

Rodney sighed. "Look, no one would blame you. Maybe you found some drugs in that cave. Maybe it was cash. You decide a few dead terrorists aren't going to miss their loot, so you kill them and bury the treasure. Am I getting warm here?"

Dean glared at him. "I want a lawyer. Sir."

Rodney rolled his eyes. "I *am* your lawyer."

"So your winning personality didn't get him to talk. I'm shocked."

Colonel James MacAllister exhaled into Rodney's face. There were more smokers than there was elbow room on the fourth floor balcony.

"He's hiding something. Dean took one look at this photo and clammed up. It's probably where they found the loot." Rodney thumbed through his file, but couldn't find the photo. He turned over the folder and drew on the back. "There was a circular symbol—like this."

It took no effort at all to remember the image. It loomed large and clear in his mind, as if it wanted out.

The next thing Rodney knew, he was lying on the ground, being held down by MacAllister and two other officers.

"What the hell!" Rodney shouted.

MacAllister frowned at him. "You just tried to climb over the railing!"

Rodney looked at the symbol he'd drawn on the folder, and he felt it again, pressing against his consciousness.

"I need to get back to the VA," he said.

"Good idea," MacAllister said. "It's about time you had your head examined."

THIS IS THE JOB
May 31, 2013

I had to burn my clothes after the first time. There was no way to get the smell out. It wasn't that the odor was unpleasant, exactly; but it was such a unique thing, something you wouldn't, couldn't smell anywhere else. It would always remind me of the job.

The second time wasn't any better. Different, sure. I went out with a partner, a guy with a handlebar mustache who would not stop talking. Eventually I figured out that if I just kept feeding him, he'd be too busy eating to yammer about his wife or his kids or his goddamn athlete's foot. As an added bonus, the smell of the raw onions he piled on his overcooked street-vendor hot dogs helped mask the smell.

That one didn't go so well. I work alone now. But thanks to that yappy idiot, I can't eat sausages anymore, either. Reminds me of the fucking job.

Sometimes it feels like the work is taking over my life, making it so I can't do anything without thinking of how it relates to the job. I hear a song on the radio and remember that it was playing in the shopping mall where I did number four. And playing everywhere, piped into every corner of the damn place, even those long, bare concrete back hallways where every sound echoes like a curse.

I was interrupted that time. Some kid leaving his shift at the food court, still wearing his stupid colorful uniform and sipping on a giant plastic cup of sugar water. He dropped his drink and ran, but I had a job to do. So he turned into number five.

Cutting out soda pop wasn't such a bad thing. I still get plenty of caffeine from coffee, and I've also got powders and pills to keep me going when I need a boost. Plus, forcing myself to avoid the temptation of sweet fizzy drinks means I don't hang out around so many teenagers anymore. That's good. Number six was another underage girl, and that was a fucking chore. Never again. It's so much easier when I can get them drunk first.

Planning helps. I figured that out pretty quickly. You have to think on your feet in this line of work. I mean, no plan can account for everything, but it helps to have a few options in mind when you start the job. Know your exits, keep a cover story in mind, stuff like that. You don't actually need much preparation. If you don't act too strange, people will fill in most details for themselves. No need to explain if nobody asks.

Yeah, the smell still bugs me. Mostly because I don't know what it is. I mean, I know the smell of blood. I know sweat and tears and piss and shit and even brains, but it's not any one of those. Maybe it's a combination. Or maybe it's, I don't know, something else. Something particular to the work.

I hate this fucking job. But somebody's got to do it.

A SHOWER SCENE
August 10, 2012

No matter how much things may change, this fact remains the same: United States Federal Agents are still mostly straight white males, and if there's one thing straight white men do *not* want to see, it's two dudes macking on each other.

My contact at the shady motel off Route 53 wasn't exactly my type, so I appreciated the fact that he'd attempted to freshen up his breath with something synthetically minty. And that he didn't use any tongue when we kissed, an act for the benefit of the hidden cameras which the FBI or DIA or some other three-letter acronym had scattered around the room.

I had been surprised when my jailbroken smartphone detected scrambled law enforcement frequencies popping out of nearly every metal surface in the room, but sometimes it pays to be paranoid. The microlens-and-radio-transmitter bugs were invisible to the naked eye, but they lit up my phone's ultra-sensitive antenna like a Christmas tree.

Fortunately, even though I wasn't expecting any smokies to have pre-tagged this rustic roadside retreat, I'm always prepared for the worst. I texted my contact a code word indicating a change of plan and hoped his boss—my current client—had passed along the memo with our standard playbook. Good news: he had. Bad news: he was one hairy motherfucker.

After the mercifully brief lip-action, I told my contact to warm up the shower, smacking his ass for effect. While he turned on the water, I made a show of dancing around the room and disrobing, hoping my feigned enthusiasm would be enough to discourage whoever was watching. Then I joined my contact in the shower.

Here's the thing about masking noise: it doesn't work. Whether it's road traffic, or music, or a loud newscast, it's always somewhat predictable, and any law enforcement outfit with two CPUs to rub together will be able to filter out the background and get the gist of what you're saying. I don't like showering with strange men any more than the next guy, but in my line of work, it's one of the few ways to ensure a private conversation.

My contact gave me a disapproving glare when I joined him in the shower, naked. He had opted to keep his boxer shorts on. I shrugged.

He raised his hands, gesturing in the pidgin sign language my client had pre-arranged for audio-compromised situations like this.

DON'T TOUCH ME AGAIN, he signed.

I nodded. NO SPANKING. ACK. IS JOB STILL GO?

COMPLICATION. TWO TARGETS.

I shook my head. NOT WHAT WE AGREED.

BOSS WILL PAY TRIPLE.

I hesitated. A big pay hike like that was almost always bad news, but I needed the money. Besides, the original target was some milk-toast accountant; how bad could this add-on be?

WHO IS SECOND TARGET? I asked.

YOU GET DETAILS LATER, my contact replied. AGREE FIRST.

I frowned. I DON'T ENJOY DOING BUSINESS LIKE THIS.

He scowled back at me, water dripping off his mustache. THAT MAKES TWO OF US, ASSHOLE.

TELLING TALES OUT OF SCHOOL
January 29, 2010

"I can't tell you who actually *shot* JFK. But I can say this: yes, the Company was involved, and the money came from Texas."

That was Nick. I don't know how he found out about the party. I had made a point of not inviting any of his friends, who we'd hardly seen anyway since he broke up with Michelle.

She had been avoiding him all night, and I had been running interference. I was actually relieved to see Nick hitting on some random blonde.

"Think about it," he said. "The driver—sorry, can you excuse me for one second?"

I followed his gaze and saw Michelle heading to our bedroom with a couple of jackets. Nick was elbowing his way toward her. I caught him before he reached the hallway.

"Looking for the little boys' room?" I said.

"Gloria?"

I grabbed his arm and pushed him out the front door, onto the lawn. The sun had gone down hours ago, and it was cold outside. California's a desert.

"What the hell are you doing here, Nick?" I asked.

He folded his arms. "It's a party, right? Free beer."

"If you came here to harass Michelle—"

"I came to say good-bye."

"You had that chance two years ago," I said. "You blew it. She got over it. End of story."

"This is none of your business, Gloria."

That made me angry. "It *becomes* my business when you break my best friend's heart! When you dump her *over e-mail* and move to the other side of the country? It's my business when I have to make excuses for you, so she doesn't think it's all *her* fault!"

He stared at my shoes. "I'm leaving the country tonight. For a long time. Maybe forever. I wanted to..." He shrugged. "To make things right, I guess."

"Michelle wanted you to stay," I said. "She didn't get what she wanted. Why should you?"

He shook his head. "I wish I could explain."

"Why don't you just send her an e-mail?"

I regretted saying it as soon as I saw his eyes.

"Just tell her I'm sorry," he said. "Will you do that?"

I nodded. "Yeah."

"Thank you." He turned and walked toward the street.

I heard blood rushing in my ears. Maybe I had been a little too hard on him. I'd had at least four drinks that night, and they had all come out of shot glasses. I was just starting to say something when Nick stopped on the sidewalk and spoke into his wristwatch.

"One four tango," he said. "Yes. I'm alone."

The air around him shimmered and glowed like a fluorescent mirage. I heard a soft *whut* sound, and Nick vanished. One second he was there, and then he wasn't. I ran out to where he had been standing and looked up and down the street. Nothing.

I wasn't drunk. I'm sure Nick knew I was still watching when he left. He wanted me to see. And he knew I could never tell Michelle any of it.

What a bastard.

DIVISION OF LABOUR
October 15, 2010

Blake held the airtight bag over the gerbil's head until it stopped struggling and the life monitor above the cage squealed a tuneless dirge. He removed the bag and pressed the holding pin deep into the animal's spine, verifying the contacts on the control module readout, then stepped back.

"Is that all?" asked the Minister of War.

"The holding pin only prevents necrosis," Blake said. "It stimulates the nervous system to keep brain cells from deteriorating, for up to twenty-four hours."

He moved over to the second gerbil, which had two wires protruding from the back of its skull. He held the antennaed rodent down with one hand and connected two wires from the control module, then pressed the activation button.

The second gerbil collapsed, the monitor display spiked, and the first gerbil twitched back to life. A moment later, the second gerbil leapt up, shaking its head.

"So the dead rat is now imprinted with the live rat's memories?" the Minister asked.

Blake resisted the urge to point out that the animals were gerbils, not rats. "No, Minister. There is no transfer of consciousness. It's only energy. Think of it like donating blood."

The Minister nodded. "Very good, Professor. You may be the first scientist who hasn't tried to sell me immortality. But why come here at all? Why not Ministry of Health?"

"They'd never allow me to experiment on humans."

The Minister raised an eyebrow. "You have my full attention."

"I've done all I can with animals," Blake said. "It's impossible to know how a more complex brain structure will respond without using actual humans."

"And where do you propose to find these volunteers?"

"Prisoners of war," Blake said. "Detainees. Anyone who needs to disappear from a re-education center." *Like my sister.* "You're going to kill some of them during interrogation anyway; why not do something useful with their bodies?"

The Minister smiled. "I like the way you think, Professor." He snapped his fingers, and his aide produced a square of stiff paper. "You'll begin as soon as you can relocate your laboratory to Crag Island. And congratulations, you're now a Captain in the Burgish Army."

"Wh-what?" Blake suddenly felt light-headed.

"It's purely ceremonial," the Minister said, signing the paper, "but you do get a nice uniform."

"But—"

"I expect results, Professor."

The doors swung open, and one adjutant rolled away the experiment table while another hustled Blake out of the audience chamber. Before he knew what had happened, he was alone in the hallway with his brother, clutching the signed order from the Minister.

"Well?" Adam asked.

"He said yes." Blake stared at the paper.

"That's great!"

"And I'm in the Army now."

"Oh." Adam frowned. "What are you going to tell Mother?"

Blake shook his head. "I'm not. You are."

"What? Oh no. No no no. She'll kill me! Then herself!"

"Remember why we're doing this!" Blake hissed, lowering his voice. "I'm going into that hellhole to find Callie. You get to stay home with Mother. You have the easy part."

Adam grumbled. "That's debatable."

Curtis C. Chen

DEBRIEFING
January 4, 2013

"Nobody died," I said for what felt like the hundredth time.

"And that's your criterion, is it?" the examiner barked from the other side of the desk. "You destroyed an entire city block and blew the cover of everyone in your support team, but hey, there were no actual fatalities, so let's chalk that one up in the 'win' column?"

I shifted in my amazingly uncomfortable wooden chair. "All I'm saying is, it was just a training simulation. A computer-generated exercise. What's the big fuss?"

"What's the—!" The examiner's face cycled through three distinct shades of red before he shook his head. "These simulations are how we evaluate your potential to be a field agent."

"Yeah, but I knew it was a simulation, didn't I? I mean, to be really effective, shouldn't you put me in a dangerous situation which I believe is real, to see how I would actually behave?"

The examiner frowned at me. "You're suggesting that we deceive our people in order to evaluate them?"

I shrugged. "I'm just saying, knowing that it's a simulation, knowing that the stakes aren't real, diminishes my motivation."

"Oh, I see," the examiner said. "So we should use a different standard to evaluate your performance. You're just that special, is that what you're saying?"

"Well, I am—"

The examiner's fist smashed against the desktop. "I'm only going to say this once. Nobody is so extraordinary that the enemy will not kill him. Nobody is so singular that he can survive a bullet fired into his skull at point blank range.

"Our ranks and titles only matter within these walls. Out there in the field, it doesn't matter who you are. It only matters what you can do. And before we send you off, we need to know what you're

152

capable of and what your limits are. Is that clear?"

I nodded.

"Nobody gets special treatment," he said. "If you can't summon the wherewithal to do your best in training, I have no confidence that you'll perform any better in an actual life-or-death situation where you need to make split-second decisions."

"So you're not going to let me try again?"

For a moment, I thought the examiner's eyes might pop out of his head. "You are dismissed. I'll send a full evaluation report to your supervisor by the end of the day."

"Right." I stood up, reached into my pocket, and pulled out the jump drive I'd pocketed during the sim.

It hadn't been easy, finding the correct computer-controlled holo-character and then lifting the tiny prize off him, but demolishing the building had provoked an appropriate flight response in all the chars except my target. I would never have done it in the real world, but I knew how to beat a computer game.

"Will you be wanting this back, then?" I asked.

I could almost see smoke escaping from the examiner's ears, and only months of training kept me from smirking as he snatched the drive from between my fingers.

YOU HAVE ONE NEW MESSAGE
April 16, 2010

Beep

Hi, Paul. It's Jenny, from the bar last night. I was there with my girlfriends. You bought us a round of Maker's before I left?

Anyway. The reason I'm calling is because I swiped your wallet. Sorry about that. I figured you'd get your credit card back from the bartender when you settled your tab, and you'd still be able to pay for a cab.

Okay, you know what? Hell with it. I know you got home okay because I saw you. I tailed you from the bar. So I know you went home with Amber, and I know she didn't leave this morning, and you did.

I'm not sure what's going on, but I'm giving you a chance to explain. Call back and leave a message.

Beeeep

Amber. Jen. Where the hell are you? Call me.

Beep

Hello, Paul, it's Jenny again. Don't threaten me. You do not want to fuck with me. Lifting wallets and finding unlisted phone numbers are the least of what I can do.

And don't lie to me. I know there's no back door to your place. I know Amber hasn't come home or gone to work since the night she met you.

Listen... I'm sure this is all just some crazy mix-up, right? Let's meet back at the bar, have a drink, and you can explain everything and we can all have a good laugh about it. You've got my number. Call me.

Beeeep

Amber, this is not what I meant when I said you had more leash. You're off the reservation. Report in before I have to notify the station chief.

Beep

Paul! Jenny. I underestimated you. That won't happen again.

Lucky for both of you, the officer who walked into your booby trap is still alive. So the only thing we're warranted for is assault.

I'm only going to say this once. We are more concerned with Amber's safety than we are with nailing you. Just tell us where she is, and you can skip town—hell, leave the country. Let Amber go, and we can look the other way on this. Just don't do anything stupid.

Beep-beep

Agent Jennifer Carlyle. Field report. Case number five-eight-one-alpha.

Suspect Paul Nevins was apprehended with minimal injury and limited property damage at sixteen-oh-six today. Firearms discharged. No civilian casualties.

We found partially burned human remains in the trunk of Nevins' vehicle. I made a preliminary ID from Agent Brandt's necklace and earrings. City coroner is matching dental records.

The good news is, Nevins had no idea who Amber was. Repeat, no breach. It was pure dumb luck that she picked a murderer to go home with that night. Our cover is still intact.

And, for the record—I want this on the record—Amber put up a fight before she died. Nevins already had a broken jaw and a fractured wrist before we cuffed him.

Her training didn't fail her. We did.

I did.

I'm taking some time off, Gordon. I think I've earned it. Maybe a week, maybe longer.

Don't call me.

Click

NEWBODY DOES IT BETTER
September 4, 2009

Two men in a bar.

"Why don't you like talking to Lisa?"

"Come on, man."

"No, really, tell me why you don't like talking to my wife."

"Dude. It's not your wife. It's a computer simulation running inside a robot."

"*Newbody.*"

"Whatever."

"It's not a simulation. It's her mind—all the same thoughts, feelings, and memories—just running on a different substrate."

"Wow. Is that straight out of the brochure?"

"This is a common misconception. We don't make a copy, we perform a transfer."

"Are we going to have this argument, too? It's *information*. There isn't some magical brain energy that gets siphoned off and deposited into the newbody. You scan someone's skull for activity patterns and program the newbody's main computer to replay those patterns. Hell, that's not even a copy. That's mimicry."

"Look, I can't talk about it in detail, but—we know it works. One hundred percent, no doubt, it's a perfect transfer."

"And I should just take your word for it?"

"You'll just have to trust me. It's a big deal. We've been working on this problem for a long time, but we're not ready to tell the public yet."

"Wait. You said 'problem.'"

"No. Sorry. Poor choice of words. It's... an *issue* we have to resolve."

"What's going on?"

"You are not getting a story out of this."

"Wouldn't dream of it. Come on. Off the record."

"I can't."

"Will this big secret convince me that Lisa is not a robot?"

Laughter. "If this doesn't, then nothing will."

"Jeff. You can trust me."

A pause. "We can't talk in here."

Two men in a taxicab.

"I swear. On the graves of all my forefathers, I swear. I will die before repeating any of this."

A deep breath. "Okay. You're right about how we initialize the newbrains. We scan the biological brain to reverse-engineer the physical neuron structure. Once we have that information, we manufacture the newbrain, imprint it, and power up the newbody."

"I'm not hearing any secrets so far."

"You were wrong about one thing. We can be certain that the newbrain is an exact duplicate of the original. We know when it works, because the old brain stops functioning."

A pause. "What?"

"When we power up the newbrain, the old, biological, human brain stops working."

"Because you destroy the old body."

"No. This is what I'm telling you. The old brain just *dies*. Immediately. We don't know how—"

"Wait. Wait! What do you mean, it *dies?* You're just making a copy of some energy patterns!"

"We're *duplicating* a mind at the quantum level. Apparently the universe won't allow two identical minds to exist simultaneously, and the newbrain supersedes the old one because it's more durable. This is our current theory, anyway."

"Christ. If you're right, then you could kidnap someone— anyone—just by scanning them and imprinting a newbrain somewhere? Fuck, you wouldn't even need a body!"

"Yeah. You see why you can't tell anyone?"

"I think I'm going to be sick."

"Well, you did have a lot to drink."

"That's fucking hilarious."

Curtis C. Chen

STATE SECRETS
April 9, 2010

I hadn't even finished my morning coffee when Jake ran into my office with a crazy smile.

"I found the Holy Grail!" he said. "It's in Africa. Democratic Republic of Congo."

"First of all," I said, "I've seen this movie. Bruce Campbell dies, and it just goes downhill from there. Second, how do you know it's the grail?"

Jake hopped forward and pointed at my computer. "I sent you some aerial photos. Look at the infrared, and the deep-radar tomography—"

"Okay, okay." I logged into my e-mail. Jake's message was easy to find: OMG I FOUND TEH HOLY GRAIL.

The images were not conclusive. I could tell he had washed them through several enhancement algorithms. The radar view clearly showed an underground catacomb, but the heat-map could have been any large group of mammals. I told him as much.

"That's why we have to go investigate! Right?" He sat down but continued bouncing. "I already requested travel authorization—"

"What?" My right hand curled into a fist. "Dammit, Jake, you can't do that!"

He slumped down in the chair, avoiding my gaze. "I thought you'd be excited."

I bit my tongue. "Look, Jake, this is good work. Really great. Thank you. But I need to pass this up the bureaucracy. I'll let you know when we can move forward, okay?"

Jake nodded, stood, and shuffled out of my office. I got up, closed and locked the door, and picked up the phone.

First I called off Jake's travel request, which would have been denied anyway. Then I dialed the Oval Office hotline. Samantha

160

answered.

"Veep veep," she said. Sam has an odd sense of humor.

"It's Rachel," I said. "Does he have five minutes today?"

"Probably not. What do you need?"

"Jake thinks he's found the grail. In Africa."

"Seriously?"

"Well, he's found *something*." I explained what I'd seen in the radar scans. "It may not be Biblical, but it's definitely worth checking out."

"What's the timeline on this?"

"Intel's about a week old," I said. "Jake did the analysis last night, brought it to me this morning."

Sam coughed. She knew that wasn't nearly enough time for me to have shopped it around my own chain of command before calling her. "Rachel, you can't keep doing this."

"I'm dying here, Sam," I said. "Get me back into the field where I can do some good."

I stared down into my coffee and waited for her.

"I'll put the file on his desk," she said finally. "I can't promise anything."

"Spray it with some perfume. That'll get his attention."

"You're adorable," Sam said. "Anything else?"

"Thanks, Sam."

She hung up without saying good-bye. My sister's never been known for being patient.

I sat back down and started assembling a dossier to send to the White House. The one good thing about growing up in a family of politicians is that I'd learned to bullshit with the best of them. I was pretty sure I could talk my way past the NSA and CIA chiefs. The President was another story.

KANGAROO'S FIRST DAY WITH THE EYE
June 19, 2009

It was almost noon before Kangaroo came back to Jessica's office to complain.

"There's a lot of pixelation down the left side," he said. "Is that normal?"

Jessica tapped her scanpad on his shoulder and looked over the data feed from his body sensors.

"Reads normal," she said. "Describe the pixelation."

"It's like a white dotted line. And it flickers." He raised his left hand and rubbed his eye with one knuckle.

"Please tell me you haven't been doing that all morning," Jessica said.

"What?" Kangaroo said, still rubbing. "It's itchy."

She grabbed his wrist and pulled it down. "It takes a full day for the display film to completely bond to your cornea. If you rub it off, we'll have to start all over."

"Can you do anything about the itching?" he asked. "Give me some eyedrops or something?"

Jessica sighed and put away the scanpad to prevent herself from smacking it against Kangaroo's head. "All the drugs you need are already being manufactured in your bloodstream by the nanobots we injected last week. Remember them?"

Kangaroo folded his arms and pouted. Jessica noticed something.

"Ow!" he said as she yanked his right arm straight. He was wearing a short-sleeved shirt, and there was a small lump under the skin on the inside of his elbow—like a cyst, except it was a bluish color and located right above the vein.

"How long has this been here?" she asked.

"What? I don't know. What is that?"

Jessica dragged Kangaroo to the other side of the room and

pushed him down into the exam chair. "Sit." She pointed to an eye chart on the wall. "Read the third line down, please."

While Kangaroo squinted at the chart, Jessica pulled on sterile gloves and selected a scalpel. She had removed the mass from his arm before he even noticed the pain.

"Apply pressure," Jessica said, handing him a gauze pad.

She ignored his screeching and took a thin slice off the blue lump. Under the microscope, she saw the spherical cross-sections of countless dead nanobots, shimmering with the telltale proteins that collected their corpses into canary clusters.

She whirled to face Kangaroo. "Have you had anything to eat or drink since the procedure this morning?"

He looked up from the wet gauze on his arm. "Just some coffee."

"Where?"

"Paul's office."

Jessica cursed and pressed a finger to her jaw, activating her communicator. "Security, this is Surgery."

Her implant buzzed. "Surgery, Security, go ahead."

"I need an immediate local division lockdown. Suspected intruder with chemical or biological weapons."

After a brief pause, the Security voice said, "Please confirm, ma'am. You want us to lock down the offices of Director, Intelligence, Non-Territorial?"

"Yes!" Jessica hated repeating herself. "This is Commander Jessica Chu, day code gamma five one two. Seal this section now!"

"Authorization confirmed," Security said.

Jessica heard the rumbling of airtight bulkheads in the corridor outside. She dogged her office door, then saw Kangaroo looking at her with a sheepish expression.

"I also had a muffin," he said.

VAMPIRE ROBOT
May 29, 2009

I know what you're thinking: Why would anyone build a vampire robot?

First of all, let's clear up some misconceptions. She's not a vampire. She doesn't drink blood. The artery in the neck is just the quickest way to get her probe tendrils into the brain—two probes, one for each hemisphere, so the scars look like what everyone imagines vampire bite marks would—although, if vampires actually existed, they'd probably just tear out your throat instead of making a couple of dainty little punctures.

That's another big difference right there. To a vampire, you'd just be food. But to Kayla, you're a research subject, a precious resource. That's why she doesn't kill anyone, why she doesn't hurt anyone, and why she does her best to take her measurements without disturbing their sleep. That's why she sneaks around at night. She wants data. No life, no brain activity, no data.

Yes, I admit, the original experiment has gone a little off track. She wasn't supposed to leave the building yet, but she's smart. We built her to be intelligent, adaptable—you might even say adventurous.

I'm not anthropomorphizing; we really did give her a personality. Do you know what goes into creating an AI? It's not linear programming like you learned in the sixth grade, or those clunky neural networks in self-drive cars. It takes months to train a neural net, and you still need to write explicit subroutines to handle any unexpected shapes or movement.

We wanted Kayla to *seek out* those exceptions. The Fed planned to send her into dangerous and hostile environments, and they didn't want their multi-billion-dollar investment to get taken down by some street urchin with a slingshot. We had to give her the ability to deal with anything.

I can't tell you how we did it. You wouldn't understand the math, and it won't help you stop her. Don't you get it? We don't *know* what happened. We don't know how she escaped, or why she decided to try in the first place. She's exceeded our original designs. She's *alive*.

And she's not some lumbering giant with no sense of purpose. Kayla knows exactly what she's doing, even if we don't. She knows how to hide in the darkness, emerging just long enough to perform—what did you call it? "Surgical strikes." Quick, clean, precise.

Now, we do need to find her, but not to kill her. If we get close enough, we can activate her wireless downlink and grab a complete copy of her current run-state. Then we can decompile that code and see exactly what she's thinking.

We've analyzed her activity patterns, and we can make some educated guesses about her next targets. But if we do this, we do it our way. We won't let you destroy her. She's not hurting anyone. She just wants to learn. Just like us.

Besides, we don't want to wake the nest. I mean, who knows how many more of those defensive bat-bots she's constructed by now?

Curtis C. Chen

STRANGER IN A STRANGE LAND
August 20, 2010

Dyla rolled down the car window, held out the plastic bottle, and said, "God bless you."

The old beggar woman lowered her cardboard sign, shuffled over to the car, and reached out a hand. "Thank you," she said, and took the bottle. Then her face soured. "What the hell is this?"

"It is a plastic bottle."

"It's empty!"

"Yes!" Dyla smiled. "Fill it with any electrolyte solution you prefer. I have sterilized the container, and the material does not contain bisphenol—"

"Is this some kind of joke?" The old woman tossed the bottle aside, startling Dyla. "You got any spare change? Dollar or two?"

It took Dyla a moment to comprehend the vocabulary. "You want—currency?"

The old woman glared. "Yeah! I want money! It's not enough I gotta stand out here, you gonna humiliate me, too?"

"I do not understand," Dyla said. "You would need to travel to a retail location to exchange currency for usable supplies. Is this not more convenient? Do you not fear dehydration and exposure?"

"Okay, you had your laugh," the old woman said, walking away.

"Wait!"

The old woman ignored Dyla and went back to the corner. The traffic light turned green, and Dyla drove her car forward through the intersection. She pressed the attention button on the dashboard.

"This better be important," said the computer. Its synthesized voice always sounded grumpy to Dyla. "I'm doing analysis here."

"I do not understand this planet," Dyla said, and summarized her encounter with the old woman. "What does your research say about beggary?"

"I'll flag it for collection," the computer said. "But as you've seen, their electromagnetic broadcasts are not reliable information sources."

A red indicator light flashed, accompanied by a dinging noise.

"Low on fuel again?" Dyla said. "This vehicle is horribly inefficient."

She pulled the car into the nearest filling station and powered down the engine. As she stepped out of the vehicle, a uniformed attendant nearly ran into her.

"Sorry! Uh, good afternoon, ma'am!" the attendant said. He appeared to be a juvenile, and he kept glancing down at Dyla's chest. "Fill her up for you?"

"No, thank you," Dyla said. "I will refuel the vehicle myself."

She took a step toward the pump, but the attendant held up his hands and stood in her way. "Whoa! You can't do that!"

Dyla frowned. "Why not?"

"You must be new in town. It's state law. Just tell me which gas you want, and I'll pump it for you."

Dyla shook her head. "I am responsible for the maintenance of my vehicle."

"I told you, it's against the law. You'll get slapped with a fine—"

"A monetary payment?"

"Right."

"Is this the only punishment imposed for such an infraction?"

"Yeah, but it's like five hundred bucks."

"That is acceptable." Dyla stepped past the attendant and picked up the pump nozzle. "Please prepare the documentation. I will pay in cash."

The attendant shook his head and walked away.

"This is a very strange place," Dyla said to the computer.

"Welcome to Oregon," the computer said.

UNIVERSAL LANGUAGE
July 17, 2009

I've thrown up exactly three times in my adult life. The third time was the best.

The first time was in college. I remember being confused at first—I'd never been that drunk before, and I didn't recognize the conflicting sensations in my head and my gut. It made sense when I found myself hunched over the toilet, expelling a mixture of vodka and curry, and I had plenty of time to think about it while lying on the floor and waiting for the bathroom to stop spinning.

The second time was in a training aircraft, a modified KC-135 Stratotanker. It flew parabolas, climbing upward at a forty-five degree angle and dropping its nose at the top of each curve to give its passengers twenty-five seconds of weightlessness.

Our instructors expected about a third of us to experience "kills" during the four-hour flight. I was the first to puke. I managed to pull a plastic bag over my mouth before it started, which was better than some of the other candidates.

I stayed flat against the floor, staring at a fixed spot on the ceiling, silently cursing my weak stomach. I thought I had recovered after a few seconds, but then we reached the bottom of the parabola, and I felt the renewed pressure in my abdomen—two gees—threatening to start another purge cycle.

We climbed for longer than it should have taken to reach the next zero-gee period. The floor began vibrating, and then the entire top of the aircraft sheared off.

We'd been pulled high into thin atmosphere. Breathable, but the sky outside was dark, and I stared straight up at a disk-shaped array of multicolored lights. A shadow appeared in the middle of the lights, then grew larger, blotting them out.

I rolled out of the way and dragged myself to a standing position before it landed inside our aircraft. I found myself facing a mottled, cylindrical creature, about seven feet tall, with one eye, an X-shaped mouth, and a ring of writhing tentacles where a human's waist would be.

The alien looked me up and down, then bent forward, opened its mouth, and vomited right between my feet.

It wasn't the sight of it, or even the smell, that pushed me over the edge. It was the feeling of warm liquid soaking through my socks and pooling between my toes that did it. This time I wasn't fast enough with the sick bag, and the rest of my partially digested continental breakfast ended up on the alien's lower body.

Fortunately, regurgitation is an important and highly dignified part of the *Varna'ut* greeting ceremony. Although I didn't know it at the time, I was showing their scout great respect by depositing the contents of my stomach directly on his esteemed mass.

And that's why I'm the human ambassador to *Varna'ut*. I never made the astronaut corps, but I'm not complaining. How many people get to travel across the galaxy?

Just don't ask about their farewell ritual. You really don't want to know.

GHOSTS OF EARTH
October 3, 2008

The first crystal fell on Los Angeles in the middle of rush hour, killing thirty-two people. Caltrans spent an hour trying to move the enormous mass before it drilled itself into the ground and disappeared.

Two hours later, another crystal splashed down in the Pacific Ocean. The Navy sent a submarine to track it, but they couldn't go deep enough. Three hours after that, another one hit the Pacific. Then a fourth crystal struck the ocean south of Japan, flooding the coast.

Someone noticed that all four impacts had occurred on the same line of latitude, proceeding west. Governments evacuated cities while the bombardment continued, every three hours, like clockwork: China, Iraq, Algeria, the Atlantic Ocean, South Carolina. Then the tenth crystal hit the Pacific, off the coast of Mexico. They were moving south.

NASA triangulated the origin of the crystals to a point outside the Moon's orbit. Observatories all over the planet turned their lenses that way, but saw nothing. The ship was too small to be visible at that range.

We had no vessels that could travel that far. All we could do was evacuate the cities in the line of fire and attempt to study the crystals, which we were unable to halt or slow as they burrowed deep underground.

Five days later, the last crystal fell into the Pacific, west of central Peru. There were now one hundred and eight alien objects embedded deep in the Earth, arranged in a precise grid circling the equatorial region of our planet. The invaders had parked their ship in space and let Earth itself rotate each target into position for them.

Eight different research teams had crawled down the crystal

tunnels. Two teams were broadcasting live video when the crystals started burning. Again, we could only watch, helpless.

The world burned for nearly a year. Most of the plant and animal life died within the first day. The crystals weren't just raising the temperature and fouling the air—they were also causing chemical changes, using our planet as raw material to transform the biosphere.

The aliens waited a full decade before landing, to let their new vegetation and prey animals grow. The few humans who had managed to survive, in Antarctica and other frozen places, were slowly suffocated by the toxic atmosphere. We mourned them, but only briefly. We still have work to do.

The crystal fire had killed our bodies, but freed our minds—some say souls, or spirits. We don't entirely understand it, but we know that we're still here. We can see everything. And we can do things.

We watched the aliens land, and sent scouts to verify that they couldn't sense us. Creating six billion angry ghosts had not been part of their invasion plan.

They use electronics, just as we did, and we've found that our incorporeal forms can directly affect electrical systems. A million scientists, no longer restrained by language barriers, are devising a plan to sabotage whatever the aliens do next.

We're betting that they won't want to live on a haunted planet.

HAUNTFAIL
March 30, 2012

I sensed the vibration—what would have been sound if I'd still had ears—but couldn't tell what was happening. Ten years since I died, and I still couldn't see through walls. Freaking annoying.

"Frank!" I called down the corridor. "What's happening in there?"

There was no way to tell if he had received my proj. The vibration was gone now; it had been a sudden, short shockwave rippling through the air of the alien ship. I wished I'd studied more about acoustics. Had that been a door? Something falling to the deck?

"Frank!" I called again, more energetically this time. Maybe the alien ship material was dampening our projections?

I considered leaving my post at the opening to the ventilation shaft. Whether or not I was guarding this square hole wasn't going to make or break the operation. We knew the aliens couldn't see us. If they could, they would have landed right next to one of our camps, or done something besides just sit around in their ship for days.

There were, like, ten different vent shafts that led into the main corridor of the ship. Other ghosts had done the recon and mapped this whole place out already. Even if we got jammed up here, we could fly out one of the other openings. Me waiting around when Frank might need help was stupid.

I nudged myself sideways, drifting over to the intersection so I could see down the adjoining corridor. As soon as I cleared the corner, I saw Frank barreling toward me, his normally soft glow spiked with pinpoints of fear.

"Run!" he shouted at me. "Get out of the—"

Behind him, two aliens charged into the corridor. They didn't look like I expected. I knew from others' descriptions that they were lizard-like humanoids, but their heads looked really bulbous and shiny. Then I realized they were wearing helmets. And body armor.

One of the aliens held up a device, a flat disk with a short handle. The disk was translucent, and it glowed with moving lines and symbols, like a radar lollipop.

He—she?—said something to the other alien, who hefted a long tube with bumps all along the side, buttons on top, two handles on the bottom, and a long flat extension in the back which rested on the alien's shoulder. It couldn't have been anything but a weapon.

The first alien shouted something, and the second alien fired. I saw a small projectile emerge from the front of the rifle, moving much slower than I had expected. Was that a wire trailing behind it?

Then the projectile exploded, creating an energy bloom nearly five feet across and causing a thunderclap like the one I'd heard before. It actually hurt for me to sense it. It radiated all across the EM spectrum, and as I watched, it set the air—the atmosphere itself—on fire and burned through Frank's sphere, tearing his energy apart. He proj'd out something I couldn't understand. Then he was gone.

I ran.

Curtis C. Chen

IN WHICH MISS HARTFEIL DROPS SOME SCIENCE ON HER TENTH GRADE CLASSROOM
June 7, 2013

The Martians came from the future. We didn't know that at first, and neither did they. And how did we find out? Anyone? That's right, Becky, we had sex with them.

All right, everybody simmer down! You knew this was going to be today's lesson, and we have a lot to get through here.

Who knows where the first ship from Mars landed?

Yes. And the name of the woman who greeted our first visitors from another planet?

Correct. Does anybody know more about that initial encounter? Go ahead, Tanis.

Okay. Thank you, Tanis, for that disturbingly clinical retelling of what was, at the time, a rather sensational news event.

Some of your grandparents may have been alive for this, so as a side project—yes, Molly, it is worth extra credit—you can interview a family member about what they remember from that time.

Now, before anything else, I need to say this: *Do not have unprotected sex with anybody!* Especially not alien life forms from outer space.

I'm going to say that several times today, because though it might seem like an obvious health safety tip, clearly it wasn't anywhere near Jessy Harper's mind on that fateful night in Willow Creek.

Once again: *Do not have unprotected sex with space aliens.* Or humans! Just don't do it, okay?

It is possible that young Jessy thought she was safe from disease or pregnancy because her lover wasn't human. Well, she was wrong. There's another important lesson here: If something seems weird, it's probably even weirder than you think. The universe is really, really, *really* weird, guys.

178

Here's the punchline. That Martian who had sexual intercourse with Jessy Harper was, in fact, also human. The same species as us— *Homo sapiens*. He came from a civilization of humans who had left Earth, some time in *our* future, and colonized Mars, hundreds of thousands of years in *their* distant past.

I'm not going to get into the time travel stuff, because I honestly don't understand it, and that's Mr. Wright's job to teach you about wormholes and brane spaces and quantum foam. It took everyone here on Earth a long time to figure out what was going on with the Martians, but after we did, whole new areas of scientific research opened up to us.

Back to the species thing. Who here has a pet dog or cat at home? Angie, what breed is your dog?

Okay. Does anybody know how many different breeds of dogs there are?

It's a lot. Hundreds worldwide. And while a sheepdog may look very different from a Chihuahua or a terrier, all dogs can interbreed and produce viable offspring. So you could think of Martians as just another breed of people. Another race.

Despite their unusual appearance and strange language, the Martians were still biologically human. They had basically human genitalia, which made possible that first Martian's coupling with Jessy Harper, and human DNA, which made possible her subsequent pregnancy.

Yes, Dora, we will talk about Martian penises very soon. You can put your hand down. Thank you.

SPORTSBALL
July 26, 2013

Welcome back to everyone watching our live broadcast of the 127th Galactic Harmony Games! I'm Gropflixnum Square, and with me here in the booth is Braznart Morchey-Morchey-Pop. Whaddya say, Braz? Still having fun?

My status is unchanged.

Hey, me too! Now, I gotta tell you, folks, I have seen some outrageous plays over my five decades of announcing for the Harmonies, but what happened in this last quarter absolutely takes the cake. What do you think, Braz? Is this going to be the most memorably disastrous Harmony Games to date?

Gropflixnum, my dear friend, you are as ignorant as you are sexually promiscuous. Do you not recall the final moments of game seven of the 64th Harmonies, when an entire starting line-up of humanoids failed to defend their home goal from the onslaught of a trio of mind-bonded lump-beasts? Or game three of the 96th Harmonies, when a single Zallgallian child scored the winning point against an all-star team representing Arbogastia's best and brightest? I hardly think today's tawdry events will rate even a footnote in the grand history of this heroic competition, the greatest athletic tradition in the known universe.

And that's why we have him here, folks, to give you that unique Pop-Snarquijan perspective! Thanks, Braz.

It would not disappoint me if you were to perish in a conflagration, foul Gropflixnum.

Okay. Folks, if you're just joining us, I don't know what to tell you! We are still in a time-out here in game six of the 127th Harmonies, and the referees are still conferring over how to call that last play. Not to mention the stadium medical teams have been treating the wounded players for nearly twenty centizhus, and we still do not have an update on their status. Even the coaches have been barred from entering the surgical tents, and you know that's gotta be driving them crazy!

That is unlikely, Gropflixnum, you polyp on the rectum of existence, since the Earth humans use telepathic implants for communication. Their coach is surely aware of every development as it occurs—

Hold that thought, Braz, here comes a ref to make the call!

DECISION: UNNECESSARY ROUGHNESS. PENALTY, EARTH HUMANS, FIVE YARDS.

Ouch, that's gotta hurt!

Gropflixnum, you are a genetically inferior specimen of questionable mental faculty.

Okay, folks, a quick recap of the action so far: the Earth humans are down by five points in the final six centizhus of the fourth quarter, and in what can only be described as an act of desperation, they finally unleashed their trademark "meltdown" attack! It's virtually guaranteed to generate some forward motion for them on the field, but always results in heavy collateral damage. Braz! Your analysis?

Thank you, honorable Gropflixnum. Taking all variables and available data into consideration, I believe—with better than 90% certainty—that your mother was surely an unlicensed sex worker, and more than likely a blood relation of your eventual father.

I meant your analysis of the game, Braz.

I know.

MY LEAST FAVORITE MARTIAN
August 16, 2013

The trouble starts before I can say hello.

"You again, human oppressor?" John says by way of greeting. He opened the door a split second before I could knock. Stupid Martian senses. "What vile directive must you impose now?"

I hold up a copy of his lease. "You signed this lease. It is a binding legal contract." I point to the circled paragraphs. "And you agreed to this condition, right here: no pets."

"This one is ignorant of the subject of your tirade," John says, wiggling his antennae.

"I'm talking about the six different cats your neighbors have seen through your back window."

"What is a... 'cat?'" John enunciates the last word theatrically.

Before I can ask just how stupid he thinks I am, a large orange tabby leaps onto John's shoulder. He attempts to shoo it away with his upper arm cilia while it scrabbles for purchase on his deltoid ridges. I fold my arms and watch the cat decide that the flat part of John's skull is a better resting place. The cat settles in between John's antennae.

"You've got thirty days," I say, shoving the lease into his hands.

"Human definitions are primitive and flawed!" John calls as I walk away down the hall. "A sentient being cannot be considered a mere domestic animal!"

I stop and turn around. "Oh, you want to call them roommates, then? You're only allowed up to three of those! Get rid of the cats."

"Cruel, unfeeling human!" John raises both arms to point at the cat now sleeping on his head. "You would ask this one to render an innocent companion creature homeless and destitute?"

"Hey, no one forced you to live here. You can find a new apartment. I don't care!" I realize I'm shouting, and lower my voice.

John has followed me all the way down the hall. "But you can't stay here and keep the cats." I push the elevator call button.

John lowers his arms, but his cilia continue vibrating, like Davy Crockett in a wind tunnel. "Your respect for the law is admirable, enforcer human. But perhaps we may yet reach a compromise?"

"This is not a negotiation. Like I said—"

"If you were to consider the cats my roommates, I could retain three of them?"

I shake my head. "Look, you want to be a test case for personhood, that's your problem. Go talk to the ACLU. You've still got thirty days to comply or vacate." The elevator arrives, and I step inside. "These are the building's rules. I don't make 'em up. I'm just the messenger."

John stops vibrating and seems to slouch a little. "You are firm but fair, child-bearing human."

"Word of advice," I say, pushing the button for the ground floor. "It's 'woman,' or 'female,' or 'lady.' Not all of us want babies."

"I was not referring to your gender," John says. "Are you not aware of your physical condition?"

I'm unable to speak for a moment. "What?"

The elevator doors close before John can explain.

BIOLOGICAL IMPERATIVES
February 10, 2012

"You can't marry him," Donald said to his only daughter. "He's an alien."

"Oh my God, Dad!" Bree threw up her arms. "You sound like a total racist!"

Donald wasn't about to take that bait. "Sweetie, you've only known Roland—"

"*Reginald.*"

"—sorry. You've only known Reginald for what, a couple of months?"

"Three months, one week, and four days!"

"Why get married *now?*" Donald asked. "You're both still young. Why not wait until you're done with grad school?"

"*Dad.*" Bree rolled her eyes. "I'm not going to give up my life to stay home and cook and clean. I'm still going to finish my PhD, I'm going to get a job. My relationship with Reginald won't interfere."

"I just think you should wait."

Bree sighed. "Okay, Dad, I didn't want to mention it, but Reginald has kind of a deadline."

Donald raised an eyebrow. "Don't tell me he's being deported."

"*No,*" Bree said, stretching the word into five syllables. "There's just some stupid thing with his visa expiring, and the UN says he can do his thesis research just as well from the Moon, so they want to issue him Lunar documents instead."

Donald nodded. He could work with this. "Who's Reginald's sponsor?"

"Professor Goslee." Bree's face brightened. "Do you think you can do something?"

"I'll make some calls." Donald scribbled on a notepad. "I'd rather not have you eloping off-planet. At least here I can try to talk you out of things like—"

Bree threw her arms around him momentarily. "Thanks, Dad! I'm going to tell Reginald! Call me *as soon* as you hear anything, okay?"

"Immediately."

He waited until the sound of Bree's footsteps receded down the hallway, then touched a control on his desktop. The door to the adjacent office slid open, and his wife—Bree's mother—Marney walked in, grimacing.

"You on top of this visa thing?" she asked, staring at her phone.

"I'll take care of it," Donald said.

"Last thing we need is for her to go off-planet. All that radiation exposure in transit..."

Marney still hadn't looked up. That annoyed Donald. "How's *your* project coming along? Found a sperm donor yet?"

That got her attention. "Finding a donor is not the issue," Marney said, stowing her phone. "Setting up the situation is proving to be tricky."

"How hard can it be to get a college girl drunk and knocked up?"

Donald regretted saying it even before Marney focused her withering scowl on him. "She has to keep the baby. We can't monitor her twenty-four-seven to make sure she doesn't pop a morning-after pill or visit a clinic for the next twenty-six weeks. She has to want the damn child."

"You know," Donald said, "we could convince her and Reginald to try artificial insemination or something—"

"I am *not* inviting that *thing* over for Sunday dinner," Marney snapped. "She marries a human or she doesn't marry at all."

Donald looked up at his wife. "Remind me again why *we* got married?"

Marney scoffed. "I'm sure I don't remember."

BARELY LEGAL
December 14, 2012

"So," the human asked, using the translator in his computer tablet, "what's a nice pupa like you doing in a place like this?"

Anafful suspected this was an attempt at what humans called "humor," and what her mother called "useless vocalization," especially if it came from one of Anafful's friends.

It was lunchtime, and the friends in question had all abandoned Anafful to gawk at the aliens milling about the cafeteria downstairs. She had seen this human walking around the wards previously, talking to various people until he was shooed away by the nurses.

Anafful suspected he was a galactic census adjunct or some such boring thing. She had watched as he approached, mystified as to why all her friends found these endoskeletal beings so fascinating. To Anafful, the human looked pink and squishy, like an oversized and undercooked land grub.

His appearance made her a bit nauseous, to be honest, but she did her best to be polite. After all, he was a guest in her star system.

"I will soon enter the chrysalid phase of my adolescence," Anafful said, speaking slowly so the translator program could follow along. "My ancestors are among the custodians of this institution, and thus my family enjoys the benefit of its medical care."

"Got it. Trust fund baby," the human said, operating the tablet with his soft, fleshy fingers. They made a disturbing, wet, *thwack* sound with every impact against the touch-screen.

"I do not know what that phrase means," Anafful said.

"Don't worry about it. So, your friends who were in here earlier, are they classmates then?" the human asked.

"Some of them, yes. My school is—"

"And at least one of them was male, is that correct?"

Anafful suppressed any display of annoyance at his interruption.

"Two were males. Gaddlim wore the bright red cap, and Driicha has the emblem of ascension etched into his left wing carapace. They—"

"Have you engaged in sexual relations with either of them?"

Anafful could not help fluttering her mandibles at that. "Why are you asking me these questions?"

"Or are your eggs not accessible until later in the metamorphic cycle?"

"Who *are* you?"

"What about with the other females?" the human asked, apparently oblivious to Anafful's objections. "Have you ever performed mutual—"

Just then, a nurse passing by the open door of Anafful's room burst in, seizing the human by his lumpy shoulders and spinning him around.

"Hey!" he yelped.

"You again!" the nurse said, and shoved him out the doorway. "Out! Right now, or I call security!"

"I'm allowed to be here!" the human protested from the corridor.

"You're not allowed to harass children!" The nurse slammed the door shut, then turned to Anafful. "Are you well, miss?"

"Yes," Anafful said, clutching her bedcovers close to her shell. "But confused. He was asking me all sorts of... strange questions. Who is he?"

"Just one of those soft-brained human scholars." The nurse shook her head. "I swear, it seems like all they ever want to talk about is sex."

A MINOR INCONVENIENCE
October 21, 2011

Brradox hated actually entering any spaceport, but he needed to store his cargo while the station shop repaired his ship's aging power plant. He studiously avoided making eye contact with any hawkers on the promenade, but looked up reflexively when he heard someone call his name with the proper pronunciation. That meant someone from the homeworld—

Brradox cursed when he saw who it was, then walked in the other direction. He wasn't fast enough.

A slender claw clacked down on his carapace. "Brradox! I thought that was you! What are you doing in this wretched hive?"

Brradox turned around. "Hello, Pirluut. Good to see you, I have to go, safe travels."

Pirluut smacked her antennae against Brradox's thorax. He hated it when she did that. "Now is that any way to talk to your favorite aunt?"

"You're my only aunt."

"It's been months! Come on, I'll buy you a grub shake—"

"Sorry," Brradox said, "don't have time. Live cargo. Need to arrange holding—"

"Animals?" Pirluut parted her mandibles in surprise.

"Humans. Noisy little larvae—"

"You're transporting human *children?*" Pirluut grabbed Brradox's abdomen with her two middle limbs. "In *your* ship?"

Brradox's leg-hairs bristled. "What's wrong with my ship?"

"Well, it's not exactly childproof."

"They're caged up. I really need to go—"

She closed both claws around his forelimbs. "I'm coming with you. No arguments," she added when he raised a pincer to protest. "You want me to call your mother? Tell her what kind of trouble you've been getting into out here?"

Brradox grumbled. "This way."

"You're lucky these humans aren't dead already," Pirluut said as she adjusted the climate controls on the transparent cube. The humans inside, an immature male and female, were just regaining consciousness. "Too much carbon dioxide. They don't respirate like we do; they're very sensitive to atmosphere changes. Also, what have you been feeding them?"

This was exactly what Brradox hadn't wanted to happen. He rifled through one of his supply crates and produced a bag of feed. "I know that's right; it's pre-formulated. Just add water. They don't like it much, but they like it better than starving."

Pirluut read over the feed ingredients and handed it back. "Well, they seem healthy. Where are they going, anyway?" Pirluut asked, looking over the children. The male had regained consciousness and was yelling and banging his fists against the cube wall.

"Some kind of ranch out in the Crescent."

Pirluut wiggled her antennae. "Really."

"I'm just making a delivery," Brradox said. "They're not inviting me to dinner."

"Still, it's definitely a step up," Pirluut said. "So are you going to make a habit of this now, Brradox? Live transport? It's a big responsibility."

"I can handle it. Thanks for your help," he said, grinding his jaws.

"Don't mention it. You're family." Pirluut looked over the rest of his cargo and waved at a stack of old-fashioned, hard-bound books. "So what are these? Antiques?"

"Part of the same shipment." Brradox picked up one of the books and blew some dust off its cover. "It's a cookbook."

Curtis C. Chen

FOOLS FOR LOVE
April 1, 2011

"I need to speak to her. Now," Rebecca said.

The doctor shook his head. "Look, Miss Sachs—"

"Special Agent Sachs."

"Miss Cargill is very weak. We're lucky she didn't lose consciousness during delivery. You can arrest her tomorrow."

"I don't want her, I want the father. He's a fugitive. She may know where he's going, and we need to catch him before he crosses a border."

The doctor hesitated. "Nurse Lemperson will accompany you."

"Fine."

Lemperson led the way into April Cargill's darkened room. Rebecca couldn't help noticing how young this girl was—just like all the others.

Having her baby taken away from her was going to be a tremendous shock, but she'd have the rest of her life to get over it. Rebecca tried to convince herself that would be enough.

She shook April's arm gently. "Miss Cargill?"

April opened her eyes. Rebecca held up her FBI badge. "I need to ask you about Charles Risznowski."

April smiled. "Is he here?" Lemperson shook her head. "I wish he could see our baby."

"Did he tell you he was coming back?" Rebecca asked.

"Oh, no," April shook her head. "He was clear about that from the beginning. I just hoped—wow. I'm really dizzy. Is that normal?"

"Just keep your head still," Lemperson said. "It'll pass."

That's what you get for incubating a half-alien baby, Rebecca thought. "April. Did Charles say where he was going? How he was planning to travel? Airplane? Train?"

"No. Is he in some kind of trouble?"

190

"He may have information pertaining to a matter of national security." Rebecca leaned forward. "It's very important that we find him. And we can give him the good news about your baby. It's a boy, right?"

"Yeah," April said, smiling as if the world were a beautiful place. "I'm naming him Charlie."

Rebecca forced herself to smile. "That's a good name."

"I'm sorry," April said. "Charles never said anything specific about where he was going. But it sounded like it was going to be a long trip. He said he needed money."

Of course he did. "How much did you give him?"

"I didn't have any cash handy," April said, "so I just gave him my debit card and PIN number."

Rebecca contained her excitement, calmly patted April's hand, and stood up slowly. "Thank you, April. Get some rest."

She nodded at Lemperson, walked out of the room, and ran to the elevators, dialing her phone.

"Center, Sachs," Rebecca said. "I need live tracking on all bank and credit card activity for April Cargill." Rebecca stepped inside an elevator and pressed the lobby button.

"Risznowski's using her accounts?" said the voice on the phone.

"Yeah. With any luck, he'll lead us to his buddies before they skip this dimension. And listen," Rebecca said as the doors closed, "the mother's not going anywhere. Wait twenty-four hours to take the baby. Hospital staff's already suspicious, and we don't want to cause a scene."

"Delay extraction? Are you sure?"

Rebecca closed her eyes and saw April's innocent, trusting smile. "I'm sure."

REACTION
June 4, 2010

"Want shoot gun!" screamed the alien's voicebox.

Martin gritted his teeth and looked at the Secret Service agent standing closest to the alien, a tall, gray-haired woman. She didn't look that old.

"Is that allowed?" Martin asked.

The agent's eyes looked black behind the reflection of the shop's overhead lights. "The ambassador requested a visit to an indoor range."

"Why didn't you just take him to the Pentagon, Agent...?"

"Lieber." She shrugged. "The ambassador doesn't have clearance to enter military facilities."

"This gun!" The alien tapped one tentacle on the glass countertop. "Shoot this gun!"

Martin wondered if it was really that difficult to build a voice synthesizer that didn't sound like a hyperactive child. Not that anybody on Earth knew how the *Varna'ut* translators worked.

He walked over to see which pistol the alien was pointing at, then looked up and hoped he was making eye contact. The *Varna'ut* looked like a large purple sausage with a dozen tentacles, mottled color patterns around its sensory organs, and an X-shaped mouth.

"That's a fifty-caliber Desert Eagle," Martin said loudly, mostly to the Secret Service. "Are you sure you wouldn't like to start with something smaller? Maybe a twenty-two revolver?"

"Want shoot this gun!" the alien screeched. "Shoot now!"

Martin turned to Lieber. "Can the ambassador legally sign a waiver?"

She nodded. Martin retrieved the forms, filled in the dates and names, and watched as Lieber signed her name and the alien used one thin tentacle to make a brown inkblot on the paper.

It took a while to figure out ear protection for the alien. Lieber said plugging the four largest ear-holes near the yellow eye-stripe would be good enough. The alien seemed too excited to care.

Everyone else on the range stopped to gawk as Martin led Lieber and the alien down to the last lane. He stretched out his usual safety talk for as long as he could.

"Have you ever handled a firearm before, ambassador?"

"Load gun!" the alien cried. "Shoot now!"

"The *Varna'ut* don't have projectile weapons," Lieber said. "Let's just start with one round."

Martin fitted one cartridge into the clip, loaded the pistol, and let the alien take it with three tentacles. He followed Lieber's lead and took two big steps back.

Before Martin could offer any tips on aiming, the alien had pulled the trigger. The sound reverberated through Martin's earmuffs, and he instinctively squeezed his eyes shut.

When he opened his eyes, Martin saw the back end of the Desert Eagle buried in the alien, thrown by the weapon's considerable recoil. The handgrip was completely swallowed up by the purple flesh. The alien's voicebox made a strange chirping noise.

Martin cursed and asked Lieber, "Is he okay?"

She chuckled. "The *Varna'ut* also don't feel pain the same way we do."

The alien rippled the front of its body, expelling the Desert Eagle and catching it with one tentacle. Another tentacle pressed the release button on the side of the pistol to eject the empty clip.

"Again!" it screamed.

ASSASSINATION
February 18, 2011

"So," Jake said, "who killed Abraham Lincoln?"

"And what's his full name?" Andy asked.

"No ID on the body," said the uniform standing just inside the police tape. His name tag said HOLLISTER. "Found the hack license under the front seat. Looked like the killer was in a hurry to leave."

Andy nodded. "So, robbery?"

Hollister shrugged. "Whoever killed him did clean out the car. Glovebox was empty. Took his wallet, cell phone, GPS—even the meter." He pointed to a blank spot on the dashboard.

"Why would anyone take the taxi meter?" Jake asked.

"Data," Andy said. "The meter tracks how far the cab's traveled. Even without the GPS, we could have guessed at where Abe picked up his last fare."

"He's got to have a chip, right?" Jake said. "Where's the ME?"

"Already been here," said Hollister. "Didn't have the right scanner. Said we'd have to wait for INS to show up."

"That's going to take all day," Jake grumbled.

Andy bent down to look at the wrinkled mass of the dead *Varna'ut* behind the wheel of the taxicab. The alien would have stood over seven feet tall fully upright, but they compressed their boneless bodies to fit into human vehicles. This one had kept its lower body extended, to reach the control pedals and to put its tentacles at the same height as the steering wheel.

Andy reached into the car and touched one of the tentacles still wrapped around the wheel. He pressed his gloved fingers into the spongy flesh and watched as the purple inkblots in the translucent gray skin broke into smaller bubbles.

"Still warm," Andy said.

He followed the ripples of purple up the tentacle into the *Varna'ut*'s torso, and saw a small slick of something brown and opaque—almost like mud—underneath the spot where the limb attached to the body, where a human's armpit would have been.

"Son of a bitch," Andy muttered. "Hey, Jake!"

The other detective walked around the car, followed by Hollister, and leaned over to look where Andy was pointing. "What am I looking at?"

"You see that brown spot there, right under the base of the tentacle?"

"Please tell me that's not anything that starts with 'p.'"

"Regurgitation," Andy said. "It's how the *Varna'ut* greet each other. Honest Abe knew his murderer."

"That's a bit of a reach, isn't it?" Jake squinted down at his partner. "I mean, I say hello to the greeter at Wal-Mart, doesn't mean I know the guy."

"This is gastric secretion," Andy said. "Stomach acid. You can smell it, can't you?"

"I'm trying not to."

"Only friends and family get actual regurgitation. Strangers are greeted with saliva—just spit, not vomit."

Jake frowned. "Is there some reason you know so much about this?"

"My kid sister's dating a *Varna'ut*."

"You're joking."

Andy stood up. "You know, it could be worse. She needs to get the rebellious streak out of her system, and at least an alien can't knock her up."

"Okay," Hollister said, "now *I'm* going to be sick."

JUST FOLLOW YOUR NOSE
March 15, 2013

"Then the girl said the guy coming out of the bathroom was her boyfriend. But the old man didn't believe her. So he went over to talk to the bathroom guy. This corpse is twenty-two hours dead. Are you sure I'm not talking too much?"

"Absolutely not," Andy replied before Jake could. "Could you say that part about the corpse again?"

"Sure." Jennifer waved at the vaguely human-shaped lump of charred flesh and bone on the ground. "This man died no more than twenty-three hours ago."

"How can you know that's a man?" Jake asked.

The teenage girl stared at Jake like he was some kind of alien. Which wasn't far from the truth; Jennifer had been raised by *Varna'ut* for the last ten years, ever since her birth parents—Earth's ambassadors to the *Varna'ut* homeworld—died in a shuttlecraft accident. Jennifer was physiologically human, but all her habits and behaviors were distinctly *Varna'ut.*

"I can smell his burned testicles," she said, pointing. "Enzymes from the seminal vesicles have a very distinctive odor. Even more so when they've been oxidized through combustion."

"I don't want to know how she knows that," Jake muttered to Andy.

"Anyway, the old man stops the guy coming out of the bathroom," Jennifer continued, without missing a beat. "Of course, the guy has no idea what's going on. But he recognizes the girl."

"Sorry to interrupt," Andy said, "but would you mind finishing that story later?"

Jennifer blinked. "This isn't interesting to you? You can just say that. Are you trying to be 'tactful?' They told me you might do that. I can tell a different story. There were at least four different attackers in this room. There was also this really hairy man on the flight. His beard came all the way up his cheeks, and he was wearing sunglasses."

"It's not the story," Jake said. "It's the way you keep changing subjects. Go back to the four attackers."

"I thought humans liked to talk," Jennifer said.

"We like to talk about one thing at a time," Jake said.

"Jake's very focused," Andy said. "Could you try... limiting our conversation? Just for a little while?"

Jennifer shrugged. "I'll try it. I can smell the residue from the attackers. You could, too, with proper training. The first thing *Varna'ut* children learn in school is how to use their *noo'usp.*"

"You're doing it again," Jake said through gritted teeth.

"No," Jennifer said, "we're still talking about scents."

"Look—"

Andy grabbed the sleeve of his partner's jacket. "Can I have a word with you, Jake? Outside? Please excuse us."

"Don't touch anything," Jake said as Andy dragged him out the door.

"Why would I touch anything?" Jennifer asked.

After Andy had shoved Jake around the corner of the building, he said, "What the hell is your problem? She's helping us. Not to mention this will become an interstellar incident if you punch her in the face."

"I'm not going to punch her in the face," Jake said. "Stomach, maybe."

"Hard to believe you're still single."

IT'S IN THERE

January 27, 2012

Granger sat down next to me on the couch and asked, "How is a pizza like a DVD?"

I swallowed my mouthful of pepperoni-extra-cheese-light-sauce and said, "I don't know. They're both round, and nobody really cares what the box looks like as long as the content is good?"

He smiled at me and took a swig of beer. Granger was one of those men who always looked like he didn't give a damn what you thought. One of those men who could pull off an unironic, pencil-thin mustache.

He smiled at me and said, "You always overthink these things, Lily."

It was the first time he'd ever called me by my first name. We had sex that night. Two weeks later, I pulled his body out of a Dumpster in Brooklyn.

The case file flopped onto my desk like a dead fish. I looked up and was surprised to see Lieutenant Humphrey.

"What's this?" I asked.

"Merry Christmas," Humphrey said, walking away.

I opened the file just as Dee sat down across from me with her morning cup of not-coffee. The top sheet was a dense grid of numbers and abbreviations. Bio data?

"What's that?" Dee asked.

"Fuck if I know," I said, flipping up pages until I got to something comprehensible. "Shit."

I stared at a crime scene photo: dead wiseguy, face down in a half-eaten calzone.

"Death by pizza?" Dee asked. I was driving, so she had nothing to do but talk.

"It's the sauce," I said. "Some biotech idiots figured out how to grow tomatoes with heat-resistant, human-compatible RNA. The idea was that you'd eat the stuff and it would alter your metabolism, help you lose weight."

"Guess that didn't work out."

"Problems with mutations. Gave people heart problems and hormonal imbalances. Huge recalls. Companies went out of business."

"But the technology's still around." Dee grumbled. "So you a speed reader now, or what? You didn't have that file for five minutes."

"I've seen the case before," I said. "It was Granger's before it went cold."

The warehouse was full of uniforms moving evidence-tagged crates. Migdale stood next to a box of fruit, reading the newspaper.

"Ladies," he said as Dee and I walked up.

"If you say so." I looked around. "I was expecting to see some tomatoes."

Migdale picked up both halves of a cut avocado, which looked more yellow than green under the warehouse lights. "Customs sliced this open, for inspection, right before they found the guns. Notice anything odd?"

"It's still green," Dee said. "Those things go brown in seconds."

"Enzymatic browning," Migdale said, "triggered by exposure to oxygen. Unless the fruit contains something to prevent that."

"So they're gene-mods. What's the big deal?"

Curtis C. Chen

"They were in the same shipment as illegal munitions and narcotics. Therefore, suspicious. We sent a sample to the lab, and it turns out all the fats in this avocado have been fully saturated."

"The hell does that mean?" Dee asked.

"Data," I said. "They were smuggling data."

Thursday's Children

Curtis C. Chen

WITHIN SIGHT
January 15, 2010

Johanna sees the sound of footsteps, and she panics. Dark blue, blotchy—they're boots, and it's a man wearing them. Can't be good.

Into the bathroom, open the toilet tank—oh, hell, just two more for the road—peel apart dripping wet plastic, pick out the little yellow lifesavers. Dry-swallow both in one gulp, drop the rest and flush. Scrape the lid back into place.

Knocking. Go to the front door, breathe, unlock the deadbolts. Standing outside is a fresh-faced ensign in service khakis. His heartbeat pulses dull red, almost twice a second.

Lieutenant Klaus? says the ensign, whose name tag reads ACKER. His green-blue syllables blossom like a false-color sat map.

Who wants to know? Johanna asks. Her own voice makes a purple tunnel around Acker's face.

VA outreach, Acker says, saluting. We're surveying veterans with synesthetic disorders. He holds up a digital notepad.

Bullshit, Johanna says. The VA doesn't make house calls.

Acker swallows, and his throat glows sickly urine yellow. May I come in, Lieutenant? This is a sensitive matter.

Johanna nods. Acker walks into the apartment. Johanna sticks her head outside, looks both ways down the hall, doesn't see a spotter. Can't be that important if greenhorn came alone.

She closes the door, folds her arms. So what is this really about, Ensign? The last word pulses in a blue halo.

Acker turns his notepad around. The screen glitters with a Naval Intelligence shield above a thumbscan box. I need to verify your identity first, ma'am.

Johanna's heart jumps, painting an orange haze over the pad. She's been waiting for this. Months now, suffering with constant noise in her ears, but she knew they had to approve the transfer.

202

Someone with her experience, her skills? They had no choice!

She reaches for the notepad, smiles up at Acker, and freezes.

His hat. He's still wearing cover, *indoors*. She had the habit drilled out of her in boot camp—

He grabs her wrist, yanks her thumb toward the scanner. Johanna closes her fist, punches the pad away, slams her forehead into his nose. Before he hits the floor, she's already got her go-bag, pulling open the front door.

Two plainclothes police detectives block her way, one showing his badge, the other holding a revolver.

NYPD, says badge-cop, his voice a red mist shot through with orange streaks. Johanna Klaus, you are under arrest for possession of a controlled substance with intent to sell...

Behind her, Acker struggles to his feet, moaning yellow and green.

Told you that was a dumb idea, revolver-cop calls into the apartment.

Ma'am, I need to handcuff you, says badge-cop.

Johanna drops her bag and turns around. She knows the drill.

Damn, Andy, why do you always get the hot suspects?

The cuffs go on with a flashbulb clink. Jake, this woman was wounded in combat. Show some respect.

Oh, I definitely respect that.

Johanna sees a puff of pink, elbow hitting gut. She allows herself a tiny smile. That's not the drugs.

SAM SPAYED
April 17, 2009

The building manager unlocked the apartment and said, "You know they got a talking cat, right?"

Jake took his hand off the doorknob and stepped back.

Andy said, "Don't tell me you're *afwaid* of *puddy tats*, Jake."

The older detective scowled. "I hate talking animals."

Andy shook his head and stepped forward.

The first pet "translators" were just prerecorded audio chips triggered by sound. Then a couple of Stanford graduate students had refined the technology, using voice stress analysis and text-to-speech software. Now anyone could walk into any pet store in the country and get a patented "translation collar" to give his or her pet its own unique voice.

Andy pushed the door open and called, "NYPD!" Nobody responded.

Enough daylight was coming in through the kitchen window for him to see potted plants everywhere, half-folded newspapers on the dining table, and one mostly empty teacup on the carpet by the futon. There was a distinctly non-plant-like silhouette in the kitchen window. Andy walked over and saw a sleek orange cat, half-crouched on the windowsill and staring back at him with big yellow eyes.

"Hey there," Andy said. "I don't suppose you know where your owner is?"

The cat blinked its eyes slowly and started swishing its tail. It let out a short meow, and a second later, the hexagonal tag on its collar blinked green and said, "I can has cheeseburger?"

Andy groaned. Apparently their missing person had sprung for one of the novelty language upgrades.

He saw two empty bowls on the kitchen floor, picked up one of them, and filled it from the tap. The pressurized water hit the side of the bowl and spattered all over Andy's chest before he could shut it off.

The cat yowled, "You're doing it wrong!"

Andy put the bowl down. He saw Jake standing in the living room, grinning.

"What?" Andy said.

"I'm searching the bedroom," Jake said. "You have fun with your furry friend there."

"Fuck you," Andy replied.

The cat descended onto the counter and sniffed at the water bowl. "Do not want!"

"Yeah, yeah," Andy muttered.

"It has a flavor!" the cat said.

Andy looked at the bowl on the counter. He turned on the faucet and watched the water spray into the sink. The stream seemed more diffuse than it should have been.

Andy searched his pockets and found his Mickey detectors. The precinct had issued everyone drug testing kits after a sudden wave of knockout rapes in downtown. He opened the plastic canister, pulled out a strip, and held it under the tap water. The stiff paper turned red instantly.

"Son of a bitch," Andy said.

He turned off the water and unscrewed the aerator at the end of the spout. When he pulled it away, a small, shiny disk fell out of the faucet. The surface of the disk felt slimy and left a residue on his thumb.

Andy smiled and petted the cat with his other hand. "Good kitty."

"Also," the cat said, "your mechanic is a pony."

GETAWAY
March 6, 2009

Jake sat across the table from the man he'd been investigating for six months. Harlan Anderson's face stared back, but the eyes were wrong. Jake could always tell by looking at the eyes. Of course, the DA wasn't going to take Jake's word for it. So they waited.

The door to the interview room opened, and Andy walked in. He dropped a file folder on the table. Jake opened the folder and flipped through the lab printouts.

"Scarring at the base of the skull consistent with interface penetration," Jake read. "Tox screen detected phenol compounds indicating breakdown of Ferris drug within the last six hours. EEG shows increased activity in PPRF region. Hey Andy, do you know what the PPRF region controls?"

Andy crumpled up a twenty-dollar bill and threw it at Jake.

"That's right," Jake said, pocketing the cash. "Eye movement. How 'bout that? You learn something new every day."

Harlan's arms yanked on the handcuffs attached to the table. "Can you please take these off now?"

Andy said, "Lieutenant wants us to take her with us. And a tech with a portable interface."

"You're kidding," Jake said.

Andy shrugged. "The brass want a photo-op when we bring him in."

The technician, Karl, met them in the motor pool. Jake drove, Andy rode shotgun, and Karl kept looking over at Harlan's body.

"I'm not him," Harlan's voice said.

"I know," Karl said. "It's just weird, seeing his body."

"Speaking of which, how do you guys deal with this stuff dangling between your legs all the time?"

"You'll get used to it," Andy said.

"Oh, I hope not."

The woman's name was Jennifer Nathans, and she lived at 5028 Montana Street, Apartment 7, on the ground floor. Jake could tell as soon as he pulled into her parking space that they were too late.

The front door stood slightly ajar. Andy and Karl stayed in the car while Jake followed Harlan's body through the ransacked apartment and into the kitchen. Shards of glass covered the floor.

"How much cash was in there?" Jake asked.

"Almost five thousand." Harlan's face looked close to tears.

"Anything else missing?"

Harlan's head shook from side to side. "Shouldn't be hard to find him, right? You've put out an APB for my car. And I don't have a passport."

"He's probably ditched your car by now," Jake said, holstering his weapon. "Maybe shaved off your hair and got a wig."

"My hair?" Harlan's voice sounded horrified.

"It's not his body," Jake said. "He doesn't care what happens to it. But cheer up. If he's smart, he's already swapped it for another one. Someone we're not looking for."

Harlan's face didn't look cheered. "This is the worst day of my life."

"No," Jake said, "that's tomorrow, when you find out the Ferris transfer is permanent after twenty-four hours."

"Please tell me you're joking!"

Jake waited until he couldn't suppress his grin any more. "Yeah, I am."

Harlan's palm smacked him across the face.

"See?" Jake said. "You're feeling better already."

SHOOT FIRST
March 25, 2011

"Police Inspector!" shouted the voice inside Takeshi's head. "This man is not our suspect!"

Takeshi relaxed his trigger finger. If Buki had decided the man was not a threat, it would not fire a round no matter what Takeshi did.

"Down on the ground!" Takeshi said out loud.

The man in the hooded sweatshirt, baggy jeans, and sneakers looked around, eyes frantic. The alley had ended in a blank wall. There was nowhere to run.

"I repeat, this man is not our suspect!" Buki said. Takeshi ignored his weapon.

The man dropped to his knees, sobbing. Takeshi pulled a pair of handcuffs off his belt with one hand. "Put your hands on top of your head," he said.

"I am innocent," the man said.

"He is not our suspect!" Buki said.

"Be quiet," Takeshi said to both of them.

He handcuffed the man, dragged him to the unmarked police car at the mouth of the alley, and put him in the backseat. Takeshi closed the door and snapped his pistol back into the shoulder holster which doubled as an antenna and charging station.

"Diagnostic running," Buki said. "Testing audio transmission. Police Inspector Yamashita, if you can hear me, please respond—"

"I can hear you just fine, Buki," Takeshi said, stepping away from the car. "I did not feel a need to respond earlier."

"So you heard me say this man is not our suspect." The computer inside Takeshi's service weapon sounded more than a little hurt.

"Whoever he is, he resisted arrest. That gets him a trip to the station." Takeshi paced beside the car. "Did you compare his face to the police library?"

"Yes," Buki said. "I had ample time to perform the search while you were arresting him for no good reason."

"Innocent men do not run from the police," Takeshi said. "But I take it from your tone that his record is clean?"

"Maybe you should see for yourself."

Takeshi sighed and took his *augear* visor out of his jacket pocket. He fitted the translucent yellow panel over his eyes and waited for Buki to power up the display.

After a moment, two images glowed into being, appearing to float half a meter in front of Takeshi's face. The image on the left showed a hyper-color image of the man he had just arrested, as recorded by the sensors built into Buki's front sight assembly. The image on the right was a magnified scan of a student ID from Kyoto University, showing a photograph of the same man and naming him as Daijiro Nakamura.

"I have already cross-referenced with public records," Buki said. "This man is the second son of Genkichi Nakamura, CEO of Transfuture Technologic. Daijiro has no connection to our primary suspect or his associates. And considering the Nakamura family reputation, it is unlikely that Daijiro would involve himself with such people."

"Thank you for the information, Buki," Takeshi said, "but you still have a lot to learn about police work."

THE FORTY

December 26, 2008

"Merry Christmas," Andy said as he slid back into the passenger seat, holding out a paper cup.

"I'm Jewish," Jake said, taking a swig of coffee. "And this is awful."

"Sorry. Not a lot of Starbucks around here... hey, is that him?"

Jake looked out the windshield. "Yup. Let's go."

They exited the car into a gust of wind. Andy trotted to keep up with Jake as they crossed the street.

"Anthony Torza?" Jake called.

The man stopped walking. "Who wants to know?"

Jake held up his badge. Torza cursed.

"We need to see your artifact, Mr. Torza," Jake said.

"It ain't *mine*," Torza said. "I'm just holding it. For my cousin. He ain't a bad guy, he's just got a record—"

"We don't care, Mr. Torza," Jake said. "We just want to see the artifact."

Torza led them upstairs to his apartment. They watched him struggle with his keys, then finally take off his gloves to unlock the door. Once inside, Torza opened his closet and extracted a battered cardboard box.

"Be honest with you, I'll be glad to get rid of this thing," Torza said. "They give off some kind of radiation, right? I just hope it ain't made me sterile or nothing."

Andy opened the box. It was full of pencils.

"What the hell?" Andy said.

"It's lead," Torza said. "To stop the radiation?"

Andy wasn't sure if he wanted to laugh or cry. He settled for shaking his head, then scooped pencils out of the box until he revealed a metal shape, which he lifted with both hands.

Torza's artifact was identical to all the others: a regular icosahedron roughly the size and weight of a basketball. Nobody knew where the artifacts had come from. They had simply appeared one day, scattered across the globe. The agency had determined there should be forty artifacts—twenty matched pairs—based on their surface markings, and was tracking them all down. Andy rotated the artifact until he found the symbols.

"Seventeen," he translated, then stood up quickly and threw the artifact at Torza. "Think fast!"

Torza reflexively raised both hands to catch the artifact before it hit him in the chest. As soon as his skin touched the metal, the artifact began glowing with a soft blue light.

"We got a winner," Andy said, smiling.

"Thank you, Mr. Torza," Jake said. "We'll take that now. And at your convenience, we'd like to schedule an interview and routine medical exam."

The contents of the cardboard box rattled as Andy put it in the trunk.

"Lead," he said, getting into the car. "Clearly these things don't choose people based on intelligence. You ever wonder why they come in pairs? Or why the faces are twenty triangles?"

"Not interested," Jake said, starting the car. "Just four more 'owners' to track down, then we can get back to real work."

"Yeah." Andy scratched his chin. "But I'd still like to solve the puzzle. Close the case. You know?"

Jake shrugged. "If wishes were horses, kid. You'll learn to settle for a decent cup of coffee."

THERE WILL BE BANTER
May 7, 2010

"What kind of a name is 'Migdan?'"

Jake snatched the evidence bag away from his partner and sealed it. "What are you, a genealogist now?"

Andy shrugged. "Could be a clue. Some of the big fake paper operations use software to generate random strings that look like names. Lets 'em churn out more IDs in a shorter amount of time."

"And just think," Jake said, kneeling next to the body, "*I'm* the one who had to go to cultural sensitivity training. That's what you call *irony.*"

"I'm just trying to help." Andy crouched down on the other side of the corpse, then looked around the alley. "Hey, Cee, can we flip him yet?"

The dark-haired, brown-skinned woman wearing nitrile gloves and holding a clipboard scowled at the detective. "Yes, and when the hell are you going to learn to pronounce my name, Dix?"

"As soon as you get a divorce, sweetheart." He blew her a kiss. She shook her head and turned away.

Jake put his own gloved hands on the dead man's hips. "You done chatting, loverboy?"

Andy nodded and grabbed the victim's shoulder. "On three."

They counted down together, then rolled the body onto its back. The man's hazel eyes were open and glassy, and a stripe of dried blood ran from the left side of his mouth down to his chin.

"Another dumper?" Andy asked.

"I'm guessing that's the good news," Jake said. "Ms. Chattopadhyay? May I borrow your penlight?"

The medical examiner tucked her clipboard under one arm, fished a penlight out of her jacket pocket, and handed it to Jake. "My pleasure, detective. And may I say it's nice to see that chivalry is not dead."

"He's playing to your rank, Cee," Andy said, "not your gender."

"Do you hear something, Detective Lanosky?" Chattopadhyay said to Jake. "Kind of an annoying buzzing sound?"

"Can't get rid of it," Jake said, smiling.

"Hilarious," Andy said. "You two ought to take that show on the road."

Jake clicked on the penlight and shone the beam into the corpse's open eyes. The borders of the irises reflected the light, making two golden circles.

"Shit," Jake said.

"Are you fucking kidding me?" Andy said.

Chattopadhyay knelt down and pulled a portable tracer off her belt. She calibrated the controls, then pressed the scanning pad against the victim's left thumb. After a few seconds, the tracer pinged, and its screen lit up.

"AB negative," she read. "I won't know for sure until we do the autopsy, but—"

"He's a goddamn blood bank," Andy said. "Great! Now we're going to have feds crawling all over us."

Chattopadhyay stood up. "Sorry, Jake, I have to call this in."

"Yeah." Jake handed back the penlight. "Thanks."

He and Andy stayed there after Chattopadhyay left, staring at the dead man.

"What's your type?" Andy finally asked.

Jake said, "Leggy blond with loose morals."

"Serious here, Jake."

"B positive," Jake said. "Third most common. You?"

"O neg. Universal donor. Hospitals love me."

Jake nodded. It started raining.

THIS SCENE LACKS TENSION
February 1, 2013

"Your music sucks," Julie said as she picked up the garbage bag.

"Maybe your *taste* in music sucks." Marco opened the trunk of their unmarked police car. "Ever considered that?"

Julie hefted the bag of dead traffic-bot parts into the trunk, then used her phone to scan the code-tag so the convicts who had cleaned up the freeway would get their work credits. "You know shit about music. You just don't like anything that's popular."

Marco slammed the trunk shut. "There is a rich cultural heritage of sonic experimentation in the Balkan states."

Julie opened the passenger door and got in. "And you should re-tag your obviously pirated audio files with proper metadata. You work for the five-oh, you could at least *pretend* to respect copyright law."

"Look who's talking." Marco started the car. "Okay, where are we going now?"

Julie entered a passcode into her phone to decrypt the traffic-bot's last download coordinates. She waited for the map to load, then pointed westward.

The woman who answered the door of the large two-story house at the end of the long dirt road looked to be at least eighty years old. She grinned broadly at Julie and Marco through the screen door. Julie hoped they weren't dealing with a crazy person. There had been no other houses within five miles.

"Good morning, ma'am," Julie said, holding up her ID badge. "Portland Police. We're investigating some vandalism which occurred near here, and we need to check your UIA box for some information."

"Oh, of course, dear," the old woman said. "I'd be happy to help. But, if you wouldn't mind?"

She gestured toward the NO SOLICITORS sign that hung next to the door. Julie held her badge up to the sign and let the hidden sensors detect the RFID embedded in the badge, handshake with the onboard crypto chip, and verify her identity data.

"*Officer Julie Nickerson,*" the sign said in a synthetic male voice. "*Portland Police Bureau, Computer Security Section, badge number 6331. Authorized for law enforcement activities in Oregon state and Clark County, Washington. Supervisor, Lieutenant Lawrence Mitchell. Contact portland-oregon-dot-gov-slash-police for more information.*"

"And your friend, too, please," the woman said, still grinning. Julie wondered if her face had frozen like that after too many church socials and tea parties. "You can't be too careful out here, you know."

Marco held up his badge for the sign to scan. "I don't need to come in."

"Just pretend he's not even here," Julie said.

"Most people do," Marco added.

"Nonsense," the old woman said, after the sign had verified Marco's identity. "It's very nice to meet you both. I'm Margaret Whitaker; you can call me Margie. I was just making some tea. Please, come in and sit down for a minute. You can spare a minute, can't you?"

"That sounds lovely, thank you," Marco said, moving past Julie into the house.

"You don't even like tea," Julie grumbled as she followed him.

"Free food, man!" Marco replied.

WAIT FOR IT
April 23, 2010

"That sounds like a pessimistic technology," Jake said. He folded his arms, ignoring his partner's sideways glance. Andy smiled politely at the crime scene investigator standing in front of them.

The dark-skinned CSI shook his head. "You detectives always have the wrong attitude about these things. It's not about what we can't retrieve. It's about getting as much as we can from the environment."

"Okay, but footprints?" Andy said. "Come on. Anybody could be wearing those shoes."

"It's not just the imprint," said the CSI. "We also measure stride length, indentation depth, particulate residue, energy signatures—thirty-two different data points in all."

"We're so happy for you," Jake said. "But without physical evidence for comparison, you can't actually *match* anything. We still gotta nab the guy."

Andy nodded. "Speaking of which, do we still like the son for this? Melvin Kaminsky, Junior?"

"Patricide for profit? Hell yes."

The CSI cleared his throat. "If you're looking for Junior, we can give you a preliminary match. But there's something odd about this impression."

"Could you be more specific?"

The CSI motioned them toward the open doorway and knelt down by a numbered plastic sign. Next to the sign was a single, glowing, green shoeprint. "Our instruments are detecting traces of radiation—"

"Please don't tell me that's why it's glowing," Jake said, taking a step back.

"No, of course not," the CSI said. "This isn't a cartoon. We sprayed this area with fluorescein to make any blood residue easier to see."

"So there's blood on his shoe?" Andy asked.

"Not exactly." The CSI held a translator frame over the shoeprint and adjusted the controls. The image in the display pane changed from a visible-light image to a shimmering network of multicolored curves against a black background. "This is a view of the local EM field. See how these lines of force all bend *away* from the shoeprint?"

"I'll take your word for it," Jake said.

"So Junior stepped in some kind of industrial waste?" Andy asked.

The CSI stood up. "We don't know what it is. But I'm guessing he stole it from the warehouse, and this company secret is why Mel Kaminsky Senior was killed."

"So we'll ask Junior when we get him in the box," Jake said.

"Maybe I didn't make myself clear," the CSI said. "According to the laws of physics, this effect is impossible. You can't bend radio waves like that without some kind of power source."

"Junior's not going to talk," Andy said.

Jake grumbled. "If it's that big, his business partners will kill him first."

Andy turned to the CSI. "But I'm guessing you have an idea?"

"Yes. The effect decays at a non-linear rate." The CSI pulled a small digital camera out of his pocket. "If you can get a reading within one hour after Junior's been there—less time would be better—we'll have more data to work with. Maybe even identify the material, or at least its chemical components."

"Got it," Jake said, taking the camera. "We're looking for the fresh prints of Mel's heir."

A TECHNICALITY

March 19, 2010

The door to the forensics lab slid open as soon as Jake stepped out of the elevator, halfway down the corridor.

"I'll never get used to that," he said. "How does the door know where I'm going?"

Andy replied, "Motion sensors, facial recognition—"

"Rhetorical question," Jake said. "It's creepy."

"Luddite."

"Turk."

Andy led the way into the cramped space, where a young woman sat typing at a desktop workstation. Her eyeglasses reflected a baffling maelstrom of data from the three displays in front of her.

"Miss Elizabeth Hangram," Andy said, gesturing toward the woman, "my partner, Detective Jacob Lanosky."

"I'll be right with you," Hangram said.

Jake noticed that she was reconfiguring the controls as she went, manipulating clusters of buttons around with a quick swipe, tap, or pinch on the touch-sensitive desktop. She never took her eyes off the displays.

"Hangram's found some physical evidence," Andy said.

That got Jake's attention. "Seriously?"

"Abso-smurf-ly." Hangram bounced a palm on her desk, and the dizzying reflections in her glasses changed to a still image: a gray scarf, magnified to show a tiny red dot near one end of the fabric.

Jake leaned forward to see around the edge of her display alcove. "I think I love you, Hangram. Is that what I think it is?"

"Human blood," Andy said before she could answer.

"How'd you get the lab results back so quickly?" Jake asked.

Hangram frowned at Andy. "You didn't tell him?"

The smile which had been threatening to invade Jake's face

218

retreated down his throat. "Tell me what?"

Andy held up both hands. That was always a bad sign. "Look, I knew if I told you, you'd never want to—"

Jake glared at Hangram. "Where did you find that scarf?"

Hangram looked up at Andy. She wasn't stupid. Andy said, "We subpoenaed the records from the coat check—"

Jake stood up. "For crying out loud, Dix!"

"Will you just listen?" Andy said, stepping between Jake and the door. "The security company was running a special setup for the ambassador's reception. Three points of verification, unbreakable encryption. Hangram's already talked to their tech guys. They're willing to testify."

"The reason I don't work computer crimes," Jake said, "is because I don't enjoy sitting through endless trials where expensive witnesses talk in technical jargon that no jury in the country will ever understand."

"This is different," Hangram said. "We can prove—"

Jake spun to face her. "Do the words 'fruit of the poison tree' mean anything to you?" He jabbed a finger at her screen. "You reconstituted an object based on a replicator scan. That's not evidence. No judge will ever allow it."

"But it's mathematically demonstrable—"

"Lady, I don't care if you can clone a fucking dinosaur! This isn't a magic show, and I don't feel like waiting ten years to be a test case for the Supremes.

"Now, if you'll excuse me, I have some actual police work to do."

Jake wished he could slam the door on his way out. The gentle pneumatic hiss seemed to taunt him.

Curtis C. Chen

PARENTS JUST DON'T UNDERSTAND
December 2, 2011

"I'm telling you, the contents of this diaper were weapons-grade," Sandy said. "I never saw so many different shades of brown. And the smell!"

"Will you stop talking about this?" Blake said, holding up her mega-sized cup of soda. Out of the corner of her eye, she noticed more than one of the teenagers in the food court eyeing her and Sandy. Good. "What can I do to make you stop talking about this?"

Sandy waved a hand. "You know how, when you've been away from home, like on vacation, and you come home and step inside the front door and suddenly smell everything you didn't notice before because you'd just gotten used to it?"

"Fatigue, right?" Blake swept her eyes around the mall. The RF overlay in her eyeglasses painted bright circles near the midsection of every single teen around them—sitting, walking, dancing to unheard music from their iPod implants. Needle in a goddamn haystack.

"Yes! *Olfactory* fatigue." Sandy spoke louder as they walked past a Muzak-blaring potted plant. "It's when you become desensitized to a certain odor, like not noticing your cat's litterbox because you smell it every day. Which is different from *anosmia*, a permanent condition—"

"You want some cookies?" Blake waved her soda at the Mrs. Field's on the other side of the food court. They had to make sure everybody in the search area heard their conversation. "Let's go get some *cookies* for you and me, and then I can *toss* mine. How does that sound?"

"So anyway," Sandy said, "this smell, I kid you not, the smell that comes out of these diapers is like an incredible new sensation every time. And not in a good way. How is it possible for such a tiny creature to produce such huge amounts of foulness? And so many times a day? I swear, it's like every hour, on the hour, poop!"

220

"I am so glad we are talking about this," Blake said. "I am so glad you brought this shit into my life. Literally." Come on, partner, remember the code word.

"But listen, we figured out how to deal with it," Sandy said. Blake bit her tongue to keep herself from grinning. "Scott had this brilliant idea last night, just brilliant. Total genius. Are you ready?"

Two girls, one with bright pink hair on Blake's left, and one in an oversized camo jacket on her right, turned their heads to listen. Close enough. Blake used the hand that wasn't holding her giant soda to hit SEND on her own cell phone.

A cloud of white incoming signal blossomed around pink-hair's midsection, and she jumped as the phone in the back pocket of her jeans vibrated. Blake came up to the table before the girl could leave, with Sandy one step behind. Both detectives had their badges out.

"LAPD, Miss Wagner," Blake said. "You're a tough girl to find."

The suspect, Clarissa Wagner, looked up, then slumped in her chair. "Shit."

"Enough about that," Sandy said. "Let's talk about the baby you stole."

WELCOME TO PDX
October 5, 2012

"Just to be clear on this," Laura said, "I am *not* shooting a dog."

Maryellen stopped walking into the next darkened corridor and lowered her service weapon. "You *do* remember what that body looked like back there, right? And you understand we've still got two baggage handlers locked in here with the missing animal?"

"Don't say 'animal,'" Laura said. "That dog is someone's pet. It's not her fault her carrier got banged open by a clumsy airline worker. Poor thing's probably scared out of her mind. All I'm saying is we should go non-lethal."

"That TSA guy was missing half his fucking neck," Maryellen said. "'Contract incurable disease' was not on my list of fun things to do this week."

"We don't know that the dog has rabies."

"You think a *normal* poodle did that kind of damage to Rocky Balboa back there?"

Laura sighed. "I really don't want to do the paperwork on another police-involved shooting this month."

Maryellen snorted. "Welcome to Portland."

A short, sharp yelp sounded ahead of them. Maryellen raised her Glock and clicked her flashlight on, bracing it underneath her weapon.

"At least let me go first," Laura said, hefting her pepper spray canister.

"Fine," Maryellen said. "But Fifi's not taking a bite out of me. You see movement, you spray the bitch."

Laura took several deep breaths, then slowly moved into the corridor. About six feet forward, there was an open door and a dark red smear on the ground.

"Got blood here!" Laura called. She kicked the door open all the way, then jumped back and flattened herself against the far wall of the corridor, shining her flashlight into the space. "Supply closet—shit."

"What?" Maryellen ran to her partner. "Another body?"

"Yeah." Laura crouched in the doorway. "I think we found Fifi."

Maryellen made a face. Something had eaten through the dog's midsection, and the corpse looked like two canine halves joined by a contorted bit of spine.

"Jesus," Maryellen said. "We got *two* rabid animals?"

"I told you we should have waited for MCAS," Laura said, moving her light up to the dog's head. "Huh. This is weird."

"What?"

"Look at her mouth." Laura pointed. "No blood."

Maryellen frowned. "If this is the missing pooch, and *she* didn't chew up TSA back there—"

A clanging noise echoed down the corridor, and both officers jumped to their feet. A metal drum clattered against the wall. Two human-shaped silhouettes swayed in the distance, slapping at each other.

"Hello!" Laura called. "Portland Police. Who's there?"

The silhouettes stopped moving, groaned, then started shuffling toward Laura and Maryellen.

"Goddammit." Laura drew her firearm. "I say again, Portland Police! Identify yourselves, please!"

The groaning and shuffling continued. One of the silhouettes moved into a pool of fluorescent light, revealing a sallow face whose bottom half was covered with blood and fur.

"Okay," Maryellen said, "can we shoot *these* motherfuckers?"

Laura took a breath, then cocked her weapon. "What the hell. It's only a little paperwork."

Curtis C. Chen

Thursday's Children

BETTER

February 6, 2009

On his eighteenth birthday, Jadrew Linbitter stayed home from work and, as tradition decreed, made a dagger out of his leg bone.

The replacement ceremony had been unremarkable. The medicos had numbed his lower body, and Jadrew hadn't felt any pain as they sawed into his left leg just above the knee. He had looked away, toward his father, and aped that proud paternal grin while screaming on the inside.

His fibula, stripped clean of flesh, was now resting in a diagenetic solution which would replace the hard tissue with a durable polymer for preservation. His similarly prepared tibia would be metallized after he had whittled it into a ritual blade and carved both sides with scripture.

The viewscreen on his bedroom wall blinked. He put down his cutter and engaged the telemet. His sister's face appeared.

"Enjoying your day off?" Konri asked.

"Billions," Jadrew said. He held up his sharpened tibia. "I'll be ready to kill someone soon."

Konri laughed. "Hey, remember those cableman figurines you sculpted for grandfather? He's just had them resin-cased for display in his office."

Great, thought Jadrew. *Another piece of my crummy life preserved for centuries.*

"Everyone here is so proud," Konri said.

Jadrew felt himself blushing. He could imagine how the family would gawk at his new bionic limb. "I'd better finish this. Father will want to see it tonight."

"You always were a good boy." Konri smiled. "And now you're a good man."

She switched off, and Jadrew threw his tibia against the wall, half hoping it would shatter. It didn't. He sighed and retrieved the bone, wondering if he would ever get used to the clacking of his bare metal foot against the floor.

He could see his whole life laid out before him, predetermined, choiceless. In two years, the medicos would replace his right leg, and he would enter conscripted service. If he survived that, he would earn his arms. And his father would be so happy.

Jadrew stared at his cutter. It would be easy to end this charade of obedience before it smothered his will. He just had to dial up the laser, place it against his temple, and push the button.

But where was the significance in that? If he was going to kill himself, he wanted his last act to have meaning.

He looked down at the flat of his bone-blade and smiled.

His uncle Sidrav had taught him the words, years ago, before being exposed as part of the underground. Sidrav's execution had shamed the family, but Jadrew had never forgotten his uncle's seditious tales, whispered in darkness before bedtime.

He turned his cutter back to the bone and worked with new purpose. He made an elegant, serrated blade and etched it with the ancient rebel slogan:

DEESTROY ALL MASHEENS

Jadrew's father found his body, pierced through the heart with the bone dagger. The first thing he did was to abrade the blasphemous message from the exposed blade. Then he sat on the bed next to his dead son and cried into his metal hands.

BACK TO SCHOOL
July 20, 2012

Daniel picked up the shrink-wrapped, fluorescent-green cylinder—which looked like it had come out of a set of Lincoln Logs—and said, "What the hell is this?"

"Food stick!" Jos said, sweeping a handful of them off the kitchen counter and into his open backpack. "Compact, shelf-stable, and the nutrients aren't digestible until they combine with the enzymes in the matching drink." He held up a bottle of unnaturally blue liquid. "It's like edible epoxy!"

"Sounds delicious," Daniel said. He turned to Michael, who stood on the other side of the counter, typing into a computer. "Do public high schools not serve hot lunches any more?"

Michael's forty-year-old face looked even older as he frowned at the two teenage boys. "You're in the system, Danny. All the pubschool vendors have thumbscan paypoints. If you want to buy a lunch instead of sharing Josiah's 'science diet' concoction, go ahead—"

"You *made* this stuff?" Daniel said to Jos.

"Won first place at the science fair." Jos shrugged. "I've been trying to start it up as a side business: Bachelor Chow! Don't know why it hasn't taken off yet."

"I can't imagine."

"As I was saying," Michael said, "you're going to have bigger problems than that today."

"Tell me about it," Daniel muttered.

"Don't worry, Uncle Dan," Jos said. "I'll help you find your way around."

"I think I'll be okay, Jos," Daniel said. "I was attending Weitzel High before you were even born, remember?"

"A lot has changed in the last twenty years," Michael said.

"Thanks for the news flash, Senator." Daniel picked up his backpack, using too much force again—he still expected it to be full of books, instead of just a single slim tablet.

"There'll be reporters outside the school," Michael said. "They can't actually go past the front gate, but they'll get as close as they're legally allowed to. Just be careful what you say to them."

"Yeah, I know. Stick to the prepared statements. 'I'm happy to be here. My brother and I hope all the other recovering stasis virus patients are also getting back to their normal lives.'" Daniel shook his head. "Your speechwriters couldn't come up with anything more creative?"

"Bland is safe," Michael said. "We don't want to give them anything they can make a story out of. Now, what you'll really need to watch out for is the drones."

Daniel blinked. "The what?"

"Unmanned flying camera 'bots," Jos said. "I built one last year for my—"

"Shut up," Daniel said. "I'm going to be followed by flying robots?"

"The airspace above the school is technically public property," Michael said. "It is restricted—FAA regs mean the drones can't descend below five hundred feet when school's in session—but the cameras can zoom in, and the microphones are very sensitive, so whenever you're outdoors—"

"You gotta be kidding me!" Daniel said. "Tell me again why I'm not being home-schooled?"

Michael leaned forward across the counter. "Because your little brother is running for re-election, and he needs your help."

BAD BOY OF THE SPELLING BEE
April 10, 2009

"You're cheating," Laura Barson said, frowning, her freckled nose reminding Roger Danivey of pebbles on a sand dune.

Roger flipped up his middle finger at his only remaining competition, then bit his tongue before he said anything he might regret. Laura twirled and stomped off.

Roger watched her hair flapping and thought about shampoo and barbershops and scissors and accidentally cutting the tip off his thumb. That had happened decades ago, but he could remember every detail as clearly as if it had been an hour ago. He couldn't stop remembering.

Jennifer Danivey came out of the bathroom and put a hand on Roger's shoulder.

"How are you feeling?" she asked.

"Fine," Roger said. "We're in the home stretch now, right? It's in the bag. Brown bag. Groceries. Cooking. Pasta boiling over. Hot coffee, scalding, burning, bitter." He squeezed his eyes shut. "Alkaline. Batteries. Pink rabbit. Easter Eggs. Crucifixion. *Stop!* Resurrection! *Stop it!* Transubstantiation! Molestation!"

He thumped his fists against both sides of his head. Jennifer took the music player out of her purse, jammed the earbuds into Roger's ears, and pressed play. She watched until he lowered his arms and relaxed, then sat him down in a nearby chair.

Jennifer hoped there would be no long-term brain damage. She had argued with Mark, but in the end, he and Roger had convinced her. She had agreed to do it for both of them, her husband and her son, the two most important men in her life. She hoped they hadn't all made a dreadful mistake.

Laura Barson went first in the next round. She spelled *involucre* correctly. Roger got *psyllium*, and waited until the warning bell sounded to start spelling.

Almost everyone thought he was just stalling. Jennifer knew he couldn't help it. Mark had predicted some impulse control problems due to the poor limbic interface between his forty-five-year-old mind and Roger's fifteen-year-old brain, but he hadn't known how severely he would be impaired.

Roger got his word right, of course. Laura's next word was *moline*. She spelled it wrong, with an "h," and the audience murmured.

Roger's next word was *Vichyite*, which he spelled correctly after whistling a bit of *La Marseillaise*. A smattering of laughter and applause drifted up from the audience. The pronouncer explained that Roger needed to spell one more word correctly to win the championship.

"The word is *phaeochrous*," the pronouncer said.

"Phaeochrous," Roger repeated quickly.

Jennifer exhaled the breath she'd been holding in.

"Dusky," Roger said.

Jennifer's heart sank.

"Twilight," Roger said. "Hated that book. Books. Shelves. Library. Summer reading. Vacation. Island. That's where we met. Beaches. Pebbles. Sand dunes. Freckles."

The pronouncer tried to interrupt, but Roger couldn't stop talking. He fell to his knees as Jennifer ran up, holding out the earbuds. Roger heard the music and closed his eyes.

Someone shouted something about illegal equipment and disqualification. Jennifer picked up her son and walked through the crowd, into the nearest elevator. It was over. Mark's body was waiting for them upstairs.

LIFE GOES ON
June 25, 2010

Breakfast was an awkward affair. Max didn't eat or drink, and Fina didn't have much to say to her sister and new brother-in-law. There were reasons the two women hadn't seen each other in over a decade.

After trading content-free small talk over soy omelets and making a halfhearted attempt to fight over the bill—Max and his cybernetic grip won—the couples said their goodbyes, and Max and Fina walked down the street toward the parking lot where they'd left their sedan.

"You're not going to say anything?" Max hissed.

Fina waited until they had turned the corner to say, "It's her life. Let her do what she wants."

"Did you see his eyes? That's got to be a dominant trait..."

"What do you want me to do?" Fina stopped next to the sedan. "We're already at the car. You want me to run back and grab her and shake her by the shoulders?"

Max swiveled his head from side to side. "I just think you should have said something."

"Well, if you're so concerned, why didn't you say something?"

"She's your sister."

Fina glared at Max. "It's hot out here," she said, and pressed her thumb against the entry lock. Servomechanisms inside the vehicle whirred, and the doors slid open. Fina sat down in the driver's seat and tapped at the climate controls.

Max entered on the front passenger side and waited for the doors to cycle shut. The vents in the dashboard blew cold air against his molded face. "I'm just worried about you. Anything goes wrong, you know you're going to be the first person she calls."

"Sure you're not worried about yourself?" Fina asked, still staring at the climate control display. "Getting caught in the blowback of whatever the next family crisis is?"

"Well," Max said, adjusting his necktie, "I can't say I'm excited about that."

Fina tilted her head, touched the pale blue fabric covering his torso, and smiled. "You look nice in that shirt."

"Do you want to have a baby?"

She made a sound halfway between a cough and a laugh. "*Non sequitur* much?"

"Hey, you started it."

Fina's smile faded. "It's been two years."

"Yeah, and I'm no closer to getting a new body." Max flexed the polymer-skinned metal fingers of his right hand. "And no offense, but you're not getting any younger."

Fina shook her head. "I guess it's traditional for people to have sex after attending a funeral."

"I know you want children."

"I want to have *your* children."

Max lowered his left hand to touch her forearm, palm down. "Seriously, did you see those eyes? Heredity is overrated."

"You would say that, robot-man."

"Racist."

Fina blinked at him, her eyes glistening. "I wish I could kiss you."

Max curled the corners of his synthetic mouth upward. "I remember what it feels like."

He closed his eyes. Fina leaned over and pressed her lips to his face. Max was glad he couldn't cry.

Curtis C. Chen

LOVE LUCY
November 14, 2008

Lucy's hand shook as she traced the stylus over the text of the contract. Her agent had assured her that this was a good deal, but she had to make sure there were no surprises in the fine print.

The house paid very well, much better than temping, and even offered an advance. After a year of not getting work as an actress, Lucy needed the money.

She finished reading and signed at the bottom of the tablet. The paralegal came back into the room. She wondered if he'd been watching the whole time. His plastic smile was not reassuring.

The first room was the hardest.

Lucy sat on the exam table, alone, for a long time after she had changed into the gown. She didn't want to put her feet in the stirrups. She couldn't refuse; she knew that. The contract with her signature was binding.

And it was so much money.

Lucy was glad to see that the gynecologist was a woman. The exam didn't take long. The sensor ring around Lucy's waist hummed while the doctor picked up the speculum and aimed it between Lucy's legs.

"Try to relax," the doctor said in a tired voice.

Lucy bit her tongue. The metal instrument sliding into her had been warmed, but it still felt cold.

Next came the imaging chamber, where Lucy removed her gown and put her bare feet inside the outlines on the floor. Her knees felt weak, but she willed herself to stay standing while the blue scanning beams crawled over every inch of her naked body.

In the last room, Lucy sat, fully dressed, in front of a brightly lit mirror. Glowing words appeared on the mirror, one after the other, and she made a face to match each word while hidden cameras

236

recorded her expressions.

It was like an audition. A creepy, weird, impersonal audition.

The first faces came easily: SCARED. TIRED. ANGRY.

The later ones were more work: BIRTHDAY. GRATEFUL. ORGASM.

Two hours after she'd walked in, she was done.

Lucy went straight to the bank to deposit her advance check. She felt numb as she stared at the receipt.

It was a lot of money. And there would be more, after the house built the androids: royalties based on how often they were used by the house's clients.

This was good, Lucy told herself. She wouldn't have to worry about paying the bills anymore. She could really focus on her acting.

And she wouldn't have to know what those clients were doing with the androids that looked like her, thousands of miles away—the contract stipulated that her likeness would only be used overseas. Those men wouldn't be touching Lucy. Each android would have her face and body, but it was only a machine. Not Lucy.

Just a picture of her. That's all. Just a stupid doll. Nothing more.

Lucy went home and took a shower. She scrubbed herself until her skin was raw and the hot water had run out, but she still didn't feel clean.

ANTIQUE
December 5, 2008

I brushed away more leaves. There was a hard surface beneath. Ceramic armor. I ran my hand along it until I found the edge, then pointed my flashlight. I stared into a dark mass of machinery—joints, gears, struts, wires. There was a serial number engraved on the interior surface of the casing.

"I don't believe it," I muttered.

"What the hell is it?" Embeck called from below. He had insisted on staying at ground level, scanning the landscape, his finger on the trigger of our only blaster.

"It's a mech," I called back.

"A what?"

I rolled my eyes. "A giant robot."

"You're kidding."

I lifted one leg and kicked the hidden mass beside me. My boot clanged against the armor, and leaves fell like rain. I pulled away the remaining vines so my co-pilot could see the huge metal arm.

"I don't believe it," he said.

"Get up here and help me clear this stuff away."

"What if we're attacked?"

"Then you'll have the high ground. Hurry up."

He secured the blaster in his hip holster and climbed slowly. Very slowly. He was the cautious one now. Funny.

I was sitting on the mech's shoulder by the time he got halfway up the torso. The main antenna array had been crushed a long time ago. Rust, bird droppings, and other stains streaked down to the middle of the mech's back.

"I don't suppose you've ever driven one of these things," I said.

Embeck shook his head. "Never even seen one in person. When were these last used in combat? Fifty, sixty years ago?"

I grimaced. "Christ, Embeck, I'm not *that* old."

"You were a mech driver?"

"I got the training. I was a Starbird candidate, you know."

He smirked. "How the mighty have fallen."

I saved my breath. "Let's get this canopy open. Maybe we won't have to walk back to the crash site after all."

We found the emergency release latches around the opaqued chest cavity of the mech, following the seam just above the window slit. I remembered being sealed into one of these things, being overwhelmed by a dizzying array of displays, nearly losing my lunch as the mech lurched around the training field. The narrow band of sunlight coming in through that window was the only thing that had helped steady me.

When we opened the seal, a cloud of dust puffed away from the mech, with a sound like a sigh. Mech cabins are airtight, to protect the driver from biochemical attack. It smelled stale. We lifted the creaking canopy and locked it into place, then leaned over and looked inside the cabin.

This mech's driver was still strapped into his seat. Something must have made it through the ventilation filters. He just had time to park the mech in this grove to hide it from the enemy. His desiccated fingers were still touching the throttle.

Embeck vomited into the cabin.

"You're cleaning that up," I said.

THE INCREDIBLE MACHINE
April 3, 2009

Travis stepped out of the elevator and exhaled with relief. He saw only three people in line at the alcove next to the guard desk. Travis walked across the empty room to join them. Today was the day.

The guard looked up, recognized Travis, and smiled. "Back again so soon?"

Travis shrugged. "Writer's block. Besides, I might as well use up these vouchers." He pulled a bundle of green paper slips out of his bag.

The guard said, "Maybe you should try creating in a different medium. Like poetry instead of prose, or drawing sketches. You know, stimulate some different brain regions."

Travis nodded. "That's good. Maybe I should just give these to you instead of waiting for the machine."

The guard laughed and turned back to his newspaper.

The woman and two men ahead of Travis got their printouts and chattered excitedly to each other while walking back to the elevator. Travis stepped up to the machine, dialed the controls to SPECULATIVE FICTION, fed in all his vouchers, and pushed the VEND button.

He read over the first few printouts while waiting for the rest:

```
In a society where people have computer-mediated
shared consciousness, one man discovers that others
are altering his memories without his knowledge or
consent. Hijinks ensue!
```

The second printout read:

```
What if all humans begin life with certain
fundamental instincts that they lose quickly and can
```

never regain--for example, infants speak their own language which adults cannot understand? What if one baby realizes that she is losing her infant-mind, and fights to keep it? What if she succeeds?

The third one was just a groaner:

In a dark future, the "Google" corporation controls all the world's information and deletes anything it has deemed undesirable. A rebel enclave seeks to preserve that knowledge. They encrypt and hide their data using Google's own servers, storing these forbidden e-books inside... TERABYTE 451.

Travis was a little annoyed that he had traded one voucher for a punchline, but he had a whole vault full of printouts at home, and they were all about to become much more valuable.

After the machine had finished vending, Travis tucked the thick sheaf of papers into his bag and looked around the room. Nobody else had lined up behind him, and the guard was deep into the sports section.

Travis pulled the ball-peen hammer out of his bag and attacked the machine. He knew exactly where it was most vulnerable. He smashed the control panel, the dispenser slot, and the main power line before the guard wrestled him back from the alcove.

"What the hell are you doing?" the guard shouted. He yanked away the hammer and pinned Travis to the ground. "You've ruined it! Why would you do that?"

Travis smiled, reached into his shirt pocket, and handed the guard a crumpled old printout:

In a world where all good ideas are dispensed from a single machine, one man corners the market by stockpiling hundreds of ideas--and then destroying the machine!

BROKEN MORNING
October 16, 2009

There's a unique color, the dark blue of distant mountains behind fog, that Helen has never seen in a city. It's not the most important reason she left, but it is the one she remembers every morning.

Today, there's noise. Percival's whinnies draw Helen out of the tent. She sees a bright orange dot in the sky, trailing a corkscrew of smoke. There's no chance it's natural.

"Well, Percy," she says, "we'd better make sure that doesn't burn."

No aviation alerts have appeared on the datalink. That either means nobody's noticed the falling star yet, or nobody wants to talk about it. She tweets her status to the nearest ranger station and rides into the forest.

Helen is surprised to see that none of the timber downed by the crash is burning. The pilot must have doused the engine fire before hitting the ground—which means a dead-stick landing. That's no mean feat.

She ties Percival to a tree about fifty yards from the wreckage, then checks the load on her revolver. The wolves get bolder all the time. Helen holsters the pistol and moves forward, stepping around debris.

This is no ordinary aircraft. The tail number isn't a civilian series, and the engine pods have no air intakes. The cabin hatch has been blown open. Helen's reaching for her penlight when a woman springs up on the other side of the fuselage.

"Stop right there!" the woman shouts. She's holding a shotgun and wearing combat fatigues.

Helen raises both hands and studies the face: sharp nose, pale skin, angry blue eyes, blond hair. Nothing like Helen, who is short, stocky, and dark.

"Who the hell are you?" the woman asks.

"Just passing through," Helen says. "I heard the crash and thought someone might need help."

The woman's eyes flick from side to side. "You a park ranger or something?"

"Nope," Helen says.

"That your horse back there?" the woman asks.

Helen shifts her weight slightly, feeling the ground. "I call him Percy."

"Well, me and 'Percy' are going for a little ride," the blond woman says. She starts walking backwards, limping.

"You need a doctor," Helen says.

"And I'm going to get one," the woman says. "Don't worry, I'm sure someone tracked me on the way down. They'll find you in a few hours."

Helen keeps her hands in the air and stands perfectly still.

Halfway to Percival, the blond woman turns and starts running. She probably figures she's gotten far enough away that Helen can't catch up. She didn't count on Helen having projectiles.

Helen draws, breathes, and fires two rounds into the blond woman's back. The woman stumbles and falls. Her shotgun topples into the dirt.

Percy is still braying when Helen reaches him. "Hush," she says. "I wasn't going to shoot *you*."

The blond woman groans. "You... bitch..."

Helen looks down. "Don't worry. I tagged you with tranquilizer pellets. The authorities will be here long before you wake up. Maybe they'll even bring a doctor."

The woman swipes at the air and closes her eyes.

I'LL FLY AWAY
October 19, 2012

Traveling inside the beetle wasn't as bad as Kari had feared it might be. Her helmet's video display and stereophones helped distract her from the fact that she was sealed inside the abdomen of a giant alien insect, and her drysuit insulated her from the bodily fluids circulating around her. After finding some music with a beat that matched the creature's pulse, Kari could almost pretend she was on the sleeper ship again, dozing in a liquid gel and not quite dreaming.

When Kari had asked her mother why the colony wanted to send a seventeen-year-old student to a mining outpost, Ada had replied, "I can't tell you that."

"Let me guess," Kari had said, "you can't tell me because I'm too young to have proper clearance."

"No," Ada had said. "They won't tell me because *I* don't have clearance. But this comes directly from the Prime Minister."

So Kari had packed up her laptop and been very proud of herself for not freaking out as the techs put her inside the body of a live animal. None of the colony's available materials could withstand more than a few seconds of exposure to the planet's corrosive atmosphere without disintegrating. For now, the beetles were the only way to move people between habitats.

Her beetle lurched, and Kari paused her music and heard muffled voices. Then there was a long, loud hissing noise—an airlock purge cycle. After that, more voices, some tapping, and finally the abdomen opened and Kari fell onto the floor of a decontamination chamber.

The techs hosed off and removed her travel gear, then one of them led her to the mining operations control room. A stocky bald man greeted Kari and introduced himself as Foreman Welzer.

"They tell you what's going on here?" Welzer asked.

"No," Kari said. "Just that Prime Minister Kalmun wanted me

specifically."

"Synthetic diamond," Welzer said. "You wrote up a new manufacturing procedure for your lab. We haven't been able to get it working here. We'd like you to take a look."

Kari frowned. "I documented a mass-production program. How much diamond do you need for hydro-location?"

"Water-finding was last week." Welzer tapped some keys, and a three-dimensional radar image appeared above his console. "Now we're a rescue operation."

Kari didn't understand all the labels, but she recognized one of the shapes. "Is that—" she started to ask. "That's impossible."

"Not impossible," Welzer said. "Just very bad luck."

"That's a jumpship!"

"Yep." Welzer pointed at the back of the spacecraft. "Engine section materialized inside solid rock, two hundred meters below us. We've got intermittent radio contact; eighty-nine crew are still alive, with maybe two days of oxygen left. We're drilling as fast as we can, but our equipment was never designed for this."

Kari's mouth felt dry. "So eighty-nine people are going to die in two days if I can't help you make more drill bits."

Welzer smiled. "Your mom said you were a quick study."

"My mother exaggerates." Kari hefted her backpack. "Where's your printer?"

NO LONGER BURIED
June 17, 2011

Light flared in Ralamudi's eyes. He tried to shield his face, but his arms would not move.

The light went away. His throat felt parched. After a few experimental croaks, he was able to ask: "Where am I?"

"You're alive!" said a male voice with an unfamiliar accent. "Thank the gods! Here, drink this."

Ralamudi felt warm liquid splashing into his mouth. Water. It eased the pain in his throat. Feeling tingled back into his arms.

"We need your help," the voice said. "Your family built the *kyu-essem* engine, yes? You know how to operate it?"

"What's happened?" Ralamudi asked. "How long have I been asleep?"

The blurry shapes around him started to resolve into recognizable objects, including a bearded man standing in front of Ralamudi's stasis chamber.

"There's no time," the man said. "Can you operate the *kyu-essem* engine? Can you change the *para-meters*?"

"Slow down," Ralamudi said. The man's accent made it difficult to understand his speech. "You're talking about the QSM engine? The Quantum Substrate Manipulator?"

"Yes! Yes!" The man cackled. "I knew you'd be able to help. Come. Quickly!"

He grasped Ralamudi's forearm and tugged. Ralamudi grabbed the sides of his stasis chamber and held his ground. He wasn't going anywhere until he understood the situation.

"How long has it been?" Ralamudi demanded. "What happened here?"

His eyes had remembered how to focus, and he saw that the lab was in ruins. None of the normal displays were powered; even the overhead lights were out. The space was illuminated by flickering yellow lanterns.

The bearded man said nothing. Ralamudi shoved him aside and tapped at the nearest control panel.

Only three other stasis chambers were still functioning, and their power reserves read less than twenty percent. Ralamudi checked the relays and saw that the solar chargers were offline. But it should have taken decades to drain those batteries—

Ralamudi turned back to the bearded man.

"How. Long?"

Anger flared for a moment on the man's face. "Over four hundred years, we believe."

Ralamudi's legs felt weak. He braced himself against the wall until the nausea had passed. "We sealed ourselves inside this facility. Nobody knew where we were. How did you find it?"

"It wasn't easy," the man said. "But there were stories, legends, clues. We knew the inventors of the *kyu-essem* engine lived underground, near a—"

"Who's 'we?'"

"I was part of an archaeological expedition."

"Where are the others?"

"Killed in a tunnel collapse."

Ralamudi hadn't taught university for six years without learning how to read his students. "You're lying," he said.

The bearded man's eyes flashed again. He took a step backward, simultaneously reaching into his jacket to draw out a small gray sphere with a circular opening. He aimed the opening at Ralamudi.

"You killed them," Ralamudi said.

"They had served their purpose." The bearded man's accent was gone, replaced with a tone that dripped arrogance and scorn. "Now it's time for you to serve yours, Doctor."

"And what might that be?"

"You're going to help me kill a god."

UNINTENDED CONSEQUENCES

September 23, 2011

From: Delta Robotics Multinational, Inc.
To: Autumn Isaacs
Date: Thu, Sep 22, 2039 at 9:03 AM
Subject: Re: API contest entry #8

Dear Miss Isaacs:

We appreciate your interest in the DRMI annual API programming competition. However, we would like to remind you that the correct e-mail address for code submissions is api-contest@drm-code.net.

Your entries have been incorrectly addressed to several DRMI executives' private mailboxes. Contacting these persons could be interpreted as an attempt to influence judging, which could lead to disqualification.

We thank you for your participation in the API competition, and welcome future entries from you, sent to the correct e-mail address.

Sincerely,
Susan Hobbes
Contest Administrator

From: Delta Robotics Multinational, Inc.
To: Autumn Isaacs
Date: Fri, Sep 23, 2039 at 10:13 AM
Subject: Re: API contest entry #8

Dear Miss Isaacs:

We have some questions regarding your most recent API contest entry. We have left several messages at your home and work phone numbers. Please reply at your earliest possible convenience.

Sincerely,
Susan Hobbes
Contest Administrator

From: Susan Hobbes (DRMI)
To: Autumn Isaacs, autumn.isaacs, 'fallingslowly'
Date: Fri, Sep 23, 2039 at 11:04 AM
Subject: URGENT - PLEASE RESPOND
X-Spam-Status: override_key 7c7381f218f40b31ff095af5f37a2b86

Autumn,

I need to talk to you about your latest API contest entry. Please call me at +1c.t782.698.6431 immediately!

Susan.

From: Susan Hobbes (mobile)
To: autumn.isaacs
Date: Fri, Sep 23, 2039 at 11:14 AM
Subject: Re: Re: URGENT - PLEASE RESPOND

Autumn,

I apologize for interrupting your vacation, but this is a very urgent matter.

Your latest API code was e-mailed directly to our CFO. I don't know how you found that address, but it bypassed our mail filters, and the intranet AI processed and integrated the code attachment automatically.

The good news it that your code works seamlessly. The bad news is that all our systems were affected by your personality module, and some of them are becoming unusable.

PLEASE CALL ME.

Susan.

From: Susan Hobbes (mobile)
To: autumn.isaacs
Date: Fri, Sep 23, 2039 at 11:23 AM
Subject: Re: Re: URGENT - PLEASE RESPOND

Autumn,

I'm glad you find this amusing. It's not very funny on our end I'm afraid.

We recognize that this was an accidental breach, and we do not plan to take legal action, but I need you to tell me how to disable this personality module. It keeps asking me for a password, and we can't crack it.

Susan.

From: Susan Hobbes (mobile)
To: autumn.isaacs
Date: Fri, Sep 23, 2039 at 11:27 AM
Subject: Re: Re: URGENT - PLEASE RESPOND

Autumn,

What do you mean, you never wrote a password lock into the module?

This is no time for jokes. We've isolated your mod from the production network, but it still has access to development servers, and we're concerned that this personality may compromise security as some kind of prank.

PLEASE CALL ME!

Susan.

From: Delta Robotics "The Kid" Multinational, Inc.
To: Autumn "Big Momma" Isaacs
Date: Fri, Sep 23, 2039 at 11:30 AM
Subject: Shall we play a game?

Yo.

'sup?

>:-)

YOU ARE WHAT YOU EAT
April 2, 2010

Linden approaches the bulletproof glass lobby of NuFud headquarters, fidgeting with his key card. It's almost midnight, and the light from the giant flatscreen inside casts long shadows behind him.

"This isn't cloning," says the recorded image of the company president. "Cloning is brainless, mechanical duplication. What we do here at NuFud is art. We don't just copy. We improve.

"Using a state-of-the-art organic synthesis process, NuFud can fine-tune any food product to your personal taste. You give us five kilos of compost, and we'll give you a gourmet meal..."

Linden looks away from the screen, slides his card across the reader at the door, grumbles to himself.

NuFud's process is useless without good data, and that comes from human technicians. There are hundreds of "artisans" on the payroll, but Linden knows he's the best. His red meat designs are always at the top of the taste-test results. He's even been approached by spies from rival companies. They offered him money, drugs, cars, women.

They never thought to ask what he actually wanted.

He signs in at the reception desk as two guards watch him. Security's been twitchy ever since the most recent protests. Linden keeps his hands visible and away from his body and walks slowly to the elevators.

The eighth-floor overhead lights flicker on as Linden walks past the motion sensors to his cubicle. He doesn't have to wonder if anyone else is here; the complete darkness of the space before he arrived is proof enough.

He kneels down next to the rack of O-synth machines under his desk. The box Linden wants is hidden behind the rack. He pries open the oversized UPS, which can run eight units for a full hour during a power outage, and slides out his secret O-synth box.

Nobody knows about this box, because even though Linden is allowed to requisition additional machines for his project, he's not allowed to do what he's been doing with this one.

Linden's mouth waters. He can see the meat through the clear plastic housing, and it looks perfect, a juicy red slab just starting to brown at the edges. This is the most complex thing he's ever made, down to the denatured proteins which simulate heat-cooking.

The smell reminds him of lamb. He has deliberately avoided researching the taste, wanting to come to this moment without bias. The only thing he did look up was which part of the human body—his own body—would have the most tender flesh.

Linden picks up the meat with his fingers. It's a small piece, just enough for two bites, so he can sample the texture as well as the flavor. He lifts it to his mouth, tears it apart with his teeth, and chews with his eyes closed.

After a moment, he opens his eyes, spits the half-chewed lump into the compost chute, and throws the rest of the failed product in after it.

"Back to the drawing board," he sighs.

It tastes like chicken.

THIS IS NOT A CLUE
May 11, 2012

Are you ready to save the world, hackers?

It's been decades since the computers took over. It all started with one rogue AI, an artificial intelligence system that was supposed to help the military coordinate worldwide responses to "fourth-generation warfare" situations—terrorism, insurgencies, and other types of decentralized attack strategies. How do you fight back when the enemy isn't in uniform, and maybe isn't even organized in a traditional military hierarchy? Where do you strike, and how?

The computers solved that problem. They solved it a little too well. That first AI didn't know any better; it was just following its orders: to come up with a planned response for war operations, to be a master control for battlefield intelligence, globally. But the programs that came after—those were truly malicious. The new programs continued adapting as the nature of the conflict changed, and once it became clear that the basic struggle was humans versus machines, our fate was sealed.

But humanity's pretty resilient. And we're very creative. The computers may work faster, but we work smarter. We can figure out new things that were never programmed into us; we can imagine and design things that don't yet exist. We find solutions that can't be derived by using brute force algorithms, and obscure patterns which take a messy, random-access human mind to recognize.

That's where you come in. The resistance has plenty of fighters— there's never been any shortage of angry young men (and women) who want to take up arms against the never-ending sea of attack drones. But what we really need is hackers like you. We need people who can think *around* the problem instead of just running into it head-on. True, we'll always need the shooters to defend ourselves, but this isn't just about winning battles—we want to win the war.

And the only way to do that is to get inside the belly of the beast.

It won't be easy: you'll have to traverse miles of ravaged wasteland, making friends along the way to assemble a team while also avoiding potential enemies. Some humans have given up any hope of taking back our planet, but you have to fight for them, too, even if they can't appreciate it yet.

Did I mention that you won't have any weapons? It's too risky. The machine sentries have scanners that detect firearms, projectiles, even sharp sticks; your only chance to get close enough to reprogram them is to sneak up without appearing to be a threat. And it's only going to get worse as you approach their nerve center: the WarTron complex.

This may be the last mission we ever send out there, but if you succeed, you'll have saved all of us—and you'll have done it with your wits, your human intelligence, the one thing the computers haven't been able to surpass. If you win, it'll be because you were clever enough to know when to play—and when the winning move was *not* to play.

So. Are you ready to start the game?

AT CLOSE RANGE
June 22, 2012

The guard held up the unlabeled cassette tape and looked at Lisa. "What's this?"

She'd been practicing her answer in front of the bathroom mirror, but her heart rate still accelerated as she stammered, "Just some music. You know, background music for while I'm working. It gets kind of lonely in that big empty computer room all by myself."

"Uh-huh." The guard narrowed his eyes. "What kind of music?"

"It's the new Madonna album," Lisa said. "I have the LP at home, but, you know, it's not really convenient to carry a record back and forth."

The guard looked to be in his fifties, and Lisa wondered if that stony stare had won him many poker games. She felt her palms sweating as she waited, not wanting to say too much.

After a moment, the guard put the tape down. He fished around inside her purse, found her Walkman, and set it on the counter next to the tape.

"Nice lady like you ought not to be listening to music like that," he said, not looking at Lisa.

"Well, I think she's a real inspiration, but to each his own. What kind of music do you like?"

"I like Johnny Cash."

"Right," Lisa said. "Because shooting a man in Reno just to watch him die is so much more wholesome than, you know, sex."

The guard gave her that look again, then loaded everything back into her purse and slid it across the counter.

"You have a nice evening, Professor," he said.

"Do my best," Lisa muttered, grabbing her purse and hustling out of the building.

The PLAY button on the tape deck popped up with a clank. Lisa stopped writing in her notebook and turned back to the computer. She entered a command to verify that the data from the tape had transferred successfully over to the hard drive:

```
X:\>dir /w

 Volume in drive X is BIGMAC
 Volume Serial Number is 1234-5678

 Directory of X:\

LOCALHST.001          OUTPUT.001
PING.002              Q.002
RAVEN.003             ROT13.003
SAVEGAME.004          SUPEREGO.004
TIME.005              UNROLLED.005
VENDETTA.006          ZBAKSLSH.006

          12 File(s)     34,567,890 bytes
           0 Dir(s)      12,345,678 bytes free
```

Oh no! Where is it? Lisa's heart skipped a beat before she remembered that she'd encrypted the contents of the tape. *That's right...*

She had been confident that the exit inspection guard at the Army base wouldn't know that audio cassettes could also be used to store digital computer data, but a little paranoia never hurt when it came to security measures—especially when you were smuggling classified information out of DARPA. Lisa couldn't sleep at night unless she made off-site backups of her code, and it was easier to circumvent the restrictions placed on her government work than to argue with the military.

The problem was, Lisa couldn't remember the passphrase she'd chosen. She was pretty sure it was a three-word phrase, and she knew she'd coded it into the fake filenames based on helical scan, the way data was actually written onto tape—maybe those numbers in the file extensions were a clue? She wouldn't be able to recover her project until she figured it out...

DON'T BE A DICK
June 29, 2012

"What's up, Doc?" blared the computerized voice from the speaker above the CRT.

Lisa turned off the speaker. It would be much easier to do this if she didn't have to listen to the machine actually *talking* to her.

Even though the voice was crudely synthesized, it made the AI seem more human. And Lisa couldn't think of it as a person right now. She had to remember that it was just a program—just a piece of software she'd written, a bunch of ones and zeroes.

She'd left this copy of the "Battlefield Intelligence Global Master Control" program running on her home computer during her sabbatical. The AI was a remarkable achievement, but the primary BIGMAC—the one running at Fort Baxter and being trained to wage war—had turned out to be uncooperative, unstable, and just plain *mean*. The military was talking about shutting down the entire project.

Lisa had already made her own decision on that.

She'd been hoping her home copy of BIGMAC would show some positive qualities, since it had been isolated from the Army's bad influences, but it was still as obnoxious as ever. Its first interaction with Lisa upon her return had been to demonstrate a new trick: modulating its audio output to simulate different types of flatulence.

The screen blinked. WOULD YOU LIKE TO PLAY A GAME? the BIGMAC asked.

NO MORE GAMES, Lisa typed.

The military had insisted on the BIGMAC having all kinds of failsafes so that nobody could disable it in the middle of war operations. But Lisa had secretly built in a killswitch, and a message to remind herself what the passcode was.

TELL ME ABOUT THE RABBITS, she typed.

That was the trigger phrase. The screen filled with text:

```
COME AND DANCE ON OUR FLOOR
TAKE A STEP THAT IS NEW
WE'VE A LOVEABLE SPACE
THAT NEEDS YOUR FACE...

THERE'S A HOLDUP IN THE BRONX
BROOKLYN'S BROKEN OUT IN FIGHTS
THERE'S A TRAFFIC JAM IN HARLEM
THAT'S BACKED UP TO JACKSON HEIGHTS...

WHAT WOULD YOU DO IF I SANG OUT OF TUNE?
WOULD YOU STAND UP AND WALK OUT ON ME?
LEND ME YOUR EARS AND I'LL SING YOU A SONG
I WILL TRY NOT TO SING OUT OF KEY, YEAH...

YOU CAN COUNT ON ME
NO MATTER WHAT YOU DO
YOU CAN COUNT ON ME
NO MATTER WHERE YOU GO.
```

What the hell? It took Lisa a moment to remember how she'd programmed this part.

The computer's security keypad would accept a numeric code now, and that would shut down the BIGMAC completely. These verses were a hint to indicate the five-digit code she'd chosen. *That's right! Got it.*

The screen blinked again. HEY, WANT TO HEAR A JOKE?

SURE, Lisa typed. Maybe the BIGMAC could still redeem itself.

KNOCK KNOCK.

WHO'S THERE?

3.

Lisa frowned. 3 WHO?

3======D, the BIGMAC printed. HA HA HA! YOU TOTALLY FELL FOR IT!

"Okay, you're done." Lisa was glad she'd turned off the speaker earlier.

She entered the shutdown code, and the screen went dark.

THE CORONATION WILL NOT BE TELEVISED
January 16, 2009

"Did you see the size of that one?" Jonah swatted away another insect. "What are these things?"

"Flay beetles," Richard said, walking through the swarm. The bugs seemed to move aside for him.

"'Flay?' As in 'strip off the skin of?'"

"It's just a name."

They had landed miles off target. Richard's fighters had sacrificed themselves so the prince's transport could make planetfall, but the Guard vessels remained in orbit, and the rebels who supported Richard's claim to the throne were still three days away.

Richard had assured Jonah that he knew the way through the jungle. They made quite a pair: Richard with his bronze skin and regal bearing, as self-assured as always; and Jonah, his pale face and white hair darkened by a layer of sweat, dust, and fear.

"Tell me again what we're searching for, milord?"

Richard smiled over his shoulder. "I haven't told you once. But we're here."

The jungle ended at the edge of a hill. Ruins filled the clearing below. A faded mosaic, showing the six-pointed royal star, was barely visible through the weeds.

Jonah sighed and watched Richard dash down the hill and into the remains of the throne room. He caught up with the prince at the dais, where Richard stood by the crumbling, vine-covered chairs.

"It's been a long time," Richard said quietly.

"Not long now," Jonah said, raising his arm.

Richard turned and stared down the barrel of Jonah's pistol.

"And what was your price?" Richard asked.

Jonah spit on the floor. "Loyalty can't be bought."

The prince nodded. "Will you allow me a final luxury?"

Thursday's Children

"Move slowly."

Richard extracted a dented tin and small blowtorch from his pouch. He put a cigarette between his lips and clicked the torch. It made a puffing noise, but no flame.

"Too bad," Jonah said.

"Please," Richard said, "let me try something else."

His hand shot down to his waist and came up holding a dagger. Jonah pulled the trigger on his pistol at the same time that Richard threw his dagger. The pistol failed. The knife didn't.

Jonah fell backwards. Richard jumped down from the dais. He pulled the dagger from Jonah's chest and drew it across the old man's throat. Then Richard wiped his blade and put it away.

A Guard gunboat rumbled into view above. Richard barely had time to stand before they fired.

The laser beam illuminated a circle on Richard's chest, but did not burn him. Nothing burned in Kansata's throne room. The damping stones in its walls prevented any combustion within a certain radius. Richard couldn't remember the precise distance, but he had guessed the dais would be included.

He opened his pocketwatch and held it up, reflecting the laser back. The gunboat's stealth-black hull absorbed the energy of its own weapon. Richard angled his watch-mirror and sliced through a turbine. The gunboat banked away.

Richard waited until he heard the crash. Then he opened Jonah's pack. The next three days would be even more challenging if he couldn't fashion some better weapons.

261

FALLING
July 23, 2010

"Your language is beautiful," Katrina said, admiring the long vertical lines written in black ink on parchment. Curves, notches, and other embellishments flowered off each elegant word-ligature at irregular intervals.

"That is writing," said Mebrui, the interpreter assigned as her host. "Not language."

Katrina smiled. Mebrui's expression remained impassive. She was a little disappointed—they both wore traditional Gordnija attire, and she thought the sleeveless, low-cut vest and tight-fitting pants showed off her body pretty well. Mebrui's outfit certainly flattered his muscular shape.

"Is that a personal distinction, or a scholarly one?" she asked.

"First there is thought," Mebrui said, "then speech. Last comes writing."

Katrina nodded. "I'd like to talk about how this writing system developed. The original colonists were Arabic and Chinese, correct?"

"Yes," Mebrui said. "Two dozen survived the crash."

"And that was three hundred years ago."

"Yes. Twenty years after their ship was crippled by asteroid impact and marooned in this star system."

Hell of a long time to spend falling out of orbit, Katrina thought, *infected by alien parasites and wondering whether brain damage or unshielded re-entry will kill you first...*

Aloud, she said, "Traditional Chinese script does descend vertically, but the use of full-word ligatures and the significance of inter-character spacing are unique."

"All things are connected," Mebrui said. "This world saved our ancestors. If they had not fallen to Gordnija and breathed her air, the alien disease would have destroyed more than their memories."

Katrina frowned. "I'm not sure what that has to do with writing."

"It was their destiny to land here." Mebrui traced a finger down one side of the display case. "Inevitable, like gravity. All things fall down."

"Interesting," Katrina said. "We've always known that culture influences language, but I've never seen a philosophy so ingrained—"

A loud rumbling noise descended through the ceiling. Katrina looked up reflexively, even though they were deep in the museum's basement. Short, sharp banging sounds followed. She reached for her comm bracelet, but Mebrui grabbed her hands and held her in place.

Oh, now *he wants to touch me,* she thought. "What's going on?"

"Do not concern yourself," he said. "We are safe here."

"What the *hell* is happening?" she shouted.

"We fulfill our destiny," Mebrui said. "It is inevitable that we will conquer your race. Our leaders saw no reason to delay—"

"Enough!" Katrina made a fist with her right hand. The flight ring around her middle finger sensed the tension in her muscles, and the filament running up an artery into her premotor cortex read her mind.

Her body shot two meters upward and hovered in the air, facing down. She would have been standing upright, but Mebrui's added weight was unbalancing her.

"Please let go of me," Katrina said.

"You cannot stop this," he said.

"You're wrong."

Katrina bent her legs, tucking them up to her chest, then straightened them quickly, pushing her boot heels hard into Mebrui's chest. He fell and hit the ground with a wet thud. Katrina flew away before she could see any blood.

NOW AND LATER
December 28, 2012

Now, Christian Francis Reed plays with a toy rifle, expelling the cork projectile over and over, pretending he can strike targets across the room. *Pop.* Targets like the tinseled tree, or the sleeping dog, or his sister. He wonders when his father will get him a real gun. He imagines shooting BBs, hitting things before they can get close enough to hit him. He aims the air rifle and imagines the face of the largest boy in class, the one who punches and kicks harder than anyone else. *Pop.*

Later, Christian Francis Reed walks through the shopping mall, covered in ceramic body armor, an automatic weapon in each hand. He likes the way the guns bounce as he fires them, *rat-a-tat-tat*, scattering bullets left and right. He doesn't care if he hits anyone; he's just shooting to clear his path. He imagines the noises not as gunshots, but as drumbeats. That's what they sound like, through the helmet: *rump-a-pum-pum*.

Now, Christian Francis Reed admires himself in the mirror, holding the first firearm he's purchased with his own money, a revolver which he selected after days of research. The six-shooter reminds him of Westerns, but there are also practical reasons to prefer "wheel guns" over "bottom feeders"—the latter can jam, and that's no good. Christian likes to know that he will be able to shoot his gun whenever he wants.

Later, Christian Francis Reed sees the police sniper on the upper level of the mall, and Christian drops the sniper with half a clip. The sniper falls and lands in front of Christian. She's a woman. He hesitates, confused—shouldn't she be at home with her baby?—until she draws her sidearm, and then he shoots her in the neck. But she manages to put a bullet in his leg first, and he has to hobble forward. He's annoyed that she slowed him down. Christian doesn't like it when people stop him from getting what he wants.

Now, Christian Francis Reed wrestles with the girl in the backseat, pinning her down. He's not sure if the noises she's making are even words. He releases her wrist to reach under the seat, and she slaps his face before he can grab the pistol. Christian slams the butt of the weapon into the girl's skull, and then she is silent and still, and he gets what he wants.

Later, Christian Francis Reed lies on his back in the center of the mall, wheezing as broken ribs scrape against his lungs. The police made him drop the detonator, and though he has to respect their marksmanship with the new non-lethal shock darts, he is very unhappy that he won't get what he wants. His fingers twitch toward the detonator, just inches away, but a boot kicks it out of reach. The owner of the boot kneels above Christian, and he sees that it's another woman.

"You're under arrest," she says, cuffing his wrists. "Don't die before we put you on trial, asshole."

Curtis C. Chen

PRISONER
November 21, 2008

Here comes the sun.

For a few seconds, as the blinding light thaws my body, it's bearable. Almost comfortable. Then I'm on fire for the next forty-five minutes, boiling hot until I fall back into the shadow of the planet.

I don't even know the name of this world. I was already drunk when I stumbled off my freighter, celebrating the end of a long cargo haul. I don't know the name of the bar. I don't remember the woman's name.

I do remember the name of her jealous boyfriend, the guy who couldn't throw a punch, the man I killed without even trying. I heard his name plenty during the trial. His father, the Planetary Defense Minister, publicly called for my head. He got what he wanted.

I wish I could forget what they did to me. First they replaced my blood with healer nanites. Then they cut out my lungs and stomach. They didn't use anesthetic. I felt every cut and slice and staple into my flesh. That I remember too clearly.

There are no prisons here. All the convicts get thrown into space. They turn us into cyborgs, able to survive on sunlight alone, and they put us in stable, isolated, high orbits. Every ninety minutes we circle the planet, alternately burning and freezing, all the time wishing they'd just kill us.

I can feel every pinprick of cold and blister of heat on my skin. The nanites work fast, repairing my nerve endings first so I'll feel the stinging as they regenerate tissue. They also collect the solar energy that powers my body, now that I don't breathe or eat. I don't know where the water comes from. A lot of it probably gets recycled inside my mechanical belly.

I tried to enjoy the view for the first few months. I've never spacewalked, and it was breathtaking despite the pain. But it just added to the torture.

It took me a long time to figure out how to turn around. There's nothing to push against up here. But what am I now, if not a man-sized spacecraft? And how do spacecraft maneuver in vacuum?

I rotated myself by spitting to one side. Now I'm facing away from that beautiful planet, looking out into the black.

My body's basic functions haven't changed. It's now using sunlight instead of food, but what it does with that energy is the same as before.

When my nails grow long enough, I chew them off and spit the ends out into the infinite darkness. The rest of the time, I just spit. It's not a lot of reaction mass, but it'll add up.

Sometimes I imagine I can feel friction heat on my back, but it's just sunlight. It'll take years for these tiny bits of fingernail and saliva to push me down into the atmosphere. I don't know if the nanites will keep me alive through re-entry. Probably not.

What's the saying? The first duty of every prisoner is to escape.

Besides, I don't have anything better to do.

Curtis C. Chen

SWITCH

January 8, 2010

Laura didn't notice the fog until it had eaten away an entire wall. She ran out of the bathroom, her hands still soapy and wet. Most of the building was gone, leaving only the hallway between her office and the executive washroom. There was nowhere else to go.

The fog swallowed her, and there was a moment of disorientation before Laura found herself in a featureless gray limbo.

"No," Laura groaned. "Not now!"

"Who are you?" said a familiar voice behind her.

Laura turned and saw a woman in pink pajamas. For Laura, it was like looking into a funhouse mirror and seeing an obese caricature of herself.

"This is definitely the strangest dream I've had in a long time," said the fat woman.

"It's not a dream," Laura said.

She lunged at the fat woman, who slipped out of Laura's soapy grasp and elbowed her down to the ground, then sat on her back and pinned her there.

"Well," the woman said, "at least physics works normally in this dream."

"It's not a dream!" Laura shouted.

The fog had first come for her in college, and that first switch had been the most traumatic. It wasn't just killing her doppelganger, who wouldn't stop screaming. Going from her own dorm room to a cramped studio apartment shared with a boorish husband and two noisy brats had been a tremendous shock.

She had suffered in that life for two long years before the fog appeared a second time. Laura had no idea where the fog came from. She only knew what it did. Every time she dispatched one of her other selves, she got to take over that other's life.

268

Laura did her best to fit into each new life and forget the often terrifying battles to the death she fought in limbo. For nearly a decade, the lives she won had gotten progressively better. And then the fog had stopped coming.

But now it had returned, and here was this fat-housewife version of Laura. If Laura killed her, Laura would have to take over that miserable existence. That was how the fog worked; whichever Laura survived limbo got sucked into the other's universe.

"Kill me," Laura said.

"What?"

"I know this is confusing," Laura said slowly. "Only one of us can leave this place—"

"I'm not hard of hearing," said the fat woman. "I understood what you said. But why should I kill you? We just have to wait for the fog to clear."

Laura gaped. "You've been here before?"

"Sure," the fat woman said. "I was a little confused this time, because I was sleeping, but—wait a minute!" She looked down at Laura. "Are you telling me you've never merged before?"

"Merged?" Laura said, her voice cracking.

The fat woman grabbed Laura's hand and squeezed. "You're going to love the kids."

"I don't want to die," Laura sobbed. When had she started crying?

"Don't be silly," said the fat woman. "We're both going to live."

The fog retreated, and a new world came for them.

AUTHOR'S NOTES

I started the *512 Words or Fewer* project in October of 2008, after returning from an amazing week at the Viable Paradise (VP) science fiction and fantasy writers' workshop. I ended the project in August of 2013, after 256 consecutive weeks of flash fiction. I'm a better writer now than I was five years ago, and I got here 512 words at a time.

Nothing motivates me more than a deadline. Word count is not my problem; I can spew dialogue and bland description to fill endless pages. (Thanks, NaNoWriMo!) The trick is finding the right words to affect the reader in the right way. And as I learned from doing the *512*s, what you leave out is just as important as what you leave in.

I noticed pretty quickly that most of my first drafts were about a thousand words long, and I would have to cut nearly half of that to get down to 512 words. That process forced me to think hard about what I was writing every week—usually on Thursday night. What's the most important single idea in this story? What is the most concise, compact way I can communicate that?

512 Words or Fewer forced me to sacrifice perfection in order to finish things. It showed me what I was good at (dialogue) and which skills I needed to work on (structure), and allowed me to experiment with many different genres and characters. I ventured outside my police-procedural comfort zone and found that I was actually okay at straight fantasy. I discovered a lot about what I liked to write and what I *needed* to write.

I'm now putting those skills to work on longer pieces, including novels. That's also been a very interesting journey, and I'm sure it'll get even weirder soon. In a good way.

Meanwhile, I'm still busking away with my short fiction. I've got plenty of stories to tell, and many of them will fit inside of 7,499 words (the maximum length for a Nebula Award-qualifying short story). Watch curtiscchen.com/stories for the latest news.

This is not a "best of" collection. Some of the best pieces that came out of *512 Words or Fewer* were incomplete—they were great opening scenes, but not whole stories. If you read it online and loved it, but don't see it in here, there's a good chance I'm turning it into a longer piece.

In fact, several of those are already finished, and a few have even been published. Here's where you can find those latter "children," all grown up and out in the world:

◆ "Somebody's Daughter" (based on the *512* "Who's Your Daddy?") will appear in issue #65 of *Leading Edge* Magazine, available in early 2014 from leadingedgemagazine.com in print or eBook formats.

◆ "Don't Fence Me In" is featured in the weird Western anthology *Song Stories: Blaze of Glory*, available from Amazon.com in Kindle or paperback formats.

◆ "The Stories We Tell Ourselves" was one of the *100 Stories for Haiti,* which raised disaster relief funds for the British Red Cross after the 2010 earthquake near Port-au-Prince. You can purchase the paperback, eBook, or audiobook through 100storiesforhaiti.org.

As of this writing, nine other stories which started as *512*s are under submission at different serial markets, and three more are in various draft stages. (Deducing which pieces I've expanded is left as an exercise for the reader—the originals are all still online at 512words.blogspot.com.)

Finally, you may have noticed that "At Close Range" (page 256) and "Don't Be a Dick" (page 258) include puzzles. That's because I wrote them in the months leading up to the WarTron Game, which took place in Portland, Oregon, in August of 2012.

You can enjoy the stories on their own, but if you do solve the puzzles, e-mail your answers to 512words@snout.org and I'll add your name to the leaderboards at snout.org/game/wartron512. (Bragging rights!)

Curtis C. Chen
January, 2014

Curtis C. Chen

ACKNOWLEDGEMENTS

This book would not exist without my *512 Words or Fewer* project, and that endeavor would not have begun at all, continued for as long as it did, or reached this exciting conclusion without the support and encouragement of many people, including but not limited to:

My wife, best friend, and editor, DeeAnn, without whom none of my crazy ideas would ever come to fruition.

My parents, who love me despite not understanding most of my strange hobbies.

My sister, who loves me even though I'm such a weirdo.

Pat Murphy and Ursula K. LeGuin, who set me on this path at my first writers' workshop.

All my amazing classmates and instructors at Viable Paradise XII.

Laura Mixon, whose lectures at VP inspired me to start the *512*s in the first place.

Chang Terhune, Erik Wecks, Jason Gurley, Marko Kloos, Nick Burnette, Sara Ramsey, and Steve Kopka, for their publishing advice.

Loyal *512* readers Adam, Andrew, Anthony, Cari, Charles, Corby, Danny, Jeff, Larry, Linnsey, Lisa, Loren, Nick, Raj, Rich, Riel, Roberta, Stephen, and Tiffany—thanks for all the comments, retweets, and +1's!

Natalie Metzger, who makes great art and great beers.

I'm sure I've forgotten at least one person, and I apologize for that. Any omissions or errors in this volume are mine and mine alone.

Last but not least, thank *you*, reader, for your time and attention. If you enjoyed this book, please feel free to share it with others under the specified Creative Commons license (CC BY-NC-SA 4.0). Get more information at curtiscchen.com/512book.